BRONX ANGEL

Also by Ed Dee

14 Peck Slip

For Hal—
Hope you enjoy my Bronx Tale,
Ed

BRONX ANGEL

ED DEE

Ed Dee

WARNER BOOKS

A Time Warner Company

Grateful acknowledgment is given to reprint from the following:

"A Little Tooth" from *The Drowned River* by Thomas Lux. Copyright © 1990 by Thomas Lux. Reprinted by permission of Houghton Mifflin Co. All rights reserved.

Warner Books, Inc., 1271 Avenue of the Americas, New York, NY 10020

Printed in the United States of America
First Printing: August 1995
10 9 8 7 6 5 4 3 2 1

Library of Congress Cataloging-in-Publication Data

Dee, Ed.
Bronx angel / Ed Dee.
p. cm.
ISBN 0-446-51774-7 (hardcover)
I. Title.
PS3554.E32B76 1995
813'.54—dc20 95-2280
CIP

For Nancy

Acknowledgments

I am indebted to every cop I ever worked with, or had a drink with. It is their stories that demand to be told. I am particularly grateful to Don McGuire, a great cop who remains an even greater friend.

Thanks to Gail Hochman, for being in my corner.

And to Joe Heiner, Kathy Heiner, and Dan Bond for another spectacular cover; to Sona Vogel for, again, skillfully wielding her red pencil; to Anne Hamilton for keeping it running smoothly; and especially to Maureen Egen for guiding everything with such a caring hand.

Finally, to my family for being so extraordinarily supportive and proud; and my friends for being so generous and unsurprised.

Thomas Lux

A Little Tooth

Your baby grows a tooth, then two,
and four, and five, then she wants some meat
directly from the bone. It's all

over: she'll learn some words, she'll fall
in love with cretins, dolts, a sweet
talker on his way to jail. And you,

your wife, get old, flyblown, and rue
nothing. You did, you loved, your feet
are sore. It's dusk. Your daughter's tall.

BRONX
ANGEL

1

In a freak April snowstorm they found the body of an off-duty cop on a Bronx back street, his throat slashed, his pants pulled down to his knees. He'd been dead for over two hours, and I was still crawling in three inches of wet snow on the Cross-Bronx Expressway.

"It's four A.M., New York," the radio DJ said, her voice a husky, intimate whisper. "And it's still coming down."

Police Officer Marc Ross had been discovered in his own car, an alleged prostitute seen fleeing the scene. The key word here was *prostitute*. The brass at One Police Plaza wanted the straight story, all the sordid details, undiluted by precinct loyalty. The NYPD does not bang the drum for all its slain comrades.

"The eighteenth snowstorm of the season," the DJ said. "Are we being punished by God?"

My Honda fishtailed as I swerved around a muffler in the middle of the exit ramp. I slid through the stop sign sideways and came to a halt in the middle of Tremont Avenue. Salsa music blared from a corner bar. Not a car in sight. I turned the Honda around and made the right onto Boston Road. That's when I saw the crowd.

"Can't be," I said. Not just for a homicide. Not on a night like tonight.

The crowd, mostly women and children, carried flashlights and food they shared with each other. They were lined up single file, up the entire block, then around the corner and down into East 179th Street. I stopped at the corner of East 179th, a short dead end with a steep drop ending at the Bronx River. The Bronx River flowed south out of the Bronx Zoo and eventually into the East River.

At the bottom of the hill I saw the flash of turret lights; NYPD cars filled the circle at the end of the cul-de-sac. The roadway was broken and slippery, the carcass of a dog stuffed in a pothole. Protective metal barriers separated the pavement from the grassy hill leading down to the river. Grainy shafts of light rose from the riverbed below.

The Bronx saddened me. I'd been a rookie cop on the streets of this brawling borough, and my good memories outweighed the bad. These days, except for the occasional high-profile homicide, the only reason I returned was out of loyalty to the Yankees. But the Yankees, like many of the cops I'd worked with in the last thirty years, were in the warm Florida sunshine. And I was in the snow, in the burned-out Bronx, with nobody but myself to blame. Cops like me hang around too long, destined to revisit the past.

I parked behind Joe Gregory's new Thunderbird. Detective Joe Gregory, my partner off and on for two decades, had come all the way from Brooklyn and beat me to the scene. But the grim crowd I'd been following didn't stop at the murder scene. The line stretched along the riverbank, into the darkness, well past the last police car. To them, the cops searching a crime scene were only a curious sideshow, like jugglers working a theater line. Murder is not a blockbuster event in the Bronx.

The breath of two dozen cops puffed in the frigid air and floated in the glare of floodlights. My brother officers worked quickly. Wet weather erases evidence.

"Detective Ryan, Chief of Detectives Office," I said, showing my shield to a tall, red-haired policewoman at the barriers.

"Hey, Mr. Ryan," she said. "How's it going?"

"Great," I said. "How about you?"

I had no idea who the hell she was. As I worked my way down the slippery bank, I figured I'd probably worked with her father somewhere; an extraordinary number of sons and daughters of cops were on the job. Her name tag said "Antonucci," which didn't ring a bell, but I'd worked with a lot of cops.

At the bottom of the hill, a dark gray BMW sat inside a border of yellow tape, the front end barely dipping into the icy river. All around the car the ground had been trampled. Fresh snow fell into a thousand footprints. Inside, slumped over on the passenger seat, was Police Officer Marc Ross, his jeans and white boxer shorts pulled down, his shirt dyed crimson. I shaded my eyes from the floodlights as I knelt to look at his butchered throat.

"Jesus Christ," I said.

"No, the Blessed Virgin, you heathen bastard," a gravelly voice said. My partner, the great Joe Gregory, stood with his suit pants rolled up, ice crystals on the cuffs. "You here for the homicide or the miracle?"

"What miracle?" I said.

"You didn't see the line of people?" he said.

"I saw the line."

"Down the whole goddamn street," he said. "See where the line ends? By the wall there. Look at the spot above all those flashlights. See her?"

"See who?"

"You can't see her? On the rocks? What kind of Catholic are you, you don't know the Mother of God?"

"Where?"

"Look where my finger's pointing," Gregory said. He moved next to me, his bulk blocking the lights.

The wall Gregory pointed to was fifty yards away. It looked like a stone retaining wall for the bridge over the Bronx River at East 180th Street. Water running down the stones had frozen into a mass of icicles forming one large striated figure, a mass of long vertical lines of ice like the folds of a cloak. The figure was lit by flashlights held by people who had climbed down to the riverbed. Some knelt on the side of the hill, some knelt in the snow at the river's edge.

"Looks like Lourdes, don't it?" Gregory said.

"Looks like a big chunk of ice," I said.

Gregory blessed himself. "City says it ain't from the river; some underground pipes must've busted."

"How long has this been going on?" I said.

"Started last night, according to the Five One Precinct cops."

"Then we must have witnesses."

"We got more freaking witnesses than Carter got liver pills," Gregory said.

Up close I could smell gin on Gregory's breath, and his clothes reeked of smoke. I knew he was half-drunk.

"Story is this," he said. "Oh two hundred hours,

BMW stops up there. Driver, this dark-skinned woman, drives around the barriers onto the grass. Then she gets out, reaches in, releases the brake. Car rolls straight down here. Nobody saw the body till some kids started to strip the car." Gregory rocked back on his heels, then steadied himself as if on a balance beam only he could see. "Cop's name is Marc Ross. Uniform cop. Three years on the job. Works in the precinct combat car. Three-man car, supposed to make the drug problem go away."

"Married?"

"No, thank God. I wouldn't want to explain this one to a wife. Works steady six-to-twos. Off Sundays and Mondays."

"He was off tonight, then. What was he doing here?"

"Beats the shit out of me, pally. They say he's a musician. Moonlights in some band in Manhattan on Sunday nights. His trumpet is in the trunk."

"Maybe he met this woman there?"

"The squad thinks it's a hooker murder," he said. "I think they got another think coming."

"Why would she drive him here and dump the car with all these witnesses?"

"They're saying she didn't know the church crowd was here. She drives in, sees the crowd. Surprise, surprise! She panics, dumps the car. Personally, I think that's a crock a shit."

"You're thinking she wanted it to look like a hooker rip-off."

"Actually, yeah," he said. "I'm betting it's a girlfriend, a barmaid, someone he knew. That's my take, but I'm in the minority."

A makeshift canvas covering had been constructed over the dark gray sedan. We stood out of the weather as the tech man, using curving strokes, dusted the roof with the fine, sooty black powder. If the car had been any darker, he would have needed a silver or white powder, for contrast. Every few strokes he'd step back to see if any powder had stuck to the grease left by a human hand. If a print was found, he would photograph it, then lift it with simple, transparent tape and place it on an index card.

"After she dumped the car," I said, "where did this mystery woman go?"

"Walked away. Up the hill, then toward Tremont."

"Just walked away?"

"Affirmative. Cool as ice."

"Description?"

"Dark-skinned Hispanic. Slender build. Five foot to five four. Black hair, styled big. Black coat, red dress, red shoes, white gloves."

"White gloves in this weather? Sounds like your date book."

"I don't know from gloves," he said. "But slender ain't my style. I still like 'em zaftig. Meat on the bone."

"So what do you think?" I said.

"Blow job that went very wrong," Gregory said. "Ended up a slice and dice."

"No possible way it could be a hooker robbery?"

"Guaranteed," he said. "The only thing missing, far as the squad can determine, is his gun. Holster's empty. But she left his watch. Not a Rolex, but not a cheapo. Two rings, wallet, credit cards, about seventy bucks in cash."

"Maybe she saw the crowd and panicked, forgot the money."

"Hookers don't forget the money, pally."

Officer Marc Ross had been cut very deeply, an artery, perhaps. Blood had pooled on the passenger seat beneath him and dyed the leather a dark red. But the driver's side was also brushed with blood. Wide red streaks slashed across the driver's side door, steering wheel, and center console. Marc Ross had probably been slashed as he sat on the driver's seat, then moved to the passenger seat.

"Pretty strong woman," I said. "To pull him over the console."

"He ain't a big guy. Looks like he only goes about one fifty. Lot of women could handle one fifty, easy."

"Not dead weight," I said. "Not easily. Tell me this: If it was a girlfriend, why didn't she leave him where she killed him and run?"

"Because she iced him near where she lived. Maybe in the parking lot of a bar where she worked." Gregory pointed to the body with a crooked index finger, yellowed from nicotine. "Look at the wound," he said. "All that ripping and gouging. Classic overkill. My money says this is personal. We got an adrenaline factor working here."

"Who caught the case?" I asked.

"The Ivy League detective over there with the shit-eating grin." Gregory pointed to a young, balding guy smoking a pipe. "Asshole rookie third-grader. Wouldn't make a pimple on a real cop's ass."

Sergeant Neville Drumm was talking Ivy League through the search. Sergeant Drumm had been the squad commander when I was in the precinct. His hair, now completely white, gave him the look of a kindly plantation butler in an old Civil War movie.

"Anyone talk to Ross's partner?" I said.

"Partners," Gregory said. "Three men, remember? POs Verdi and Guidice."

"Not Sonny Guidice?"

"One and the same," Gregory said. "He just arrived, some blonde on his arm."

I hadn't seen Sonny Guidice since I'd left the precinct twenty years earlier. Not that I gave a shit. He was in civilian clothes, standing in a circle of young uniformed cops, his arm around a woman. A very young, very blond woman, her eyebrows so white and thick, it looked like snow clinging to a ledge.

"Drumm says he'll interview Sonny and the other guy," Gregory said.

"Suits me."

Sonny Guidice had small black eyes, puffy cheeks, and pointy features that made him look like an overweight rodent. He'd arrived in the precinct from the academy shortly before I left. He shot and killed a seven-year-old boy, Martin Luther Hopkins, in the bedroom of apartment 4C of 1645 Bathgate Avenue, at five minutes after six on a warm evening, June 23, 1968. The grand jury declared it to be accidental. I was a witness.

"Where the hell were you tonight?" I whispered to Gregory.

"Auto Crime retirement racket out in Flushing. I told you I was going. I just got home, the chief calls. What'm I supposed to say: 'Sorry, Chief, I'm shit-faced'?"

I stepped back away from him. No need to whisper. The precinct detectives were giving us a wide berth, pissed off because we were "downtown" invading their turf.

"I grabbed two coffees on the way," Gregory said. "What can I say? I ain't ready to do brain surgery, but I can sleepwalk through this scene."

"What makes you think the woman was Hispanic?" I said.

"Not me." He pointed up at the line. "That's what Ivy League tells me the people say. Personally, I don't think he could find a brother in Harlem. These cops today, I'm telling you, we're in deep shit."

"Looks like everything is under control to me."

I climbed back up the hill. Within a few minutes I found an interpreter: a friendly, bilingual woman dressed in an air force parka. We started working the line. It didn't take long to confirm the old truth that too many witnesses were worse than none. The kids knew all about the car, the model, year, and accessories. The women noticed her clothes and hair. They all thought the hair was a wig. The dress was red, the gloves were long and white, spotted with blood. She walked away carrying a black coat. But the more I asked, the more the range of age, complexion, height, and weight increased.

It was near dawn when the Crime Scene Unit finished and began lugging gear up the hill. Morgue attendants yanked the body out of the car. The smell of burning tires wafted from the junkyards of Hunts Point. Gregory scrambled up the slippery bank, burly and agile as a grizzly bear.

"For the sake of argument," I said, "let's say our killer chose this location purposely for the presence of the Blessed Virgin. Who are we after now?"

Gregory was breathing hard as we walked to our cars. Down the block, women were lighting rows of candles set in paper bags, creating a fiery path to the vision.

"A whore, an angel," he said. "It don't freaking matter, pally. Either way we're looking for a psycho."

2

The snow stopped and the sun came out when they tossed Marc Ross to the back of the morgue wagon. The body bag screeched across the metal floor and stopped against a former Bronx resident who'd OD'd while making Egg McMuffins in the borough's newest McDonald's. Joe Gregory exchanged notes and fuck-yous with Ivy League and the Five One Precinct squad while I sat in Sergeant Neville Drumm's car and talked old times.

I felt oddly comfortable, a peaceful sense of place . . . a place more familiar than I wanted to admit. I thought about quiet mornings when I was a foot cop working school crossings, the sun coming around the corner, warming my back as I joked with the kiddies, smiled at the mamas.

"Mallomars?" Drumm said, offering the open box of cookies. I waved them away. "Better take one now. They don't ship them to the stores in summer. Come July you'll be begging me for one."

Drumm bit into the cookie, then examined it, as if counting the layers.

"Sonny Guidice still looks the same," I said.

"He's still an asshole, if that's what you're hinting at. But he knows the streets. Works hard. He's got balls."

"What about Marc Ross?"

"Good kid. Liked to talk about music. Very thorough cop. Meticulous with reports."

I thought carefully about how to phrase the next question, trying to remember that I represented "downtown" and in the eyes of ghetto cops lacked the simpatico of the scummiest local street thug.

"You know what they're going to say downtown, Neville."

"Yeah," he said, seeming tired and distant. "They're betting he was trying to get a blow job on the muscle. Tells her he's a cop, says, 'I ain't paying you shit.' Hooker goes berserk, starts slashing."

"It's happened before," I said.

"Tell me about it."

"What do we tell downtown about it?"

"Tell them like it is," he said. "You think I'm going to cover this up? Uh-uh. Those days are long gone. Long gone. You've been away from the bag too long, Anthony. We don't protect nobody out here anymore. Cop screws up, it's his tough shit. Moral is, don't screw up."

Cops sense they're being watched. It comes from years of being in uniform, feeling eyes upon you. I'd been aware of a hulking, bearded man across the street. He was kneeling at the side of the hill, facing the Blessed Virgin. Wood scraps crackled and burned in a barrel behind him.

"You recognize that guy?" Drumm said. "With the rebel hat. Staring at us."

"The bum with the beard?"

"I think he remembers you."

The bearded man wore a long black raincoat, a Confederate Civil War cap. A large wooden cross hung around his neck. When I finally acknowledged him he raised his fist and smiled through stained teeth.

"That's Francis X. Hanlon," Drumm said.

Instantly I remembered. "The cop fighter."

Francis X. Hanlon was a name burned into the memory of every Bronx street cop. Cop fighter. I knew of only two or three persistent cop fighters in my career. Guys who'd get drunk in some local bar and wander the streets looking for a cop and a battle. I'd always thought cop fighters had to be desperately seeking punishment, because that was surely what they received. Francis X. was the most prolific and feared. Sometimes it would take a dozen cops to subdue him.

"He's wasted. Mind's gone," Drumm said. "Cops today don't know who he is. They call him the Padre."

Sergeant Drumm and I agreed to split the legwork. He'd do the Bronx, canvass the area around the scene; I'd check the Manhattan bar where Officer Marc Ross played trumpet on Sunday nights. I reassured him it was still his investigation, that "downtown" wasn't out to take over the case. I expected a sarcastic response, but he said nothing.

The morgue wagon left in a puff of blue-black smoke. Then we left in separate cars as the pilgrims shuffled slowly to the ice Madonna. A high in the upper forties was being predicted. I didn't want to stay around to see the temperature rise.

Gregory pointed his T-bird east toward the Throgs

Neck Bridge, a circuitous route he claimed would save time. He was circling around to his house in Brooklyn, the house he'd inherited from his ex-cop father. He was going to clean up and grab a quick nap while I inched down the Major Deegan Expressway in the morning flow of commuter traffic into the East Side of Manhattan.

Our boss, Lieutenant Delia Flamer, had notified me to meet a Roderic Ahearn, who played sax in the PM Ramblers, Marc Ross's band. As I sat in traffic, three letters kept running through my mind: BMW. Nice car for a cop.

I swung off the highway and crossed the Macombs Dam Bridge into the streets of Manhattan. Traffic always moved much faster on the Adam Clayton Powell Jr. Boulevard, even at the height of rush hour. Most New Yorkers avoided the route because it took you through the center of Harlem. Cops knew it, used it.

After thirty years I was an encyclopedia of cop knowledge, some of it useful, most of it destructive. I knew shortcuts like ACP Boulevard and that traffic lights worked on a ninety-second sequence: the avenues stayed green for fifty-four seconds, while the side-street traffic had just thirty-six seconds to get across. But I also carried the memory of the day Sonny Guidice shot Martin Luther Hopkins. I knew the moment I saw the hole in the boy's chest he wouldn't live until the next green light.

Twenty-eight minutes after leaving the Bronx I parked in a taxi stand on Park Avenue and Fifty-second Street. I flipped the "official police business" plate onto the dash, made sure the doors were locked. The NYPD bureaucracy was hot on official parking plates. The laminated cards were being stolen from the windshields of unmarked police cars or borrowed and creatively photocopied.

The Park Avenue Plaza was impressive, two security guards in the lobby, bookends for an indoor waterfall. Roderic Ahearn's firm, Mohawk Associates, took up three floors: nineteen to twenty-one. I'd waited with the receptionist for less than three minutes when Ahearn jogged up an inner staircase.

"Lieutenant Ryan," he said.

"Detective Ryan," I corrected.

He was about six two, slender, late twenties. He wore suspenders over a white button-down shirt and a tie with huge hand-painted lilies and kept running his fingers through his moussed sandy hair. He motioned for me to follow him back downstairs.

Ahearn's office was on the corner, cut on an angle as if they'd tried to make two corner offices out of one. His desk, centered to the rear of an Oriental rug, was a long glass table. On it, only a white legal pad, a black fountain pen, and a banker's lamp.

"Sit, please." Ahearn pointed to a studded leather armchair. "Marc's uncle called me this morning. This horrible thing really happened, didn't it?"

"I'm afraid so."

"You got here so quick. I'm still walking around in a daze. I keep thinking this isn't real." Ahearn's hair stuck up in back as he nervously mussed and finger combed. "I'm sorry," he said. "I'm not normally like this. But this isn't a normal day, is it?" He put his hand in the air in a stop gesture and took a deep breath. "You want to know about last night. Last night . . . last night we were at Millard's Red Garter, Fifty-first off Madison.

We've had a standing engagement for four years. Sunday nights only."

"Marc play last night?" I said.

"Both sets."

"What time did he leave?"

"We finish at twelve-ten. Marc left maybe ten, fifteen minutes after the last number."

"Alone?"

"Far as I know."

On the walls, framed oils and watercolors, beach and marsh scenes that looked like the Hamptons. A vase of fresh-cut flowers stood on a low table. Ahearn took off his glasses and rubbed his eyes.

"How well did you know Marc?" I said.

"Since high school. Power Memorial. All the original band members went to Power. That's what the PM means."

"Tell me about the band."

"Nothing to tell, we were a one-gig band. Millard's Red Garter was it. Nobody was going to leave their day job for the music life. It's more of a night out. Make a few bucks, have a good time while we're doing it."

"Were you having a good time last night?"

"We all sucked down a few brews, had a few giggles. But we weren't wild men."

"What about wild women? Any women with you last night?"

"Dixieland groups aren't known for attracting groupies, Officer."

"I assume that's a no," I said. "How about between sets? Could Marc have met a woman on the way to the men's room? At the bar?"

"Anything's possible, but between sets we stayed in the back room. Watched the Rangers game."

"Perhaps one of the other band members saw something," I said.

I stood and walked to the window while Ahearn spoke to his secretary through an intercom. He gave her the names of the other band members, asked her to list addresses and phone numbers. Floor-to-ceiling windows looked southeast across Park Avenue, toward the squat round-domed beauty of St. Bartholomew's Church, a priceless gem dropped into an erector-set village.

"Are you saying a woman did this?" Ahearn said.

"No, I'm not. Did you all leave together?"

"Marc left first. But within a few minutes we were all out on the sidewalk. Snow was starting to come down. Marc wasn't there; apparently he'd already started walking home. Let me get back to this woman thing. We have a standing rule. Three of us are married. We didn't want it turning into stag night."

I sat back down on the studded leather chair. "You said he walked?"

"Always walked, there and back."

"You're sure he didn't bring his car?" I said.

"You kidding? Where the hell you going to park over there? It wasn't that bad a walk. Just to Sixty-second Street. Opposite Lincoln Center."

"We found him in his car last night."

"He didn't have his goddamn car."

"A 1989 BMW 325i, gray in color, license KAM-626, New York."

"Christ, my heart is pounding." Ahearn took a deep breath. "I can't swear that he didn't have the car with him. He usually kept it in a garage directly across the street from his building. But, Christ, I don't know. I can't even remember the last thing he said."

Ahearn put his hands to his face. I waited for him to look up, then walked him through the usual questions: What about enemies? Did he seem worried? Anything unusual happen last night or in the recent past? His head kept shaking: No. . . . No. . . . No. . . .

"Mr. Ahearn," I said, "we have a description of a woman seen walking away from his car: slender, young, possibly Hispanic. Dark skinned. Does that sound like anyone Marc would know?"

"I'm sure he knew all kinds. From his job. He dealt with those people all the time."

"Have you ever known Marc to be involved with a prostitute?"

"Whoa, please, Officer. Let's not drag his memory through the gutter quite yet."

"Is that a no?"

"Absolutely." He glared at me across the desk. "I don't understand what you're driving at."

"Would he have dated anyone who answers that description?"

"I don't think he'd let the color of someone's skin bother him, if that's what you mean."

"Have you known him to date black or Hispanic women?"

"No," he said quietly.

When his secretary came in with the list of band members, I stood up to leave.

"Nice office," I said, gesturing around the room. "For a sax player."

"I live to play, but I litigate to live."

I thought about asking further; I had nagging questions about money. Ross's BMW was expensive, but young people extend themselves financially for cars. His Columbus Avenue address was harder to explain: rent had to be into four figures, and the parking garage had to go for three hundred a month. Money created a trail that begged to be followed. But there was no rush. Money left deep tracks.

3

I parked in a No Standing zone on East Fifty-first Street next to the parish office for St. Patrick's, then banged on the door of Millard's Red Garter. The place didn't open until four, but you'd think they would have a porter getting an early jump on mopping the floor. A business card from Spillane's Distributor of Fine Spirits was wedged in the door; I slipped my card next to it with a note to "call Lt. Delia Flamer," underlined.

The only other thing I knew for sure was that Ross had picked up his car. I checked my watch, then began walking west, trying to retrace Ross's walk home. Trying to connect the dots on the time frame.

I walked north on Fifth; all the sidewalks were clean of snow. On Fifth Avenue, men with long shovels materialize as soon as the first flake hits the ground. The sun was bright, and everything was melting fast. I thought about the ice Madonna.

I couldn't get Sonny Guidice out of my mind. What

the hell was he doing still working uniformed patrol? He could have wangled some special assignment, maybe checking guns at the outdoor range or stacking stolen TVs in evidence bins in the basement of the Property Clerk's Office. Somewhere. With over thirty thousand NYC cops, there had to be one boss dumb enough to recommend him.

It took me nineteen minutes to walk to Marc Ross's parking garage near the corner of Columbus and Sixty-second. I walked down a steep incline to a small green booth. A sign above said $12.67 for the first hour or part.

The attendant was a muscular West Indian with the name "Hubert" sewn into his uniform. "Alberto is the night attendant," he said. "Ask him. I don't know a ting, mon."

Hubert flipped through a stack of time clock cards. I squeezed past him into the booth. A bottle of Guinness Stout and a copy of *Jugs* were open on the desk. Taped to a post was a smudged list of addresses and phone numbers. The booth reeked of marijuana.

"Is Alberto Restos the night man we're talking about?" I asked, reading from the list. Alberto Restos lived off Linden Boulevard, in St. Albans, Queens. I copied the address and phone number, then inked out the number on Hubert's list, just in case he got a bright idea to call Restos after I left. If Alberto Restos was an illegal alien, he'd vaporize before I got halfway through the Midtown Tunnel.

Hubert handed me Marc Ross's time card. I held it under a grimy gooseneck lamp. Alberto had apparently checked out Marc's BMW at 1:03 A.M. I took the card by the edges and placed it in a clean envelope.

"Alberto be in at midnight," the West Indian said. "I

don't know nothing else to help you." He picked up the bottle of Guinness and went back to his reading.

Alberto Restos, the night parking attendant, was not an illegal alien. He was a junior-year religious studies major at St. John's University and the son of a Queens fireman. A copy of the *Summa Theologica* was open on his kitchen table. Restos said that Marc Ross was with a woman: dark skin, bright red dress, red shoes.

"Prostitute," he said. "No doubt in my mind."

"Is a man who reads Aquinas reliable when spotting whores?"

"C'mon," he said. "All she needed was a neon sign."

On the drive back to Manhattan I looked for a working phone. I stopped at a Queens street corner known for heavy crack action. Telephones on active drug corners are never vandalized or out of service. Surrounded by guys wearing gaudy jewelry and beepers, I called my wife. Leigh is a diabetic, and her blood sugar numbers had been out of whack lately. I blamed the stress of our daughter's upcoming marriage.

Leigh wasn't at her desk, so I left a message. I called Joe Gregory's home number, let it ring twenty times: no answer. Then, feeling eyes on my back and hearing the word *cop* spat onto the sidewalk, I called Lieutenant Delia Flamer.

"I don't want Gregory screwing up this case," Delia said.

"He won't," I said. "If anything he'll make the case."

Delia had not worked with Gregory before. Their career paths had been going in far different directions. Delia had just returned from a year's study at Harvard. While she was gone I collected on an old contract and had Gregory transferred back into the building. He'd been in exile in Bed Stuy for years, mostly because of the sins of his late father, Liam, a legendary detective who spent the last year of his life ducking a bench warrant. He died, under a cloud, in Ireland.

"The autopsy is at Bellevue at two," Delia said. "I'll meet you there. Gregory is en route to the Manhattan Marina. The nightwatchman said Marc Ross was there last night, with a woman. Better get up there, make sure your suave partner doesn't fall into the Hudson."

The Manhattan Marina was a small, exclusive operation just north of the Seventy-ninth Street Boat Basin. The Hudson River smelled raw and bitter cold. Gregory was just getting out of his T-bird as I pulled in. His gray hair was slicked back, his shaven face as red as an open wound. In his hands was a large manila envelope.

"Campaign pins came in," he said.

Joe was running for president of the NYPD Emerald Society. He'd worked on the design of the pin for a month. They were gold replicas of the NYPD detectives shield, about half the size of the actual shield. In the center, instead of the city seal, was a green shamrock with "NYPD EMERALD SOCIETY" in orange block letters. Around the shamrock, in white, was the signature *Joseph P. Gregory, President.* The badge number was 1994.

"Looks like the Dublin PD," I said, pinning one on my jacket. "What did all this cost you?"

"Money is no object."

Such largesse from a guy who'd once had his Honor Legion medal melted down when the price of gold was high. But money had been no object for Joe recently. He'd bought a new wardrobe, the T-bird, even squared his tab in Brady's bar. He'd inherited the Brooklyn house and money from his father.

The guard shack was overheated and smelled of Chinese food.

"How's the health?" Gregory said, slapping Larry Stanky, the nightwatchman, on the back.

Stanky had a bubble gut and bulging blue eyes. He was an ex-cop, fired for drinking and still carrying a chip the size of a keg on his shoulder. His uniform pants were covered with cat hair.

"Ross parked at the dark end of the lot," Stanky said. "Way over there where I couldn't see him. Near his uncle's boat. Dark as hell over there."

"What's his uncle's name?" I said.

"Rosenberg," Stanky said. "Dr. Rosenberg. Cardiologist. I always figured Ross was a lawyer or some shit."

Stanky handed me the visitors log. White carry-out cartons with wire handles filled the trash basket.

"You eat yet, pally?" Gregory said. "Chinese sounds good to me."

"If we have time," I said. But I didn't want to eat before going to the morgue.

Marc Ross and one guest were logged in at 1:14 A.M., eleven minutes after he'd picked up the car. Great time in Manhattan, but possible at that hour. Stanky logged the car out twenty-seven minutes later: 1:41 A.M. Nineteen minutes after that the BMW was dumped near the Virgin Mary in the Bronx.

"It was snowing like a bitch last night," Stanky said, "and it's dark where he parked. Over at that far end."

"You said that," I said. "Did he bring women here often?"

"Sometimes. Sometimes they went on the boat. Last

night he stayed in the car, then *whoosh*, tore ass outta here. I had my back turned. Went by like a shot."

"Did they get out of the car at all?" I asked.

"I thought I saw the light come on once. I figured it was to take a piss or something."

"They both get out?"

"I saw a light, heard the door slam. That's all. Look where it is, way over there. Who knows who the hell was over there?"

"Was anyone else here?" I said.

"Not that I know of."

I looked down at the log book. No one else was signed in during that period. Stanky kept staring at my face. Staring, with those popped-out eyes. I wanted to tell him to blink occasionally.

"I never knew he was a cop," Stanky said.

"Who was driving when they left?" I asked.

"My back was turned. I told you that."

My bullshit detector buzzed in the back of my head. I tried to push him in another direction, maybe one he wasn't prepared for. I said that I was surprised he let hookers use the parking lot.

"Don't give me that horse shit," Stanky said. "No way hookers get in here. Better believe it."

"Funny," I said. "Even a religious studies major made her as a hooker."

"I made her as a serious bimbo."

"Then it's possible she was a prostitute."

"You're putting words in my mouth, champ," he said. "I say he came here with a hooker, I'm out on my ass, period. I don't let hookers in here. No way, Jose."

Everybody lies to cops, something in the American rebel spirit. I thought Larry Stanky would want to prove that he had been a sharp cop, that he still had cop's eyes. But he was being too defensive, trying to cover his ass. The tight job market telling him, "Don't blow this one, asshole."

"Were they drinking?" I said. "See any beer bottles, cans, wineglasses?"

"What the fuck," he said. "It's dark, right? They got the music blasting."

"What kind of music?" I said.

"Rock, some kind of rock. What do I know, I'm Joe the Glom in a booth."

Gregory looked up from his note pad. "Cut the shit, Larry."

"I didn't see no booze," he said. "All I saw was this hard-looking bitch. Wild hair, bright red dress, a ton of makeup. You see what I'm saying?"

"What the hell are you saying?" Gregory said.

"Alls I'm saying is not a hooker, but not an ordinary bimbo. Not dumb looking, not goo-goo looking, you know? Bimbos wear the clothes, and walk the walk, but ain't got the stones. The hard look in their eyes. You know what I'm saying?"

"Don't get yourself involved in a perjury situation," I said.

"I ain't fucking lying."

"You know she was driving when they left," Gregory said. "You're lying about that?"

"You can't lie about something you didn't see." Stanky wiped sweat from his face with a paper towel. "Guys like you make me glad I'm outta the job, you know that? Coupla humps, think your shit don't stink."

"Hey, Lar," Gregory said. "I can guarantee you'll keep your job here. Nobody gets screwed for doing the right thing. Only way you'll lose this job is for not cooperating, understand? You got my word on that. Just call me if you get flack from anybody."

He flipped him a shamrock detectives badge.

"Listen," I said. "We know you couldn't see what happened in a car parked over at the far end of the lot. But you're a sharp guy, Larry. I think you knew something was wrong when they left. And we both know you're the type of guy who jumps right in when he sees a cop in trouble."

"Fucking A," Stanky said. "He should've told me he was on the job."

"She was driving, wasn't she?" Gregory said. "On the way out."

"Some of the shit that goes on here," Stanky said. "In the cars, and the boats. You wouldn't fucking believe. I mind my business." He wiped his neck with the paper towel. "I couldn't tell for sure who was driving. They went by fast. It's possible. Yeah. Maybe I saw the hair."

"Could you identify her in a lineup?" I said.

"I ain't the square badge schmuck you think I am," Stanky said.

I walked across the lot to the spot where Stanky said Marc Ross had parked. Where he probably died. The blacktop had been plowed, snow pushed into the river. I turned over the only trash can and pushed junk around with my toe. Newspapers, coffee cups, fast-food wrappers. No knives, no bloody rags, no bottles or cans. It was becoming impossible to find an unexplored trash can in this economy. Urban prospectors rushed to lay claim, sifting for deposit bottles as if they were gold nuggets.

Traffic roared on the Henry Hudson Parkway, up the

hill behind us. The hill was dense with bushes and trees that hid the parking lot from the highway. The ground and foliage were covered with new snow. I was thinking about the possibility of a setup. It would have been easy for a third party to cross the highway and come through the bushes. It's called the Murphy game: the woman lures the man to a spot where, instead of sex, he's ambushed and robbed. Men who do report it never mention the woman; it goes in the books as a straight robbery. But then I remembered Ross picked this location himself.

A dozen cars were scattered around the parking lot, windshields covered with a sooty layer of ice. I tried all the doors, just in case. I made notes of the license plates, but they were stored cars. Even the rich schemed to avoid paying indoor parking prices in Manhattan. Gregory sat in the T-bird, writing. When he rolled down the window I could feel the heater blasting on high.

"So what do we got so far?" he said. "What's the scenario?"

A Circle Line tour boat passed. Going south toward Forty-second Street, the end of the line, the hull battered and scraped. A few bundled-up tourists stood out on the deck.

"Ross leaves Millard's Red Garter," I said. "Walks straight to his garage. But he meets this woman. Somewhere close by. Front of Millard's . . . on the street . . . maybe in front of his building. In his mind she's not good enough to bring up to his apartment. But she's okay for a quickie in the car. He drives here, a nice secure location. He pulls his pants down."

"You thinking hooker yourself now?" he said.

"A street pross would never stray this far from the

stroll. I think it was a woman who knew where to find him. She drove him to the Bronx, to the precinct he worked in. Why did she do that?"

I checked my watch; it was time to go to the morgue.

"That one's easy," Gregory said. "She lives in the Bronx. You wouldn't want her riding the subway at that time of night."

4

Lieutenant Delia Flamer met us in front of the Office of the Chief Medical Examiner. The office was located above the morgue, at Bellevue Hospital. I was glad I hadn't eaten; I felt a tightness in my chest.

"We struck out on the hairs Crime Scene found," Delia said. "It was a wig. A cheap, generic nylon wig."

We went in through the lobby, which was decorated with framed photographs of New York City landmarks: Grand Central Station, the Woolworth Building, City Hall, others. Low tables in the seating area outside the identification room held religious pamphlets and boxes of tissues.

"Anybody check Ross's past cases?" Gregory said.

"He arrested three women in his career," Delia said. "One is dead. The precinct squad interviewed the other two. Both had solid alibis."

"What about his apartment?" Gregory said.

"Done it," Delia said. "We're going through his phone messages and address book."

The morgue smelled of ammonia and cigar smoke, both props to disguise the smell of death. I hated the morgue and I hated autopsies; I'd never kept that a secret. And the cops who joked about a greasy lunch while the cutter's saw crunched the cranial bone of someone's child were practicing a bravado so transparent that it rang with the brittle peal of a whistle in the dark. It was during autopsies that I reminded myself that detectives worked for God.

"We have an artist with the witnesses in the Five One Precinct," Delia said as we walked down the stairs to the autopsy room. "Hopefully we'll have a sketch for you tonight."

"What's tonight?" Gregory said.

"Tonight you two start talking to prostitutes."

"Pissing in the wind," Gregory said. "It ain't a hooker, guaranteed."

"The chief says look for a prostitute," Delia said, "I look for a prostitute. You want to argue with the chief, be my guest."

Delia Flamer, like Joe Gregory, was a cop's kid. She was the daughter of Junious Flamer, a first-grade detective killed in Brooklyn by a kid with a Walther PPK purchased that same day in Virginia. Her mother was Irene Rosenthal, a Supreme Court reporter and the last woman in New York still wearing white go-go boots. Delia's complexion was café au lait but her skin thin as gossamer.

"That's your job, to argue," Gregory said.

"I'm not taking grief from you, Gregory," she said. "You don't like it, pack your bags. Go back to the boondocks anytime you want."

Delia had always been assigned to headquarters units and thought most street cops too crude to work in One Police Plaza. But it went both ways. Cops from the outside boroughs considered the testosterone levels of headquarters cops as suspect. I'd been at parades and riots with cops from Brooklyn, Queens, or the Bronx who smirked at brother officers wearing letters, rather than numbers, on their collar, absolutely certain that underneath those too clean, too sharply creased blue uniforms, hid French-cut panties.

The hall outside the morgue room was littered with abandoned stainless-steel gurneys. An attendant in green scrubs wheeled an occupied gurney from the direction of the storage lockers.

"Is this the cop?" Delia asked the attendant, her voice echoing in the concrete hallway. When the attendant didn't answer, Gregory lifted the sheet and confirmed. We followed the gurney to the autopsy room.

Bluish green ceramic tile covered the walls of the autopsy room, which was furnished with eight stainless-steel tables. A perforated steel sheet covered each table. At the foot of each table was a sink with hot and cold faucets; at the other end, a grooved wooden pedestal, for the head. Above each table was a bank of fluorescent lights, a smaller high-intensity lamp on a flexible neck, and a microphone. A scale hung directly over the sink, the same kind of scale used for weighing broccoli at the A & P.

Gregory spread Polaroid pictures across the first table. A tiny young woman in a white lab coat scanned them quickly. Dr. Zita Linn, a Filipino, was the rising star of the ME staff. The body should have gone to the Bronx medical examiner, but the chief of detectives, citing the possibility that the crime originated in Manhattan, personally requested her services. Dr. Linn turned to the newly arrived body, whipped off the sheet, and picked up the arm of Marc Ross and dropped it.

"Rigor gone," the doctor said.

Gregory scooped up the pictures and shoved them in his jacket pocket. He was wearing one of his own shamrock lapel pins. He looked directly into my eyes and said, "You got paperwork to catch up on, don't you?"

Gregory and I had one of those division of labor agreements most partners had. I wrote all the reports, he handled all autopsies. Most of my investigations these past few years have been older, unsolved cases, the autopsy long over. I'd forgotten how bone deep was the chill this cold room imparted. I shrugged and murmured that I'd do it later.

"Dr. Linn presiding," Gregory said, gesturing. "Don't tell any Marcos jokes."

Gregory helped shift the body from the gurney to the table. I took a deep breath and bounced on the balls of my feet. The checkered floor was a soft, expensive tile. The fluorescent lights lurched on. I needed a drink of water.

On the other side of the table was the lab assistant, Freddie Sorrentino, a ghoulish little man whose office walls were papered with celebrity toe tags. He lined up jars and vials and probes. Freddie once told us that the city's crime problems would disappear if we'd pump poison gas in all the basketballs. I leaned over and whispered to Delia, "Watch Gregory work."

It began with the snap of surgical gloves. The ME and the assistant wore two pair, under another pair of steel mesh gloves. Dr. Linn pulled the microphone closer to her and for the record noted the time, date, and names and titles of those present. Then she read the name of the deceased and the fact he'd been identified by his uncle.

The body was still partially clothed, exactly as it was found, except the hands were covered with paper bags. Paper was used rather than plastic, because plastic accelerated putrefaction.

Dr. Linn and the assistant removed the clothes, starting with the shirt. She worked carefully where dried blood had caused it to stick to the skin. Gregory requested scrapings of hair, blood, or fecal matter, which he placed in white envelopes from a stack he'd prenumbered.

When all clothes were removed Dr. Linn laid them next to the body, as they were worn, and compared the clothes to the body, matching wounds to perforations. The assistant removed the paper bags from the hands. Freddie took scrapings from the nails, hoping for skin or blood raked from the killer's body in the struggle. Ross's left hand was covered with several short, straight slices.

"Defensive cuts are only on one hand," Gregory said. "Right arm had to be tied or pinned."

The assistant examined the pubic area, looking for signs of the stiff, starchy texture of semen on the skin. Then he swabbed the body for loose hairs, foreign matter, and blood, building a collection of samples in containers. Dr. Linn looked at Ross's hands, then at his throat.

"Murder weapon a curved knife, or similar instrument," she said.

"How big on the weapon?" Gregory said.

"Maybe three, four centimeters. Approximately."

The key word in weapon size was *approximate*. Because of the elasticity of the skin, the wound was usually smaller. Cutting wounds were normally longer than deep, and deepest where the weapon first touched the skin.

"Not a straight thrust?" Gregory asked.

"No," she said. "Knife apparently came at the left side of throat. Slashing motion."

"What's that string in his mouth?" Gregory said. "Freaking dental floss, or what?"

Dr. Linn's fingers worked the jawline. It seemed awkward with the gloves. Then she pulled out something small and white. At first I thought it was a tooth.

"A button," she said.

The button, and a small piece of thread, were covered with blood. The button was clearly white and more oblong than round. Gregory checked Ross's shirt.

"It didn't come off his shirt," Gregory said. "Came from the killer, guaranteed." He put it in a separate envelope, turned to us, and winked, as if the case were as good as solved.

When the external examination ended Dr. Linn summarized her findings on tape, and the easy part was over.

"It's dead in here," Joe Gregory used to say when we walked into the morgue. He was as comfortable leaning on an autopsy table as on a mahogany bar. I couldn't remember when the morgue started being a problem for me. Maybe the sight of too many children, so tiny on eight-foot slabs. After hundreds of autopsies, I no longer looked at their faces. I had enough sorrow floating in the fog of my memory.

Dr. Linn searched a metal tray for the right tool, among scalpels, ladles, forceps, serrated knives, syringes, scissors, hand saws, and Stryker saws. Gregory looked over his shoulder at me, but I was fine.

It's not death I'm afraid of, certainly not my own. Like most cops, I'm a fatalist. I believe that caution is wasted energy; fate and circumstance rule. The pain of death is only for the living, and that is to be feared. My discomfort in the morgue comes from a dream. In my dream I see a woman crying in the shadows of a room at dusk, and I feel her sobs booming in my chest. She reaches out for me, holding her baby. I don't look, I don't listen. I'm helpless, useless.

Dr. Linn began the coronal mastoid incision, slicing across the back of the head, from the top of one ear to the top of the other. Then she peeled the scalp forward until it covered the face. I wondered where the music was; usually we heard Mozart or Beethoven.

Using a small electric saw that resembled a dentist's hand piece, Dr. Linn cut a horseshoe-shaped gouge through and across the skull. The high whine of the saw compassionately drowned out the sound of quickened breathing. When the whine stopped, Dr. Linn pulled, and with a sucking noise the horseshoe came up, exposing the brain. Brain on the half shell, Gregory used to say. Then, using both hands, she pulled the brain itself from the skull cavity, examined it, and placed it on the scale. Freddie took tissue samples from the spongy, gray-brown mass.

Gregory pulled a cigarette from his pocket and offered it to Delia. Dr. Linn said, "No smoking, please."

Delia let the unlit cigarette dangle from her lips, honoring the doctor's wishes. But if ever there were a time for smoking, this was the time. Get out the big cigars, the fat smoky stinkers. Turn the room into an opium den, with billowing clouds. But Dr. Linn was young; to her this was merely science.

The doctor took a large scalpel and made the Y-cut,

the thoracoabdominal incision: a curving cut across the chest from armpit to armpit. Then a straight, deep cut down the middle to the pubic bone. She cut through muscle and cartilage, exposing the ribs and intestines. The lack of blood always surprised me. At this point I embraced the concept of the immortal soul far more willingly than in all the years of Catholic school.

Dr. Linn said, "Left common carotid artery severed."

"Cause of death?" Gregory said.

"Most likely," she said.

"How long did it take him to die?" Gregory said.

"Wound indicates quick, massive loss of blood to the brain. Maybe he passed out in ten, fifteen seconds. Death maybe a minute later."

Then she took the cutter, so strong for such a tiny woman, and I tried to breathe shallow at the snap and crunch of bone as she cut along the breastplate. She pulled away the breastplate, and the wet brown stink of rotted meat, of everything rancid, flooded my nose and rammed down the back of my throat. The dark pulpy organs, the garbage, all of it laid bare. Raw meat and shit. Dr. Linn held up the heart and lungs like Julia Child displaying a particularly wonderful veal roast. The flame from Gregory's Zippo shot into the air. He lit Delia's cigarette. She inhaled deeply.

"I said no smoking," Dr. Linn snapped.

"Fuck off," Gregory said.

When the autopsy ended Delia went to find a phone. Joe pulled me into the morgue room. A dozen naked bodies surrounded us. The complete indecency of death.

"What's Delia's problem?" he said. "She don't trust me, right?"

"She's just a strong personality, Joe. You'll get used to each other."

"Not for nothing, pally, I need her goodwill. I need her to cut me some slack while I'm running for office. Work your charm on her. You got that charm with women."

"I try to avoid telling them to fuck off."

"Yeah, well . . ." He looked around at the bodies on gurneys and said, "You did good in there today."

"Statuary," I said.

The key to the job was attitude, and around Gregory my attitude improved. I understood the bodies on the gurneys were not the people whose names were declared on toe tags fluttering in the breeze of the floor fan. Those people had gone to a better place. These cold gray figures were statues, forgotten in the basement of a cheap museum.

We stepped into the hallway and waited for Dr. Linn on molded plastic chairs. Smoke hung above our heads. Delia was deep in thought. I remembered what an old cop told me on my first night on the street: Never eat a full meal before going out on patrol. In those days a stomach wound led to peritonitis and certain death. Medical science had made strides; society had not.

"I gotta get in shape," Gregory said. "Start running, hit the weights. You saw Ross in there. No muscle tone for such a young guy. They do my autopsy, I don't want my thighs shaking like that. Like freaking Jell-O."

Dr. Linn came out grim faced and waited for our questions.

"Any evidence of sexual contact?" I asked.

"None that I could detect," she said. "Perhaps the lab will find something different."

"Is it likely one person did this?" I said. "Considering the small number of defensive cuts, and only on one hand?"

"Good point, pally," Gregory said. "I was thinking the same thing. Why didn't he fight her? He's a man, she's a woman. Say she's quick and stabs him once, twice. Okay, I can buy that. But your adrenaline's pumping, your heart's going boom ba boom. I'd react out of fear if nothing else. This guy lets her cut him again and again? I'd be all over her, no way she could hold me down. It's life or death, and men have the power advantage. About the only one left, but we still have it."

In a blur of movement so quick it seemed like a movie film that had skipped a frame, the tiny Filipino snatched Gregory by the hair, snapped his head back, and pinned him against the wall, her knee digging into his right arm. I was amazed that blood was not pouring from the scalpel pressed against his neck.

"I'm sold," I said.

5

After the autopsy Delia went back to One Police Plaza. Gregory and I agreed to meet later that night to start riding hooker patrol on the West Side. I drove home to Yonkers, to our fifty-year-old Cape Cod, the red shingles fading to pink. My wife, Leigh, was still at work. She was a secretary at Sacred Heart High School, three blocks away.

I tried to get some sleep, but I'd lost the trick to sleeping days when I stopped working shifts. I jumped up when I heard the voices of my neighbor's twins playing in the yard.

As usual, I wound up at the computer. We had two rooms with slanted ceilings on the second floor: one room was our bedroom, the other we used as a den and computer room. I began entering the facts of the Ross case on the PC. I always kept my own notes separate from official records. My official reports were always brief. Any half-assed defense lawyer could subpoena all the police reports on a particular incident, spread them on his office floor, and find discrepancies: time, weather, clothing, whatever.

On a drop leaf table in the other corner were dozens of family pictures. Leigh had started running lines of family pictures up the slanted ceiling. Old black-and-whites of our parents: hers chubby and smiling in South Carolina; mine thinner, frowning in New York. My dad was the only one of the four still alive, living for golf in Florida.

Most of the pictures were of our two kids: Anthony, a part-time actor and full-time security guard in Los Angeles; and Margaret, an x-ray technician in the state of Delaware. And about to be married for the third time before her thirtieth birthday.

I typed in what little biographical information I had on Officer Ross. According to his precinct "ten" card, he was single, twenty-six years old, and came to the Five One directly from the Police Academy three years ago. No complaints, no injuries. He was involved in one shooting incident, last summer. It was ruled a justified shooting. I made a note to pull that information from Personnel in One Police Plaza.

Only one gun was listed, one of the new semiautomatics the department recently approved after a decade of study. The cops had three choices: the Sig Sauer, Smith & Wesson, or the Glock 19. Ross had carried the Glock. Now someone else did.

I'd never fired any of the new guns. I knew the nine-millimeter weapons held fifteen shots compared to the service revolver's six and were supposed to be slightly quicker and more accurate, considerably lighter, and easier to reload. Both Gregory and I still carried the old Smith & Wesson Chief's Special. Only five shots, but it could accumulate years of lint, dust, ashes, and crumbs and it would still fire.

When I heard Leigh come through the door downstairs, I entered a quick description of the button we'd found in Ross's mouth. Chances of tracing the button were nonexistent, so there was no doubt in my mind that Gregory would leap all over it. Then I turned off the computer.

From our west window I watched the youngest of the Kelly brood playing in their yard next door. The twin girls, always dressed alike in hooded parkas, walked dolls along the fence, going through the motions of family life in high, sweet voices. The boys chased each other with guns, making zapping noises. I was at an age when watching children made me melancholy; something about missed opportunities. Leigh walked into the room barefoot, unbuttoning her blouse.

"How late will you be tonight?" she asked.

I hadn't told Leigh I'd be going back to work, but I wasn't surprised she knew. Women were far more observant than men. And cops' wives acquired a special radar. She laid the blouse across the sofa arm.

"Very late," I said. "Three or four, at the earliest. Depending on how far we get. We're canvassing prostitutes. A lot of girls out there."

She let her skirt drop to the floor, then stretched slowly to touch her toes. The minute Leigh got home she stripped, as if her clothes were burning. Then she'd put on jeans and a T-shirt, no shoes. I figured it was the strength of her Southern roots. I told her we were lucky she didn't have a long commute. She placed her palms flat on the floor and stretched farther.

"Caprice Antonucci wants to talk to you," she said.

"What is a Caprice Antonucci?"

"She went to Sacred Heart," Leigh said. "She's a cop now. She called me today, said she saw you at the scene of the homicide."

"Oh, Antonucci, right," I said. "I wondered why she called me 'Mr. Ryan.' "

"Her father is Jimmy Antonucci, retired from General Motors in Tarrytown."

"The guy that named all his kids after Chevy products."

"Just the four girls. Corvette, Corvair, Chevelle. This is Caprice."

"Tell her to call me," I said.

"I did," Leigh said. "Is there a problem with this case? How come it wasn't in the paper?"

"Ross was in his own car, pants down. The squad thinks the killer is a hooker. But Joe and I aren't sure."

"I wouldn't rule it out."

I'd always discussed cases with Leigh. I knew what other detectives would say, but Leigh was always interested. Sometimes she saw things.

"Why wouldn't you rule it out?" I said as I watched her lie on the floor, across an oval braided rug her mother had made. "Because he's a cop, right?"

"Give me a break, Anthony."

I knew what she meant. It wouldn't be the first time a cop was mixed up with a prostitute. In the middle of the long night hookers and junkies were often a cop's only human contact.

"We think it's someone Ross knew," I said. "Maybe a girlfriend."

"Could be both," she said.

She did twelve quick situps, short stomach crunches, bringing her knees to her chest. Leigh, a woman who'd never broken a sweat in her first forty years, became an athlete after her hair turned gray.

"How's Gregory doing?" she said, breathing softly.

"You'd be surprised."

It was the first time she'd asked since we started working together again. My partnership with Gregory had always been a sore spot in our thirty-year marriage. She had a point. My off-and-on partnership with Joe correlated perfectly with my drinking years. I hadn't had a drink since we'd last worked together.

I said, "I'm not going to start drinking again if that's what you're worried about."

"I'm not worried about that."

Leigh picked up her clothes and walked to the mirror. I watched her suck in her stomach.

"Triceps look great," I said.

"That's not what you're looking at."

She was right. Nobody looked better in their underwear than Leigh Ryan. I kidded her about her exercise program, but she did look better than ever, and her diabetes, until just recently, was well under control. She even had me working out. Running had replaced drinking for me. I liked the solitude of it and the sense of well-being it brought. For cops, living well was not possible, so well-being was the only revenge.

"What I am worried about," she said, "is Margaret's wedding. Every time you and Gregory get involved in a case, everything else takes a backseat. I'm worried something is going to come up at the last minute and I'm going to hear your speech about how the j-o-b comes first."

"It's a month away. We'll finish this case long before that."

"I've heard *that* before."

"Nothing's going to come up," I said.

"Yeah, well . . . I know you don't like Cliff. But Margaret does. So give the guy a chance, why don't you?"

"He's a forty-two-year-old surfer."

"He has a store, Anthony. He sells and rents surfboards, bikes, skates, stuff like that."

"I never said I didn't like Cliff."

"You don't have to. I can see it. You're treating him like you did her first husband, and you hated him."

"Not as much as the second."

"You never liked any guy she went with."

"I just don't get what Cliff is all about."

"Well, try, Anthony. And quit worrying so much about every single thing. She's a big girl now."

"So are you," I said, and grabbed her as she passed by.

I held her closely, staring at her face through my reading glasses. But she moved away quickly, almost knocking over my chair. Leigh hated me to do that, said it magnified the lines on her face. But the lines and gray hair had not diminished her beauty, but given it a softer, vulnerable glow. I watched her disappear across the hall to our bedroom, reaching back to unsnap her bra.

She wouldn't admit it, but she worried about Gregory, worried about my drinking again. There was nothing to be concerned about. I didn't miss drinking. Not that much. Just sometimes, like when I go into any bar in New York with the Christmas lights up and it's packed with people laughing. Or I get a whiff of gin and tonic as Gregory brings it to his lips. Or that beer commercial on TV, ice running down a wet glass bottle, the cold golden brew splashing into a frosted glass, the head so pure and white, like a fine, smooth cream. Then I can feel that ache in the back of my throat. But I can handle it.

Leigh was great for saying she didn't worry. But our daughter was living in Delaware and getting ready to marry a forty-two-year-old surfer. Don't worry, Leigh says. But a cop's paranoia doesn't stay in his locker when he goes off duty. People just don't see what a cop sees. The world is crazy out there. Besides, you cannot overprotect someone you love. Outside, in the last cold sunlight of the day, Kelly's kids ran giggly circles around a melting snow fort.

6

Ninety minutes later, at One Police Plaza, I picked up a stack of artist sketches on Delia's desk. Our suspect had a big gypsy hairdo, small symmetrical features, thin lips. But the eyes were cartoonlike hate-filled ovals, too heavily inked. I shoved the sketches in my briefcase and took the back stairway down to the twelfth floor, the Organized Crime Control Bureau's Intelligence Unit.

Headquarters was quiet; the building empties out after six P.M. Night men, carrying coffeepots or plastic bowels, padded around like ghosts in soft shoes. I'd worked in the Intelligence Unit before, so I easily found the most recent reports on street prostitution and copied them.

I was ready to leave when I noticed a report sitting in an *In* basket. The report was in a common format called an "unusual." The text, spare, in PD fashion, didn't deviate from the guideline NEOTWY, the last letters of when, where, who, what, how, why.

From: Commanding Officer Five One Squad
To: Chief of Organized Crime Control
Subject: Double Homicide
At approximately 0600 hours on April 11, 1994, near the northwest gate of Crotona Park, the bodies of Junior Nieves M/W/22, and Jesus Colon M/W/19, were found beaten to death, apparently with a blunt instrument, possibly a piece of steel rebar. Both individuals were known to be part of the Tito Santana drug operation.

It was signed by Sergeant Neville Drumm.

The murders occurred just blocks from the spot where we found the body of Marc Ross, and only a few hours afterward. Not that the murder of drug dealers, even in multiples, was strange, but the weapon was unique. Rebar was a thin steel rod used to reinforce concrete in construction jobs. It had a raised braid running around it, sure to leave its imprint on a skull. In the days of Uzis and .50-caliber Desert Eagles, it was an unstylish instrument for murder.

I made a copy for myself, then I took the elevator to street level and walked out the back door, across to Brady's bar. A pink-and-blue neon sign shimmered behind frosted windows. A false frost. Snow spray left over from the Christmas decor.

A group of undercover narcotics cops sat in the shadows at a side table, watching me come through the door. Brady's bar was still the primary meeting place for cops from headquarters who preferred to exchange information face-to-face and sotto voce. But the place showed signs of change. It wasn't the Brady's of years ago. Jammed with guys in raincoats, talking out of the sides of their mouth, radar primed for bullshit. Those were guys who kept secrets in their hats, nothing on paper. No E-mail. No messages left at the beep, please. Much of that old crowd was retired, dead, or in Twelve Step programs. Brady's smelled faintly of roach spray. Sinatra sang "Only the Lonely."

Joe Gregory occupied his usual corner. A small herd of dinosaurs from Safe and Loft, and Missing Persons, hovered around Joe, but everybody stepped aside to let me stand next to my partner. On the bar was a mail-order knife catalog and a black-and-white close-up photo of the bloody throat of Marc Ross.

"Box cutter," Gregory said. He threw a small curved knife on the bar. "Bought it on Canal Street. My money says this is what she used. Honed down like a scalpel."

"That narrows it down," I said.

Box cutters could be found on the belt of every deliveryman and truck driver in New York, as well as in the back pockets of half the school kids. Looking at the wounds of Marc Ross, and assuming it could be honed to a much sharper edge, I thought it was possible. But in cutting wounds it is extremely difficult to be sure.

"Drop it off with Dr. Linn," I said. "Let her measure it against the wounds."

The *MacNeil/Lehrer NewsHour* was on the set above the bar, the sound turned down in deference to Sinatra. Jimmy, the barman, was working on the cash register, *The New York Times*, folded into quarters, near his elbow.

"Asshole broke the Jewish piano," Gregory said, pointing to the barman who was punching keys on the old NCR. "Trying to fix it with a butter knife. Hey, Mister Fix-It, get my partner a drink here."

Jimmy banged a club soda down in front of me, then free-poured Tanqueray over the sad lime floating in

Gregory's glass. Billy Joel sang about a "New York state of mind." Joel, Springsteen, and Lou Reed were nudging Sinatra off the jukebox. I reminded Gregory that we had to hit the street. He called for a toast to the freaking genius who invented police work. Then we left to do some of it.

We drove uptown in the T-bird. I'd signed out a portable radio, something we could carry into the street. Neither of us wore vests; for some reason we never remembered. Joe Gregory's driving method was curse and cut. He drove combatively, at war every time he got behind the wheel. Gas, horn, brake. Gas, horn, brake. The perpetual backup at the Holland Tunnel entrance annoyed him perpetually. Nights when the factories were closed he jumped the curb cut near Canal and Hudson and drove the sidewalk the length of the block, cutting back into traffic at the light.

"We should give that freaking tunnel back to Holland," he said.

"It's named after the architect, not the country."

"I knew that," he said. "Read the pross reports, tell me something I don't know."

In the city of New York there are five to eight thousand streetwalking prostitutes, most of whom work two dozen strolls. A stroll is a set of blocks where hookers strut their stuff. Strolls aren't secret places, but street theaters, where the actors pound concrete rather than board. But marquees are unnecessary because everyone, from stock brokers to street peddlers, knows where to find the show. So despite years of wholesale arrests, the strolls remain, landmarks to the lullaby of illicit sex.

We started at the stroll on West Fifty-eighth Street, near Fifth. It was the path Marc Ross would most likely have taken on his way home from Millard's Red Garter. The girls working Fifty-eighth considered themselves the high society of streetwalkers. Their john pool consisted of businessmen and tourists who wandered too far from the awning of the Plaza. Just a handful of prostitutes worked the area, and they were unusually low-key for street girls. Almost all worked for active pimps, always lurking around the perimeter.

Gregory and I parked half a block east of a Madonna-wannabe blonde in red "fuck me" shoes and belted red leather coat. She was patrolling the entrance to the Park Savoy. We waited in the car until she ambushed an elderly man in a homburg. I got out and started walking toward them.

The night air was crisp and cool, positively healthy after sitting next to the chain-smoking Gregory. As I approached "Madonna," she'd pinned her quarry against a building. People stalled in traffic watched the tableau unfold as she unbelted her leather coat and flashed her Frederick's of Hollywood working outfit: a patch of white lace and blue silk. Homburg surrendered without a struggle. She wrapped her arm around the old gent and muscled him toward Sixth Avenue, moving surprisingly well in stiletto heels.

"Police," I said. The old man stumbled backward, his face a shiny gray. "Go back to your room, sir," I said, and he waved and shuffled away.

"I don't believe this fucking bullshit," said "Madonna," and yanked her arm out of my grip. She thought she knew the story. "Fifteen fucking times this year I been locked up. Is there no end to this madness?"

I signaled for Gregory. Up close I could see the amount of makeup it took to make her marketable. She had dark, blood-lined eyes, rheumy and running in the night air. She had a twitch when she talked, kept flipping her head back, facial muscles in turmoil. More than a nervous twitch. More like the loss of muscle control common to crack addicts.

"This could go either way," I said. "Depending on you."

"Oh, right, I get it. I'm out here with 'patsy' stamped on my fucking head, right? You fucks must have my name on the shithouse wall in Midtown North."

Gregory cruised up, pushing open the passenger door.

"What I gotta do?" she said. "Blow every guy on the fucking force before you leave me alone?"

I knew that no cop in his right mind would touch her. She was trying to scam me with a psycho routine. If I thought she was going to be an Internal Affairs problem, I'd just walk away, grab an easier collar down the street.

"We just want you to identify somebody," I said.

"Somebody in your pants, right?"

"Get in the car," I said.

"I ain't doing two guys," she said. "Jesus Christ, what a city."

I pulled the bucket seat forward, wondering why we'd brought a two-door car, and shoved her from behind. She fell hard, down onto the cramped backseat of the T-bird. A stocky Latino with a Fu Manchu was coming fast toward the car, as though he had business with us. Gregory held his shield up to the window.

"Let's get out of here," I said as I wedged onto the backseat next to her.

"Rico," she yelled. "Rico!"

"What's the trouble, Officers?" Rico, with the Fu Manchu, said. "That's my fiancée you have in your car."

"We'll have her back in time for the wedding," Gregory said.

"I got the license number, baby," Rico yelled. "Don't worry, baby."

Gregory backed out onto Sixth Avenue, then straight ahead through the light on Central Park South. "Madonna" slammed her head against the window, then began to cry. She smelled of a combination of tobacco and perfume, and her ass was cold against my leg. Gregory drove past a line of horse-drawn buggies, then squeezed around the barriers blocking traffic from entering Central Park. Mounds of snow stood like guard towers at the entrance.

During the evening hours Central Park is closed to traffic, and despite patchy snow, the road was clear and crowded with people working out. We weaved around bikers, rollerbladers, joggers. The scene was brighter for neon swooshes of nylon and spandex. "Madonna" wailed, pushing her face into the crack between the seat and door. Gregory and I stared straight ahead as the screaming grew louder.

"Good idea, coming into the park," I said.

"I'm supposed to know you'd pick the craziest hooker in New York?"

Gregory drove uptown and pulled under the trees in the police parking lot across from the Two Two Precinct, which only rookies called the Central Park Precinct. "Madonna" looked up and saw the tree branches above her and let out a howl.

"We have to lock her up," I said. "She isn't giving us any choice."

"You want the collar?" Gregory said.

"Not me. You're the collar man."

"No can do," he said. "Got a racket to attend. Two, to be exact."

"Two parties, tonight?"

"And many more to come. Plus, the twenty-seventh, I got to be at the midtown Mounted stables in the morning. Eleventh and Forty-second, ten A.M. sharp."

A few joggers, running around the reservoir above us, gave quick glances down, trying to figure out where the screaming came from. But joggers need to keep moving. And nobody looked out from the precinct. "Madonna" started hyperventilating.

"What's going on at Mounted?" I said.

"Blessing of the horses. Guy I know told me they got some new Tennessee walkers. They're having a ceremony. Priest blesses the horses before they take the street."

I wondered if it was the same friend in Mounted who once put in an emergency call to Gregory. The cop's horse died in the freight elevator of a sofa factory in midtown. The cop had been sneaking a break, taking the horse to the roof. Mounted cops hid horses in strange, inventive places. It took a forklift and twenty cops to get the horse back out to the street, so the Mounted cop could properly report his demise.

"Blessing the horses," I said. "Nobody blessed us."

"Horses got no choice," Gregory said. "Listen, I got a favor to ask, pally. I need you to cover for me for a couple of hours. Eight-thirty till . . . say, eleven."

"So you can party."

"Campaign," he said. "Warrants got a bash at Rosie's South. The Two Oh Precinct has something going at a gin mill on Columbus and Nine Three Street. I got to show my face, press the flesh. Election's going to be here before you know it."

"You plan to attend every cop party in the city?"

"Drinking's good for the heart. It's a documented fact."

"How about the liver?"

"I'm drinking smart," he said. "Tall glass, watch my time. Drink stays in my hand thirty minutes, minimum."

"Madonna" stopped crying. She stared at the back of Gregory's head. I took advantage and handed her the sketch.

"Ever see this girl before?" I said. "Maybe on Sunday night. It's important."

Black, wet mascara tracks ran like plow lines down her face. She looked at the sketch, sniffling, then back up at me.

"What's she done?" she said.

"Murder," I said.

"She don't work Fifty-eighth. I know everybody."

I showed her the picture of Marc Ross's BMW.

"Now you're asking cars," she said. "I see a lot of cars. Ain't one of my dates, that's def. That dirty piece of shit. You sure we're talking about Fifty-eighth Street?"

"That car's not a piece of shit," Gregory said. "Just got a little fingerprint dust on it."

"You can go back to Rico now," I said.

"You shitting me?" she said.

I gave her a copy of the sketch and my card and told her that we needed her help. Until we found this killer we'd have to crack down on the strolls.

"I find her, I get what?" she said.

"You find her," Gregory said, "we'll give you a free year on the street."

"You can't fucking do that," she said.

"She killed a cop," Gregory said. "You help us nail her, you're eligible for a year's special consideration."

"I won't need a year," she said. "Rico ain't going to let me hook much longer. Only long enough to get money to open a bar in PR. I'll catch this bitch for you. I'll do it. You watch me. You just keep your fucking end."

"Madonna" fixed her makeup in the dark as we drove back to Sixth Avenue. She and Gregory talked about the art of working a room. Stars came out over Central Park.

7

Three nights later a hard rain washed away all but the most stubborn snow. We'd retraced Marc Ross's path. We'd covered all the strolls, uptown and downtown. Neither of us wanted to talk to another hooker. Only a few hard-core girls were out in the downpour, most of whom we'd already talked to.

"Cocktail time," Gregory said, as he followed a Greyhound bus from Washington, D.C., into the Port Authority Bus Terminal. "First I got to find a phone."

I inhaled bus fumes while Joe made his call. I felt tired and drained of blood. These all-nighters had reminded me that police work was a young man's job. Gregory was back in a few minutes.

"Drumm is working the night tour," Gregory said. "What say we ride to the Bronx and find out what the freak is going on? Her Highness Miss Delia ain't going to tell us diddly squat."

"What about cocktail time?"

"They got cocktails in the Bronx," he said.

Thirty minutes later Gregory and I were in Sergeant Drumm's office in the Five One Precinct. The office smelled of pipe tobacco and bay rum. Photos of the bloodied bodies of two drug dealers, beaten to death with a piece of rebar, were laid out on Drumm's desk. But Drumm wasn't there.

"Hey, guy," the Ivy League detective said. "We're covering the whole division tonight, the sarge could be anywhere."

"Call him," Gregory said. "I don't care if he's at some bimbo's house, or where he is. Call him, tell him I want to ask him one thing."

I read the Marc Ross file while they argued. Drumm's reports were a compilation of witness statements and a rehash of technical info. Dr. Linn said that the vicious slash across Ross's throat was probably the first wound and certainly caused his death. There was no sign of sexual activity on the body, and the only toxicological test to come back said that Ross's blood alcohol was .04. Far from being drunk. The button was mentioned only in reference to the blood and saliva scraped from it. Blood type belonged to Marc Ross.

On the wall behind Drumm's desk was a framed painting of the Buffalo Soldiers. In the trash was a yellow Mallomars wrapper. I duplicated what I needed from the Ross file and put everything back.

"C'mon, guy," Ivy League said, offering a conspiratorial smile. "Sarge will be back. What's so important it can't wait?"

"Screw it then," Gregory said.

It was just two A.M. when we got back in the T-bird.

"I asked that asshole when he's going to trace the

button," Gregory said. "He tells me, 'Don't worry, I'll do it.' Do shit, that's what he's going to do."

"So you took the button."

"Goddamn right I did."

"What about the chain of evidence?" I said.

"Chains can be fixed," he said. "I'll call Drumm later. C'mon, I'll buy you a club soda at your old precinct haunt. Take you for a walk down memory lane."

I wasn't sure that was a walk I wanted to take.

The Sawmill bar on Tremont Avenue was the watering hole for the Five One Precinct cops. It was a narrow, grimy place, the bar on the left, a row of coat hooks on the right. Three guys sat on the stools in the curve of the bar near the window, playing liar's poker. They gave us the glare, the ghetto cop's message: "Fuck you, suits; you don't belong here." A handful of cop groupies clustered at the open end near the back room. One of them was the pale blonde who was with Sonny Guidice at the scene of the Ross murder.

Gregory ordered a club soda for me and a Jameson and water for himself. He was drinking Irish whiskey, at least until after the election. I gazed around the bar. I hadn't been in the place in almost twenty years. It smelled as if someone had been cooking hard-boiled eggs and seemed smaller and dirtier than I remembered. The cracked two-tone tile floor was so gritty that you couldn't tell one color from the other.

I walked past the groupies into the empty back room. Four scarred red vinyl booths, two on each side of the pool table. It was a room frozen in time. I slid into the booth next to the microwave oven, which was above a small freezer that contained a handful of microwave burritos so the place could qualify as a food service and pay lower bar license fees. Rest rooms were still marked: men, women. No symbols, pictures, or cute foreign words.

It must have been someone else who spent so many drunken nights in here. Not me. I couldn't have been that stupid. But I understood the pull of bars like this at midnight when you take off your uniform, but your adrenaline is still sky high after the gun runs and the fights. No way can you go home to a quiet, dark house. First you have to wind down, relive the night blow by blow with someone who was there, someone who understands. So you stop for one drink. Just one. Next thing you know the clock has taken one of those big early morning leaps and it's four A.M. and you're telling the same story again, and you know you'll be back tomorrow.

Big Sonny Guidice blasted through the door, followed by half a dozen young cops. Sonny wore a faded U.S. Marines field jacket; the young cops, leather. He led them straight into the back room.

"Fucking Ryan," Sonny said. "Slumming, or what?"

Sonny took the seat opposite me. He set a pack of Marlboro and his red butane lighter on the table against the napkin holder. A young cop shoved in next to me. He was a big weight-lifter type, wearing a thick leather motorcycle jacket, but I could still feel the butt of his gun against my ribs.

"Paul Verdi," the weight lifter said, extending his hand. "I saw you at the scene. Down there. . . ." He pointed east. I knew he meant the scene where they'd found Marc Ross.

"Anthony Ryan," I said, shaking his hand. It surprised me that he didn't try to turn my hand to dust. He began combing his hair with a rattail comb. The pale blond groupie set a pitcher of beer on our table. Sonny grabbed her ass. Verdi patted her playfully.

"It was a shame about Ross," I said.

"Sad, man. Sad," Verdi said. "Worked with him three years. Regular guy. I forgot he was a Jew. Sent a mass card."

Verdi held his palms upward and shrugged. I thought they were both handling their partner's death a bit too well. Sonny clicked on the booth light, examining a three-color NYPD commendation ribbon. The lamp-shade had never been changed: shamrocks on a once white background, turned orange yellow from years of nicotine.

"I hope you guys are being careful," I said. "We still have a cop killer out there."

"We got nothing to worry about," Sonny said, handing the ribbon to Verdi. "We watch each other's backs. This kid"—he pointed to Verdi— "let me tell you, Ryan, this kid Paulie Verdi got five years on the job, got thirty-seven excellents and now a commendation. Best cop I ever worked with."

Verdi shrugged modestly, finished combing his hair, patted it into place, and slid the comb into a pocket in his leather jacket and pulled the zipper closed.

"How many medals you got, Ryan?" Sonny said.

"Not that many," I said.

"That's 'cause you're down in that retirement home too long," Sonny said. "The fucking puzzle palace on the East River. Home of faggots and fuzzy thinkers."

Guidice was a few years younger than I. Except for some gray hair and major bags under his eyes, the years hadn't been unkind to him. I'd always noticed that the guys who kept working looked better than those who retired completely. Guidice was slightly over six feet, with a heavily developed upper body. He had wavy, salt-and-pepper hair, dry lips, and dark circles under his eyes. He stared at my hairline.

"Your fucking hair is getting thin, Ryan," he said. "Getting old looking. Better start whipping that hair forward, cover that high forehead."

"You haven't changed," I said.

Joe Gregory leaned against the ice machine. Above his head was a Schlitz beer clock in the shape of a football helmet.

"So tell me," Sonny said. "The geniuses from downtown ever going to get off their dead asses on this one?"

Verdi pushed a beer glass in front of me, but I waved it away. The Stones sang "Satisfaction."

"They've got us chasing hookers," I said.

"Empty fucking suits," Sonny said. "If One Police Plaza blew up tomorrow, we'd never miss it. I'm telling you."

The pale blonde dropped quarters in the pool table slot, then found the rack and began to pull the balls into the triangle. She had short stubby hair, almost a crew cut, her face so pale that it was almost colorless. And those startling white eyebrows.

"What do you guys think?" I said. "Are we wasting our time on the strolls? Was Marc Ross the type who picked up hookers?"

"The type?" Sonny said. "What type we talking about, male type? Yeah, he liked broads. I'm sure they all weren't Holy Rollers. You got a problem with that?"

"Just trying to make sure we're on the right track," I said.

"The guy wasn't married," Sonny said. "So what,

then? What's the problem? Somebody going to give him a complaint? Take him to the Trial Room in the sky?"

"I'm not judging him," I said.

"I fucking hope not," he said. "I remember you, you were a fucking wildman. I saw you many a night at the sign-out book. So fucking blasted you could hardly write your name."

Gregory finished his drink and sat the glass on top of the fire extinguisher. He was watching the girls play pool. They both wore skintight jeans and tight fuzzy sweaters. Dust from the table rose up into the overhanging light.

"How's your wife doing, Sonny?" I said.

"Wifey ain't around no more."

"Divorced?"

"Better than that," he said. "Dead. DOA. Flipped over on the Palisades Parkway. Six, seven years ago."

"Sorry," I said. "I didn't know."

"I had insurance," he said. "Tell you this, though. I'll never *get* married again. I'd rather go steady with my fist. But I stumble across a broad here, a broad there."

"Just one or two, right, Sonny?" Verdi said.

The groupies were leaning way over the pool table. Gregory drained his drink again, ice cubes falling against his lips, then he leaned back.

"Still living in Pearl River?" I asked.

"Sold the house, lawn mower, all that shit," he said. "I always hated the house thing, the commute and all. Back living in Stuyvesant Town."

Except for Sonny, Gregory and I were by far the oldest people in the place, the only ones in suits, and as out of place as Bogart and Cagney, badly colorized, in a full dance production cola commercial.

"What do you guys think happened to Marc Ross that night?" I said.

"You're the fucking detective," Sonny said. "You're the first-grader. Making the big bucks."

"You a first-grader?" Verdi said. "No shit? What do you make, lieutenant's money, right? Handle any famous cases? How about Son of Sam, you work that case?"

"Don't be impressed, Paulie," Sonny said. "He never kicked a perp's ass in his life. He's a paper cop. That's his claim to fame. Always writing, always making notes. Ain't that right, Ryan?"

"That's why I'm interested in what you guys think. You know these streets better than I do. You knew Ross."

"You believe this jerk-off?" Sonny said, waggling his thumb in my direction. "Old-time detectives, the *real* detectives, wouldn't let the sun set before they'd be dragging a cop-killing bastard through the streets."

"Check out Tito Santana," Paul Verdi said. "That's who I think. He's a crazy bastard. Hates our guts."

"Who's Santana?" I said. "Drug dealer?"

"Santana's a drug *lord*," Verdi said. "He's a lot bigger than a dealer."

Sonny reached over and slapped Verdi on the side of the head. "What did I teach you?" he said. "Never talk to anyone from downtown. Not even this prick."

"What about Santana?" I said.

"It's bullshit," Sonny said. "I'll tell you exactly why that's bullshit. Tito Santana don't have the balls, number one. And two, he knows I'd come down on him like a fucking ton of bricks."

"Maybe it's worth checking out?" I said.

"Fucking Ryan," Sonny said. He turned toward Paul Verdi again. Verdi was combing his hair. "Remember that time I shot that kid? I told you about it, Paulie. Well, this here is the guy that was with me: Ryan. Stand-up guy. The Rock of Gibraltar in front of the grand jury. This guy used to piss ice water. Downtown ruined him."

Sonny shoved his hand in the blonde's crotch as she leaned over the pool table. She squealed, but I knew she wondered what took him so long.

"Let me out, Paulie," I said. "We have to get going." I stood up, and Gregory tossed me my coat.

Sonny stood up behind me and jammed up against the blond girl's ass, humping her against the pool table. Her stick skittered across the apron, knocking the cue ball off the table. It banged on the floor and rolled to Gregory's feet. The cops behind us roared.

Gregory picked the cue ball off the floor, put it on the green felt, and spun it like a top. Sonny held the blonde from behind, his hands around her breasts.

"What the fuck you looking at?" the blonde said to Gregory.

"Hardly anything," Gregory said.

"Fuck you," she said.

"Not even with a borrowed dick," Gregory said.

"Fucking perv," she said, her eyebrows of snow converging. "Fucking old enough to be my father."

"Could be," Gregory said. "What's your mother's name?"

Sonny reached over the blonde. He held his finger up in my face. I remembered he liked to jab his finger.

"Know something, Ryan?" he said. "You're a phony fuck. Come in here thinking you're better than everybody else. Drinking club soda, big fucking deal first-grader. Somebody needs to knock you right on your ass."

"Let me know when you feel up to it," I said.

Sonny shoved the blonde and lunged toward me, but Gregory stepped in between. The three of us jammed into the little space next to the pool table, Gregory's big body blocking everything. I stood there feeling oddly calm, a sense of relief, because I wanted this. I wanted Sonny to hate me.

"Let's not be stupid," Gregory said. "We're all on the same job."

"No, we ain't," Sonny said, his eyes blinking rapidly. "You know where to find me, Ryan. Anytime. Anytime."

Gregory and I walked out onto Tremont Avenue. The air of the Bronx seemed cleaner than before. Half a block west of the Sawmill the Third Avenue el once loomed above the streets. Now it was gone.

"Who's that guy that says you can't go home again?" Gregory said.

"Thomas Wolfe," I said.

"I think he was talking about this place."

We tend to remember our pasts as full of days and nights when we were kings of the mountain. Kids today can't touch our glory days, we tell ourselves. But I still remembered nights in this bar I'd rather forget. I remembered a cop named Dinny Prendergast who sat in the window of the Sawmill and went out into the street to piss rather than make the long walk to the back room. Sometimes, in the early hours of the morning, Dinny would be outside and we'd hear the train screeching through the station. Sometimes we'd get out in time to stop Dinny, who'd be standing on this very spot, pissing against a car and firing shots at the moving train.

I know guys who want to label today's young cops as different, crazier than we were. They want to say that the quality has gone downhill. But I knew better. I kept remembering guys like Dinny, and Sonny Guidice, and me.

8

"What are you doing here?" Delia said. It was midmorning; Gregory and I had worked through the night. I was at my desk, on the phone with the DEA, trying to get information on Tito Santana. I'd expected Delia to be at the Police Women's Endowment Association breakfast meeting.

"We were out all night," I said, putting down the phone.

"Where's your partner?" she said.

"In the garment district."

"Buying socks?"

"Trying to identify the button we found in the cop's mouth."

"That evidence is under the control of the Five One squad."

"Drumm knows what we're doing," I said.

"Really. Then maybe Sergeant Drumm can tell me what you're doing right now."

Delia sat on Gregory's desk, one foot on the floor. Around the office she wore flat black leather shoes, for comfort and perhaps to appear not quite so tall. She had a childhood scar, shaped like a question mark, on her left knee.

"I'm looking through a file on a drug dealer named Tito Santana," I said.

"Who made this decision, Anthony? Do this, rather than work the prostitutes?"

"Come on, Delia. That was a long shot, at best."

Her perfume was a spicy, sweet smell, an exotic sensation in a room dominated by the body odor of middle-aged men. She picked at nonexistent lint on her skirt, then handed me an equipment voucher.

"Sign this," she said.

"What for?"

"It's a beeper. I want you to carry it."

I signed the form, handed it back to her, then tossed the beeper in my top drawer.

"I realize we didn't have much time to discuss this case," she said.

"My mistake, Lieutenant. I know you must be getting pressure from the chief."

"I'll handle that pressure. I have no problem with that. I just hope you're not going to revert back to past habits, now that you're hooked up with the Great Gregory again."

"What past habits are we talking about?"

"I wasn't born on the elevator this morning, Anthony; I've got fifteen years in this building. I've heard stories about your old crew, and I bet most of them are uncomfortably close to the truth. I remember when Monsignor Dunne's team kidnapped your old lieutenant, Eddie Shick. Took him straight to the dry-out farm, right?"

"Well, actually they do take you for a last drink."

"That's thoughtful."

"Then to the hospital for detox. Then the dry-out farm after that."

"That's not my point, and you know it. It's this secretiveness, you and Gregory and your own personal rules of investigation. I think you're one place, you're somewhere else. I don't see any paper coming from you."

"That stack of DD fives," I said, pointing, "is for you. They cover us right up until today. I was going to put them on your desk before I left."

"Make sure you do that," she said, standing. "And make sure that button is returned to the Bronx, forthwith. Then you get back on the prostitutes. And carry that beeper."

Delia closed her office door behind her. Firmly.

Gregory says the best detectives are telephone detectives. I went back to the phone because Officer Paul Verdi had told us in the Sawmill that he suspected a drug dealer named Tito Santana of having something to do with the murder of Marc Ross. The more calls I made, the more it seemed plausible. Bronx Narcotics told me that Marc Ross had made over a dozen recent arrests of Santana's street dealers. Bronx Homicide said the two dealers beaten to death in Crotona Park, the rebar murders, had both been arrested by Ross. Everybody said Santana was a psycho.

I stood by the window, watching traffic on Madison Street below, wondering why Sonny Guidice was so sure Santana wouldn't kill a cop. It was too good a connection to ignore. Joe Gregory also says there's no such thing as coincidence.

The phone rang as I watched Shanahan from Missing Persons duck into Brady's bar. It was Gregory, at an outside phone. I could barely hear him from the noise of traffic.

"Get your ass up to the Blarney Stone bar on Thirty-third, across from the Garden," he yelled. "I found the guy who can ID the button."

By subway it would have taken fifteen minutes: the A train to Penn Station, two stops. But thirty minutes of cowboy driving later I parked west of Eighth Avenue and walked past the facade of the main post office, a building long enough to hold the entire motto of the U.S. Postal Service across the top, the longest message I'd ever seen carved in stone. I found a break in traffic and sprinted across Eighth.

The greasy windows of the Blarney Stone gave it a sickly look in contrast with stores on either side: an immaculate new Gap and an official sports logo store, the window filled with Knicks and Rangers paraphernalia.

The Blarney Stone smelled of stale beer and boiled cabbage and had two sections: smoking and chain smoking. On the wall just past the steam tables was a row of a dozen public telephones, all in use. A long bar on the left had a few stools with uncomfortable spindle backs, but most of the drinkers were standing, watching the ticker tape scoreboard on ESPN and nervously eyeing the phone bank.

Behind the steam tables on the right, a man in a ponytail with tattooed arms sliced meat. His customers were salesmen, pimps, garment industry movers and shakers, and mailmen, most of them degenerate sports gamblers. It wasn't even noon and the bar was packed. The Rangers and Knicks were playoff contenders.

The place was too warm with food and body heat. Within seconds, sweat trickled down my sides. I found Gregory in the back booth, sitting opposite an old man in a gray fedora, both of them under an oval mirror cracked down the center like a broken heart.

"You remember Mr. Fashion, pally," Gregory said.

Joe and I had tailed the frail, prodigious gambler many times when we'd worked in Organized Crime Intelligence. I'd never been this close to him.

"You're lucky to catch me here," he said. "I don't come in here much anymore. I hate this joint. You can smell bad luck in the air."

"That's boiled cabbage," I said.

I couldn't remember his real name, but he'd unknowingly led us to dozens of high-stakes crap games. He was a legend in the garment industry and also a major sports bettor whose code name, Mr. Fashion, appeared on the sheets of half the bookmakers in the city. We didn't arrest guys like him; they were too valuable as bait. He wet the end of a cigar and checked me over with icy blue, little dot eyes.

"I was just asking your partner if he knows the difference between a cook and a chef." Mr. Fashion jerked a thumb back toward the steam tables. "A chef don't have tattoos. Remember that, that's wisdom."

Mr. Fashion took out a pharmacy bottle and dumped a tiny white pill into his open palm. "See that dopey bastard cutting meat? I'm in here last winter and I'm on this horrendous losing streak. I'm losing football, hockey, baskets, college baskets, everything. Worst slump ever. So this tattooed bastard has a hot tip. A sure thing. He wants to go partners, but I got to lend him half a yard. Lend him, right? Tennis, he says. Can't miss. That's what they all say, am I right? I told him fuck off." Mr. Fashion popped the pill into his mouth. "He's still pissed. That's why I don't eat in here no more. Never eat in a joint where you piss off the cook. That's wisdom." Mr. Fashion held his palms face up, toward heaven. "What the hell do I know about tennis?"

Mr. Fashion wore a wool sports jacket that appeared to be cut from an Oriental rug, a blue shirt with a white collar, and a yellow tie, the widest tie I'd ever seen. His right arm rested on a copy of the *Sporting News*, a line of pencil notations next to the basketball scores, all figures preceded by pluses and minuses.

"Mr. Fashion ID'd our button," Gregory said. "I'll let him explain it to you."

"First, let's see what this genius knows," Mr. Fashion said.

"We got to get going," Gregory said, checking his watch. "We're working a case."

The crowd at the bar roared at something from the college basketball game on ESPN. Mr. Fashion jerked his head around to see.

"Never bet on a Notre Dame game," Mr. Fashion said. "That's wisdom from God." A white substance oozed from the corners of his mouth. "Okay," he said, "baseball question. What brothers have the most total home runs in the history of the Major Leagues? Natural brothers. Combined total of round trippers."

"The DiMaggio brothers," I said.

Mr. Fashion laughed a loud cackle and began coughing. We could always recognize that laugh on wiretaps or bugs. Mr. Fashion's face went deep red as he kept wheezing and gagging. Gregory handed him a glass of water, worried about the old man choking. Mr. Fashion had to be eighty; hell, he was eighty when we were tailing him. A good laugh could kill him. But he gradually caught his breath and took a big drag on his cigar.

"DiMaggio was my answer," Gregory said as he laid the white button on the table. The plastic bag was sprinkled with dried specks of the blood of a dead cop. "It's the wrong answer."

"The Alou brothers," I said. I didn't think they were home-run hitters, but I knew there were a bunch of them.

"You'll never get it," Mr. Fashion said with a smile that showed only his lower teeth. "It's the Aaron brothers. Tommy had a handful, Hank hit seven hundred and fifty-five."

Mr. Fashion laid his cigar in the ashtray and picked up the button. "What was I saying?" he said.

"The button," Gregory said.

"I was telling your partner before," Mr. Fashion said. "I remember these buttons well. See the cut, the texture, it ain't that plastic shit." He held the evidence bag up to my face. "See, not round, but oval. This is not your mass-market button." He reached across the table and put his finger in Gregory's chest. "This, he's wearing, is a cheap mass-market button. I can buy a hundred gross of those buttons for *bupkus*. But your button is ivory. Special order for a line of original cocktail dresses. Little red numbers with rolled black tiger-stripe straps. Pictured in *Mirabella*, this dress. Naomi Campbell, the *schvartzer* model, wearing it."

"What's the price of one of these dresses?"

"Let me put it this way," he said, shrugging. "If you have to ask . . . See, dresses like this they make in limited run. For the hoity-toity crowd. So Bipsy Rockefeller isn't mortally embarrassed when Boopsy Carnegie has the same dress on at the bash for hermaphrodite Nazi orphans. They say they make only two or three. That means three, four dozen dresses, tops."

"They must keep records," I said.

"You could ask."

"Who sells the dresses?" I said.

"Nobody," he said.

"Okay," I said. "Who has physical possession of the dresses?"

"You're asking me?" he said.

"What company made them?" I said.

"Billy Blass," Mr. Fashion said. "What's with you cops? You don't talk to each other? I'm sure Billy made a report."

"What report?" I said.

"The theft. I thought you guys were working on the theft."

"These dresses were stolen?"

"Ah, the light bulb goes on," he said, pointing over my head. "Yes, yes. The whole damn rack. Two *schvartzes* with knives did it, the bastards. Broad daylight. Corner of Seventh and Thirty-fifth. Last spring. During the NBA playoffs." Mr. Fashion frowned, as if he suddenly remembered something unpleasant. "That fucking Michael Jordan, he ain't human."

We walked out onto Thirty-third Street. The wind blew from the west, picking up speed in the narrower side streets. The streets seemed cleaner than in recent years, less squeegee guys and panhandlers hanging around.

"I got a sports question for you," Gregory said.

"*You* got a sports question for *me*?" Mr. Fashion said.

He reached into his pocket and pulled out a wad of money too big for his fist. The top layer was all two-dollar bills, the mark of a racetrack habitué. "Let's make it interesting. How much money you got on you? Let's go for half a yard."

"Half a yard it is," Gregory said, riffling through his bills.

"Your partner holds," Mr. Fashion said, handing me a wad of damp bills. I wanted to get in against Gregory myself. I knew he didn't know the first thing about sports.

"Fire your question," Mr. Fashion said. "Hold it. . . . This is a legit question, am I right?"

"Of course," Gregory said. "Ready? Who"—he stretched out the word—"played for the Yankees, the Knicks, and the Rangers, all in the same season?"

"This is bullshit," Mr. Fashion said. "No such person. Never happened. Give me the fucking money."

"Double or nothing," Gregory said.

"You saying *played*, right?" Mr. Fashion said, pulling out his wad again. "Not some trainer or the fucking team doctor, right? We're talking *played*, right?"

"Played, absolutely. Played," Gregory said. "You in or out?"

Mr. Fashion handed me more money. I wondered what IAD would make of this scene.

"I'm fucking in," he said, winking at me. "This is bullshit, I know, but I got to play the string. Let me have it. What's the answer?"

That was the essence of the gambler, I thought. In all the years I worked on gamblers, the thing we counted on was that they had to be *in*. The logic of a bet didn't matter; neither did the wisdom. And what especially didn't matter was whether they won or lost. Either way they'd calmly get money down on the next game or the next race. The heart of the matter was action. They had to be in the wild swirl of flying money and odds and spreads and power lines and rumors. Action was their lifeblood. Action or die.

"So tell me already," Mr. Fashion said. "Who?"

"Eddie Layton," Gregory said. "The organist."

"The organist?" Mr. Fashion said, and stopped dead in the middle of the street.

"Played his heart out," Gregory said.

9

We abandoned Mr. Fashion in the middle of Eighth Avenue, waving his arms like some drunken symphony conductor. I left my car next to the post office and sat back on the leather seat of Joe's T-bird. Sinatra sang "Last Night When We Were Young." The sound of the city seemed softer. The trip to the station house on West Thirty-fifth was only five blocks, a ten-minute New York walk, twenty minutes by car.

In the lull of traffic I nodded off and woke up disoriented. Gregory parked directly in front of Midtown South. South was a modern structure of two-tone stone: one a strong dark red, the other a wimpy beige. Inside, a banner hung across the front desk, proclaiming it the "world's busiest police precinct." We walked in without the slightest scrutiny.

Upstairs, a low metal gate separated the detectives' desks from the complainant's bench. On the bench sat a well-dressed old couple: she knitting, he dozing.

Gregory leaned over and unlocked the gate from the back.

The nameplate on the desk said "Ruiz." The guy behind the nameplate wore jeans and a black T-shirt under a black linen sports jacket. From my angle I could see an empty shoulder holster. He typed into a computer, using all fingers, as he spoke into the telephone clamped between his ear and his shoulder.

What I missed most from the old station houses was the raised desk. The sacred desk, high in the air, protected by an ornate brass rail you approached only when absolutely necessary. I had five years on the job before I went behind the desk; it wasn't about fear, it was about respect. Now the desk is at eye level, anyone and everyone running behind it. Mass confusion. Gregory says that now the station house is like a campus at some pinko liberal arts school.

When Ruiz finally acknowledged us, he said, "Whadda ya got?"

"We need to see the sixty-one on a dress heist," Gregory said, his ID in his hand. "The DD fives, all the follow-up reports, whatever you got. Location is Thirty-six and Seven. Happened June '93."

"Heist," the young cop said, smiling. "I thought only guys like Bogey, movie cops, said heist."

"Movie cops wear shoulder holsters," Gregory said. "Real cops say heist."

"Yeah, well, take a seat until the feature starts," he said. "I got some important business here."

Gregory leaned over, yanked the phone from the cop, and hung it up.

"Don't be a fucking wise guy, Bogey," the cop said.

"You a detective, Ruiz?" Gregory said.

"I'm five names away from the gold shield," he said. "Not that it's any of your business."

"Just show us where the files are," I said. "We'll look ourselves."

"The heist files," Gregory said.

"I'll take care of you," the cop said, dialing the phone, "as soon as I finish. Or maybe never."

I said, "We're working on the murder of the cop in the Bronx."

His face flushed a blotchy red. "Why didn't you say so?" He put down the phone. "All you had to do was say so. That was bullshit, man. That wasn't right."

We followed him into a back room, and all the while he kept mumbling to himself. The room had a line of metal file cabinets stretching wall to wall.

"What was that date?" Ruiz said, still shaking his head in disgust.

"June '93," Gregory said. "Complainant was Bill Blass. Dresses stolen off the street."

"You should have said you were working on the Ross case," he said. "That wasn't cool."

From the doorway I could see the old couple on the bench pouring something from a thermos. The old man held two flowered coffee mugs as the woman poured.

"June fifth," Ruiz said, pulling a thick file. "Here it is. It was closed out pending further information."

"Who caught it?"

"Fleming," Ruiz said, rolling his eyes. "Old-timer. Useless prick. Got out on three-quarters before Christmas. Nobody knew he was gone."

In the wire cage at the far end of the squad room, two men in greasy jumpsuits sat on the floor and whispered in Spanish. A cop, in an equally greasy jumpsuit with "Auto Crime Division" stenciled across the back, asked questions in English and typed the answers one letter at a time.

"I'll tell you," Ruiz said. "Most rip-offs of high-ticket evening wear are done by transvestites. Or the stuff's intended for sale to TVs."

Ruiz went to his desk and pulled his gun out of the top drawer and shoved it in his shoulder holster. "You got a car?" he said. "I know somebody maybe can help us."

Ruiz said good-bye to the old couple sitting on the benches. He told us they lived down the block and came in every day just to sit. The three of us piled into the T-bird and drove uptown. I read the file.

"This doesn't mention ivory buttons," I said.

"I don't know about buttons," Ruiz said.

Ruiz's informant was a fifteen-year transit employee, a bus mechanic who worked the four-to-twelve shift at the city bus garage on Ninth Avenue and Fifty-fourth.

"Maybe we'll catch him at home," Ruiz said.

Home was a dingy five-story walk-up at Forty-eighth and Eleventh, the northeast corner, between the theater district and the Hudson River. An area known as Hell's Kitchen.

"This guy," Ruiz said, "is not a scumbag. Know what I mean? Aside from his lifestyle, this guy is good people."

"What do we call him?" I said, assuming Ruiz didn't want us to know his real name.

"Sometimes Nathan, sometimes Natasha. Depends. He's real sensitive."

Five flights up to Nathan/Natasha's. Ruiz banged on the door. The air stung with ammonia. Worn and cracked tile floors showed streaks of a mop. The sounds of afternoon game shows leaked into the hallway. It took him/her a few wary minutes at the peephole, then he started clicking locks. Then came the unmistakable slide and clank of the four-foot-long steel bar of a Fox lock.

Nathan/Natasha was a squat, dark man with wild tufts of black hair shooting from his eyebrows and out the top of an orange Mets T-shirt. He introduced himself as Nathan. Ruiz led us into a large living room, past a tiny kitchen, bathroom, and a padlocked door. The walls were plaster.

Ruiz straddled an ottoman and motioned for the rest of us to sit. On the floor, under an empty bird cage, was a black spandex microskirt.

"Nathan," Ruiz said, "this is heavy shit. I want you to know I wouldn't bring anybody to your house for bullshit reasons. I wouldn't be here otherwise. Trust me, it's heavy."

Joe and I took the sofa, Nathan took the recliner. He wore a white chenille bathrobe over the T-shirt, and his legs were bare. On his feet were black ballet slippers. Ruiz told Nathan about the death of a cop, and his eyes began to tear.

"Nathan knows more about hot clothes than anybody in this city," Ruiz said. "Ain't that right, Nathan?"

Nathan shrugged modestly as he wiped his eyes with a hairy finger.

"Show them your room, Nathan," Ruiz said. "Go ahead. Show them the room."

Nathan turned his face away and looked out the window. The window faced west, a Hudson River view. The deck of the USS *Intrepid*, now a naval museum, was visible. Tourists walked among the aircraft on its deck.

"Nathan," I said, "we won't involve you in this. We understand your position. We won't involve you."

Gregory gave me a questioning glare, a look that said "What the hell is wrong with you?"

I handed Nathan the sketch of the suspect, then the sketch of the dress from Ruiz's file. "That person would be wearing that dress, and long white gloves."

Nathan held up his hands, thick fingers, short and swollen. The smashed hands of a mechanic. "A lot of us wear gloves," he said.

His voice surprised me. It was high-pitched and small. I'd expected something gruff, a scratchy, whiskey-soaked baritone. He studied the sketches carefully.

"I don't know this person in the sketch," he said. "But the dress is Bill Blass, from his Conga line."

"That's right," I said. "Ever see it before?"

"Sure," he said. "It's a striking dress."

"Where?" Gregory said.

"At the club, the Sweet Life, in Chelsea. Somebody was selling them. I would have loved to have one, but the big sizes go right away."

"Didn't I tell you he's a good guy?" Ruiz said.

"What about the buttons?" I said.

"What buttons?" he said.

"The ones on the dress," I said. "Did you notice anything special about them?"

"Not really," Nathan said.

"Who was selling the dresses?" Gregory said.

"Some Jamaican bitch," Nathan said. "Sorry, that's not nice talk, but she is a crude bitch. I don't go there much anymore because of that clique. I don't like all that roughness."

"Are you meaning a Jamaican woman?" I said.

"Oh, no. A man," he said. "I don't know his name. A black guy, tall. He's always there selling something."

"Where exactly in Chelsea is this club?" I said.

"Eleventh and Twenty-eighth, right on the corner," Nathan said, pointing south. "Third Tuesday of every month. Fifth floor. . . . Wait just a minute."

Nathan stood up and walked across the room. He sat on a piano stool in front of a vanity he used as a telephone table. A soap opera was on television, the sound turned down.

"I like your posters," I said.

"Thanks," he said softly. The walls were covered with framed prints of dozens of Broadway shows. Nathan pulled a paper from the drawer.

"Here," he said. "April nineteenth. Next Tuesday. It's a dress ball. Everyone will be there."

The Sweet Life's logo was a sketch of an Anita Ekberg type dancing, shaking her bosom, the movement depicted by a series of wavy lines around the bust. Contests listed this week included debutantes and most gorgeous over three hundred pounds. Tuesday, April 19. Midnight.

"I told you Nathan was good people," Ruiz said. "Go ahead, show them your room."

We followed Nathan as he opened the padlocked door. I'd assumed the door led to another apartment. We walked down a long dark hallway and through a beaded curtain. He flicked the switch and the room began to beat in pulsating red light. A wall of mirrors, feather boas, a sea of sequins, and open closets with dozens of glittering dresses. Hundreds of pairs of high heels in a wall of pigeonholes. And a dressing table, the mirror lit with a wreath of bare bulbs, like that of an old star of the Broadway theater.

"I'm impressed," I said.

"Told you, didn't I?" Ruiz said.

"One more thing," Gregory said. "We need you to identify the person who sold this dress."

"Just to us, Nathan," I said. "Then you walk away."

"I had other plans," Nathan said.

Even in the blinking red lights, which had begun to seem orange, I could see the tears running down his face. Again I promised him that we'd leave him out of it completely. I put my hand on his shoulder, and I could feel the muscles in his back tighten.

"What choice do I have," Nathan said.

10

"We treated that mutt like royalty," Gregory said. "Queen for a freaking day."

We'd dropped Ruiz off at Midtown South, then Gregory drove me to my car. Thirty-third Street was lined with empty yellow cabs, doors open, parked in a No Stopping zone. On the sidewalk a dozen wrinkled men, mostly Mideastern, milled around the cabs, talking. Cabs used to change shifts in garages. No more. Now garages were in Queens, if they existed at all.

"I'm going home," I said.

"Not a moment too soon," Gregory said. "Before your heart bleeds all over my Corinthian leather."

Gregory stopped next to my car. Stuck across the windshield, directly over my NYPD official parking plate, was a sticker that said, "You are parked illegally: by order of the U.S. Postal Service."

"We had no reason to steamroll that guy," I said.

"Please. The freak is an informant, and we got a homicide to solve. I'll bet he pulls that crybaby shit on everybody."

On the corner a group of tourists posed for pictures with a woman dressed like the Statue of Liberty. She was painted green head to toe. Face, hair, everything.

"Enough said," Gregory said. "Go. Get out. Go home. We'll snatch a snooze, get an early start. Maybe tonight we can be real cops."

I knew Gregory was right about informants, but I was tired and wondering how I was going to get that sticker off my windshield.

"Here," I said, handing him the beeper I'd signed for. "Delia wants you to carry this."

On the way home I drove peering over the sticker, talking aloud to myself, trying to stay awake. The trip to Yonkers took only twenty minutes. I was slightly ahead of the rush, thankful for bits of open road, and thinking only of my bed.

On WNYC, the former head of the Guardian Angels was interviewing PBA president Lenny Marino. Lenny, his voice rising like Martin Luther King Jr. with a Queens accent, swore that no cop would rest until we found the killer of Marc Ross. Lenny made me feel guilty. But I had to rest.

It was dark when I felt Leigh slip into bed next to me, her skin silky smooth and warm. She slept naked because she knew I liked it and she'd do anything to help me fall asleep. I was never a good sleeper, but I seemed to be getting worse with age. Lying there examining unsympathetic walls, cataloging mistakes and regrets. Just to be able to reach over and touch her skin was something very real and reassuring.

"It's almost eight o'clock," she said. I'd left her a note to get me up at eight. "I scraped that sticker off your window."

I rolled over and pulled her toward me and felt the softness of her body. In the few seconds since she'd come to bed the temperature had risen dramatically. I wondered if all women generated that much heat. I buried my face against her neck and smelled her perfume.

"What's the dynamic duo up to tonight?" she said.

"Hookers and more hookers."

"What a life," she said. "Sleep all day, party all night."

I began scratching her back. She loved to be scratched; she'd lie there blinking her eyes in ecstasy for hours, until her back was red, almost raw.

"What time do you meet Gregory?"

"Ten," I said.

"You have time," she said, and slipped her hands into the waistband of my shorts and pulled them down. I kicked them off and pushed them toward the end of the bed.

"Take your insulin shot?" I said.

"Yes," she said. "Stop thinking and relax."

I found her mouth and kissed her. Her hand kneaded my balls gently, then firmer. Leigh was an instinctive lover who sensed exactly how to make me hard. I ran my hands gently over her ageless body. A body that loved to be touched, breasts so sensitive. I rubbed and kissed, touched and scratched. She raised her leg and put it over my hip, both of us on our sides facing each other, and guided me inside her. We moved slowly in our rhythm, our pace. Then she pushed me onto my back and rolled over on top, so she could fuck me as she lifted her upper body, as if doing a push-up, and her breasts grazed my chest lightly as she raised and lowered and stared into my eyes, moving her hips. And we talked, or said nothing.

Later, our hands touching, I heard her crying.

"What's wrong?" I said.

"Nothing," she said.

"Come on, Leigh. What is it?"

"No," she said. "It's nothing. It's really nothing. That's the truth. It's nothing."

I held her tight and scratched her back in the big circles that she loved. And watched until she fell asleep.

11

At ten P.M. on Tuesday, April 19, I watched Joe Gregory from a window on the third floor of an abandoned luggage factory. He was across the street, standing on a trash can, changing light bulbs above the entrance to the Sweet Life Social Club. We'd set up surveillance well before the start of the transvestite ball, then noticed that the doorway in front of the Sweet Life was hidden in darkness. Gregory ran out and bought new bulbs to illuminate the entrance. White bulbs, 150 watts, the better to see the revelers.

"Start thinking about the security field, Ryan," Sid Kaye said as he handed me a set of keys. "Smart guy like you, they'll snap you right up. Some six-figure jobs out there just waiting for a guy like you."

Sid Kaye was an ex-cop who'd arranged to get us into the luggage factory. Sid owed us big time, and we'd never let him forget it. He was chief of security for Orion Insurance, which claimed the building as one of its real estate holdings. He was also president of the NYPD Retired Detectives and on the boards of several other ex–NYPD/ex–FBI associations. The blue underground that ran the city of New York.

"Give me a break, Sid," I said. "Six figures? Come on."

"I shit you not," he said. "This city is coming back big time. Private security is the wave of the future. Corporate America finally realized they need us. Give me a month, I'll have you in the job of your dreams."

"How come I don't hear about these jobs?"

"You can't advertise shit like this. Every useless mook who ever walked a beat crawls out of the woodwork. Word of mouth is the only way."

Gregory jumped down from the trash can and limped for a few steps. Nobody was around to see him. Eleventh Avenue was empty, not even a parked car. The stone walls of the building were covered with peeling layers of posters. Gregory, carrying the bag of old bulbs, crossed the street gingerly and entered the luggage factory.

"When we get the word about a job coming open, we keep it hush-hush," Sid said. "Phone calls get made. Badda-boom, badda-bing, by the time Joe the Glom hears about it, the position is already closed."

"Name one ex-cop making six figures," I said.

He told me about former New York City cops who had their asses on plush leather chairs on the highest floors of virtually all the city's skyscrapers. And they'd stay there as long as they remembered that their corporate value was at street level, keeping an ear to the ground. They were well organized, even published their own telephone directory. It read like class notes from an Ivy League alumni magazine: who was with Time-Warner, who with Sloan-Kettering or Citibank. Most were familiar names, good guys, good cops, the cream of the graduating class, guys you once called if you were stumped on a homicide. Now you called their secretaries, if you needed theater tickets, or security plans for a 747, or an immediate appointment with the best heart specialist in New York.

"Hey, you don't need to know all the ins and outs of an industry right away," Sid said. "Something comes up, open the directory. Call me, call another guy. Nothing somebody in that book can't handle."

Sid stopped pitching when he heard Gregory coming up the freight elevator. He'd said Joe wasn't corporate material.

"Remember this," Sid said. "There's always some guy who knows some guy who can do something for you that other guys can't."

Gregory came in bitching about his knees. Sid stood up to leave. I glanced at the entrance to the club; the new bulbs made a big difference. The entrance was clear, but the rest of the block was still a yellow haze. About twenty years ago the city went to yellowish streetlights to save money. The yellow lights were unnatural. They blurred night vision, distorted silhouettes, and compressed distances. You couldn't distinguish colors: reds looked black; you couldn't see into shadows. All that fueled the New Yorker's inherent paranoia and played hell with surveillance cameras.

"I'm outta here," Sid said. "Flying to Vegas tomorrow, seminar on terrorism. Put the lights off when you leave, don't burn the place down. Give the keys to George McGrath at my office when you're finished.

You remember George McGrath? From the Seventeenth squad. A gentleman. But what else do you expect from the Seventeenth squad?"

Gregory and I sat at the window on turned-around chairs, watching the entrance to the club. The luggage factory smelled musty, like an old attic.

"Ever see one of these cross-dressers that fooled you?" Gregory said. "Not me. I don't care what they're wearing. You can spot them. Hands are too big, Adam's apple sticks out, legs too muscular, features too broad."

"Maybe if you'd had a few drinks too many."

"I ain't never been that drunk," he said. "There's always something, the walk, the voice, the beard stubble. Something."

Delia had given us a break from hooker patrol so we could put the surveillance together. She'd said she wouldn't be surprised if the killer was a man. The plan was for Nathan/Natasha to point out the Jamaican hot dress dealer. The Jamaican would lead us to whoever bought the Bill Blass dress.

"You think Ross could have been fooled?" I said.

"Fooled, no," Gregory said. "Maybe he was a little weird, who knows. A musician, maybe he liked that shit. I don't think a cop should get fooled. If Ross went with a cross-dresser, it was intentional."

Within a short time a taxi pulled up. Two tall people in evening dresses got out, laughing too deeply.

"Here we go," Gregory said as another taxi pulled up. Then a third. From this distance some of the guests looked extremely good. The click of high heels drifted up from below; a few pairs had to be filled with the feet of actual women. Nathan had told us that some women did attend, show business and SoHo types.

Joe pointed the camera at the glittery crowd in the

spot of white light he'd created. They all acted as if they knew each other and took turns banging on the door of the club. He let the motor drive whir until the door swung open.

For almost two hours we watched for Natasha's short, stocky body while taxis, cars, and limos arrived. It looked like Oscar night, but with more cleavage. Sometimes they arrived in groups, pouring out of cabs, adjusting dresses, fluffing hair, checking each other's appearance before entering the club. Mostly they arrived alone. But no Nathan. No Natasha.

"He stiffed us," Gregory said. "And he warned off the Jamaican, guaranteed. We should have put the fear of God into that prick."

At two-fifteen Gregory began packing up the equipment. Nathan had said he'd leave the place at one A.M., meet us on the corner of Twenty-eighth Street. There hadn't been a new arrival in some time, and a few were leaving.

"You know what, pally?" Gregory said. "I've been thinking. We don't need that prick."

We locked the equipment in the trunk of the car and walked across the street to the club. The elevator was ripe; enough perfume hung in the air to make my skin itch. The doors opened onto the fifth floor, a wall of opaque glass blocks. Crepe paper hung over an archway entrance. Two bouncers, dressed like theater ushers, stood on either side of a velvet rope.

"Tenth Precinct," Gregory said, holding his shield up to the face of an usher. "Gotta check your fire exits."

We didn't wait for an okay, just brushed by, walking in the way cops were supposed to, like we owned the place. A round silver ball in the ceiling threw colored circles of light onto a factory floor that once hummed with sewing machines, presses, or lathes. We went to the left, because we always began a search to the left. Tables were empty; the crowd was down around the stage.

Someone in a dress with a shredded hemline strutted across the stage. The crowd applauded wildly. In the spotlight an announcer, dressed in a cape and floppy black hat, held a trophy high above his head. We worked our way along the outside of the hall, weaving through empty tables.

Gregory pushed open the ladies' room door. A tall black thing in a gold lamé dress leaned into the mirror, working on eyelashes as long and thick as paper matchsticks. Whoever it was, was alone, and ignoring us as Gregory swung open the door to each stall.

The men's room had a crowd. In front of each urinal stood a guy with his dress hiked and panty hose down. A tall brunette with a tiara screamed, "Strip search, strip search," as he twisted his dress around so he could piss through the hip-high slit in the leg.

We came out of the men's room one level up from the ballroom floor, behind the stage. The crowd was breaking up, people still applauding as they walked away, some heading for the exit door. It was a sea of big people in evening gowns, wigs, and size twelve pumps. I couldn't see Nathan or Natasha. Then Gregory stopped dead in front of me.

"Look," he said, pointing. "Black dress, next to Ivana Trump. Long white gloves."

I saw only one person wearing long white gloves.

"That's our woman, pally," Gregory said. "Dark skin, big hair, freaking white gloves."

The hair was right, the big black curls and swirls, and

so was the size, probably the smallest person in the room. The skin was dark, a reddish brown complexion, and the hair, and the gloves. But she seemed too drop-dead gorgeous for our sketch. She had full lips and a smile that could have replaced the klieg lights.

Gregory climbed over the rail that separated the dance floor from the tables. He jumped three feet to the parquet floor. White Gloves was in the flow of crowd moving toward the exit sign. I kept my eyes on her as I dropped to the dance floor. The floor was waxed, slippery. I felt a push from behind and stumbled over a cable that ran up to the stage. When I looked up I'd lost her in the sea of big wigs and broad-shouldered women.

I caught up to Gregory at the elevator. He was banging the button as if that would help it come faster, but it was still going down, just passing four. I took the stairs.

Five flights down I hit the door and the cold night air. White Gloves was in a black coat at the corner of Twenty-ninth Street, getting into a yellow Checker cab. She looked back at me as I ran into the street. As the cab pulled away I repeated the medallion number until it was written in my notebook.

"Where is she?" Gregory yelled.

"Cab," I said, and pointed uptown. Traffic lights were changing in sequence, the red tide coming toward us, all the way down Eleventh Avenue. The Checker was slowing to a stop two red lights away.

"Watch where it turns," Gregory said. "I'll get the car."

I started jogging down the center line, staring into the traffic ahead. I was within three car lengths of the Checker when the lights started to change to green. I turned around: no Gregory. Up ahead, the school of little red car taillights swam between the big green traffic lights. I started running again. Another three blocks. My breathing covered the sound of the clicking traffic lights. My right ankle ached.

"Get in," Gregory yelled. He threw open the car door. The pulse in the back of my head was pounding. My skin felt hot, pricked with a thousand tiny needles.

"I think he made the left on Forty-second," I said. Sweat ran down, burning my eyes.

"She's going uptown," Gregory said. "Back to the Bronx."

Gregory made a screaming two-wheel left turn onto Forty-second Street. No one was at the light in front of us. He made a wild right uptown on Twelfth Avenue. At Fifty-seventh Street he accelerated up the ramp onto the Henry Hudson Parkway and blasted through the yield sign. Horns blew, brakes squealed behind us.

"Take it easy," I said. "We're not even sure it's her."

"Oh, it's her, pally," he said. "I feel it."

Classic Gregory, I thought. God couldn't dissuade him. I'd never been good at making an identification from an artist's sketch. Plus, we'd only gotten a fifteen-second look on a crowded dance floor. We were flying on dark skin, white gloves, and a gypsy wig. But Gregory lived on pure instinct. No talking him out of it. I snapped the seat belt around me.

We caught the Checker at Grant's Tomb, lucky there were only a handful of Checker cabs still around. My breathing was starting to slow. Gregory weaved to a spot two cars behind. He settled in for the tail. The Checker moved to the right lane, up the ramp to the Cross-Bronx Expressway. We followed the cab east for a few blocks, then off onto the narrow winding streets of the Bronx. As it neared the area of the Five One Precinct, I became a believer.

"Back off," I said. "We're too close."

We were the only two cars on the street when the cab made a right off Tremont Ave. The cabdriver started to hit the brakes. We pulled to the curb. They stopped on the corner, across from Crotona Park. Gregory stayed back below the curve of the hill, opposite the Arthur Murphy Houses. Behind us was a block of boarded-up storefronts and the brightly painted Iglesia Mission de Dios.

"Let's see where she goes," he said.

I could hear Gregory breathing as she got out of the cab. She took one glance back down the street toward us, but I didn't think she could see us. The cab pulled away.

"What's she waiting for?" Gregory said.

"Maybe for us to make a move," I said.

"She didn't freaking see us," Gregory said.

She stepped off the curb quickly. Long strides, moving fast.

"She's going into the park," I said. Within seconds she disappeared into the trees.

Gregory sped to the park entrance. I jumped out and told him to meet me back on this corner. He said he'd circle the park, watch the exits. I hadn't gone ten steps when I realized I should have brought the radio.

The park was pitch black. I jogged about thirty yards, then stopped dead and listened for the echo of the click of high heels or the slap of a purse against a thigh. Nothing. Off in the distance I could see the glow of a small fire.

I knew from my days in the Five One that the park

was wider on the north side and built on hills. The longest path curved south toward Boston Road. I ran up a knoll and squatted and scanned the path in the sweep of headlights of passing cars. Again, nothing. I jogged to a shorter path that swung back toward the north end and saw her going down a small incline to the gate. My clothes still felt damp from my last run. Broken glass crunched under my feet.

Fifty yards from the gate I heard men's voices, Hispanic accents, up ahead in the darkness near the gate: "Hey, baby. Where you going so fast, baby? Come back, baby." Whistles and sucking sounds, like calling a kitten. She looked over her shoulder as she stepped into the street. I ran down the hill toward the gate.

Then, right in front of me, a large man stepped out of the bushes. He had his back to me, and I was on him before he knew it. As he turned I caught a glint of something metallic shining in his hand. I caught him square in the face with my best punch and all the force of my tumbling weight. Something crunched, bone or tooth. The silver object flew into my chest as he crumpled to the pavement.

The shiny metal object was twelve ounces of Coors Light. I picked up the can before all the beer spilled out and put it in his hand. He'd begun to piss himself. But he'd done that before. It was Francis X. Hanlon, the old cop fighter.

12

"You agree, Anthony?" Delia said. "It was definitely our suspect?"

"I can't say I'm positive. But it's definitely worth a follow-up."

"It's her," Gregory said. "Guaranteed."

We were in Delia's office on the thirteenth floor. The windows faced the City Building. Workmen on scaffolding, twenty floors up, sprayed steam from handheld metal wands. Below them, the stone was sooty charcoal gray; above their heads, a sparkling white.

"You don't know where she went," Delia said. "What building she went into."

"It had to be something just off the park," Gregory said. "I was cruising the area. If she walked far from the park, I would have seen her."

"We figure any of six buildings starting at 711 Crotona Park North, going west," I said. "Six or seven buildings tops."

Delia stood and looked at the wall map of the Five One Precinct she'd ordered from the cartography section. "Could she have turned down one of these side streets?"

"Could have," I said.

"So you're not positive about those six buildings. It could be sixty buildings."

"Could be a hundred and sixty," I said. "But I don't think so. She lives very close to the park. I'd bet on it."

Delia sat down and smoothed her skirt against her thighs. She was wearing one of her power suits, the ones she wore to important meetings.

"When are you going back to that transvestite club?" she said.

"It's a once-a-month thing," Gregory said. "Third Tuesday only."

"Yeah, but people operate this club," Delia said. "Somebody organizes these dress balls. They would know who this Jamaican is."

"Nathan scared the Jamaican off," Gregory said.

"He can't hide forever," Delia said.

"We're going back to the Bronx," I said. "Check out a woman named Tina Marquez. She was arrested by Marc Ross. Probation says she's living at 719 Crotona Park North. That's right in the middle of where I lost the woman last night."

"Tina Marquez," Delia said, looking down at her notes. "The Five One squad already interviewed Tina Marquez. Right after the Ross murder. They said she had an airtight alibi."

"Nothing's been airtight since the *Hindenburg*," Gregory said.

The Sunday *New York Times* was on Delia's desk,

open to "Apartments Unfurnished." Five or six red circles on the Upper East Side.

"That section of Crotona Park is becoming interesting," I said. "That's the spot where the rebar murders took place. Both victims in that case were drug dealers who also had been arrested by Marc Ross."

"I don't want you two going off on a tangent here," Delia said. "I'd prefer we stick to one strategy at a time. The rebar murders are Neville Drumm's responsibility." She turned to the window to see what I was looking at. She looked tired, her face puffy and rough. "Both of you keep saying 'she.' You still don't think it's possible the person you followed was a man?"

"Anything's possible," I said.

"No freaking way," Gregory said. "I had a better angle than Ryan. Eyeballed her face-to-face. And we spoke to the cabdriver, he says it wasn't a guy."

Three framed pictures stood on Delia's desk. One was a sepia-toned photo of a young black couple standing on a rickety porch. Another, an elderly white couple waving from the deck of a cruise ship. The third was a huge black cop and a tiny white woman posed on either side of former Police Commissioner Howard Leary.

"What happened to your hand?" Delia said. My right hand was cut and swollen, still throbbing from having hit Francis X. I'd surprised myself as much as I'd surprised him. I'd never swung first in my life.

"Fell in the park last night," I said.

"On your knuckles?" she said. "Better have a department surgeon look at that."

I wasn't about to report a hand injury to a department surgeon. As soon as you did, IAD red flagged you.

Hand injuries were monitored closely. I'd be labeled a potential brutality problem.

"Here's my point," she said. She leaned forward on her chair, elbows on the desk. "If it is a woman, we have nothing more than we had before. If it's possibly a man . . . then we have a new direction."

Delia knew I was ambivalent. And, to be perfectly honest, I didn't see how Gregory could be so sure. Joe Gregory thought out loud, and very often he should have run his opinion through the thought process one more time. But sometimes he saw through the muck with a stunning crystal clarity he couldn't articulate.

Delia slammed her palms onto the desk. "I don't want you two working this angle anymore," she said. "I'll get someone with an open mind. As it stands, that ivory button is the only solid evidence we have. I think we're looking for a transvestite hooker, somebody out of that club. I need believers."

"This was a woman," Gregory said. "Believe that."

Delia stood up suddenly. We took the hint and moved toward the door.

"You still have that beeper?" she said.

"Yeah," I said. "We'll work on Tina Marquez."

"No, you won't," she said. "I'll ask Drumm to reinterview Tina Marquez. You'll work the strolls. I don't want to be criticized if this turns out to be a street prostitute. Give me one more week out there."

So we went back to the strolls. Not since my drinking days had I talked to so many whores and witnessed so many sunrises. For two weeks I asked the same questions of street girls while trying not to stare at open lip sores. I kept pushing, telling myself that a cop had been killed. But it didn't matter if Gregory was with me or singing "The Rose of Tralee" at some hairbag's farewell banquet. The message from the street was the same: Marc Ross was an unknown, and our suspect sketch was as credible as the Shroud of Turin.

For two weeks the Ross homicide investigation floundered while we walked among lost children. I interviewed the night haul of prostitutes as they clambered out of patrol wagons on Baxter Street: lines of women in short skirts and high boots, chained together, filing into night court. On Houston and Delancey I saw desperate teenage hookers doing blow jobs for pocket change. On Third and Thirteenth, I questioned a nasal heroin user, who nodded until her knees buckled and she split her chin open on a parking meter. I did the uptown circuit: homeless women, doing it all for a three-dollar crack vial on upper Park Avenue under the elevated tracks. Then back downtown to the girls working the Lincoln Tunnel entrance, some of them living in canvas mail carts stolen from the U.S. Post Office.

After two weeks they recognized my car. They stopped running. After two weeks they knew the question. I stopped asking. The answer was always a fast "No, baby, don't know her, baby" as they looked past my shoulder for lone male drivers cruising slowly down the street.

I saved the transvestites around the meat market for Gregory: muscular girl-men in ten-gallon wigs, lips swathed in red lipstick, glowering down on him from five-inch heels. It seemed like justice to watch him making small talk with some begowned queen on Ninth or Tenth Avenue. It seemed like payback.

At ten P.M. on Tuesday, April 26, sixteen days after the Ross murder, I picked up my partner, Mr. Politician, at an Irish dance at Rosie O'Grady's on Seventh Avenue. Gregory took over the wheel and drove to an all-night deli on Eighth Avenue. He bought a Baby Watson cheesecake while I grabbed Wednesday's *Times* at the newsstand. Then to the Market Diner for a take-out coffee and a tea. We ate, while Gregory's sweat dried, backed up against the Hudson River. I wondered what cops did at night in cities that slept.

"What a freaking waste of time, pally," Gregory said, cutting cheesecake with a plastic knife. "A week of a thousand hookers. I say we target this guy Santana. I called the office, they're pulling all the info on his operation."

"Sonny Guidice says Santana doesn't have the balls."

"You're the one says Sonny's full of shit."

"I know," I said. "I already pulled Santana's file."

Gregory's eyes were red from booze, and his clothes reeked of smoke. Water slapped the pilings behind us. I sipped coffee through the plastic lid. Bitter tasting, it left my teeth feeling rough and grimy.

"My first collar was a hooker," he said. "I ever tell you that story? Funny story."

"For two decades, on a regular basis."

"I'm in night court, right," he said. "First time ever in One Hundred Centre. I keep getting lost in those back stairways. The pross is laughing her ass off. She's handcuffed, stumbling around in spike heels. Finally I get to the right door. But I can hear yelling in the courtroom. I peek in, see the place is packed, judge is standing up, face red as a beet, screaming at everybody. So I close the door, sit down on the hallway bench, and go over my paperwork again. Hey, I'm a rookie, don't want him screaming at *me*, right?

"To make a long story short: About ten minutes passes and guys start coming out with their prisoners about every twenty seconds, regular, like clockwork. And I notice it's quiet inside. So I go in.

"The moment I open the freaking door, this court officer grabs me, his fingers to his lips, shushing me. He checks my paperwork, puts me in line. About thirty, forty cops and prisoners in line ahead of me, but the line is moving fast. *Real* fast. Nobody saying shit. Silence, weird silence, like *The Twilight Zone*. Then I see the court clerk, he's shuffling paper like there's no tomorrow. Not even looking up, he's levying fines, handing out sentences, granting dismissals, whatever. Every cop is dropping a coupla bucks on his table, some of the hookers paying up, too. Only sound in the place is snoring. The judge was that freaking wet brain, the Honorable Harold rum-dum Doyle. He got his head down on the desk, sleeping like a baby. Most efficient night that place ever ran."

We gave the remains of the cheesecake to a city ambulance driver, then drove a few blocks south of the new Javits Convention Center, where the flashiest of the prostitutes worked. The area around the center was off-limits to streetwalkers. Gentrification and new construction around Times Square was pushing the working girls off the island.

It felt good to get out and stretch; I was beginning to get used to nights again. The air was cool and damp. Weeds were sprouting along walls and fences, and you got the feeling that the season had turned the corner. Better days were ahead.

"Yo'all find your killer girl yet, honey?" said a tall black girl in an open ski jacket, red bra, and stirrup pants. She had scabs on her nose and chin, covered by heavy pancake makeup, and she was chewing gum.

"Still looking," I said, handing her yet another copy of the flyer.

"Yo partner ain't no help," she said, pointing to Gregory, who was adjusting his damp suit. "He too busy pulling his pants outta his ass."

She threw the flyer to the ground and went back to ripping Burger King coupons from a paper that had blown against the fence. Cars were angled the length of the block, and girls leaned in windows, negotiating, or inside cars, while heads bobbed up and down. On the ground next to me were broken hypodermic needles, small glass crack bottles, and shiny wrappers from condoms.

"What about the other girls?" I said. "Anybody say anything? I don't care how silly. It might be something."

"We been talking it up, baby," she said, working the gum around in her mouth. "Believe that shit. This cop-killing shit ain't good for business. Know what I mean?"

Gregory tried to get the attention of a heavyset white girl in a fur coat. Just a fur coat. She stood in the street, blocking traffic, bending over, inviting bright lights on her ass.

"What about AIDS?" I said to the girl ripping coupons. Stupid question, but I was tired and out of cop questions. The game wears thin.

"Lemme see yo hand," she said. I held my right hand in the air. She poked her pink tongue at the green thing she'd been chewing on. It wasn't gum, it was latex. Then she bent her head and sucked my thumb down to the palm.

"Mint flavored," she said as we both looked at the saliva-covered green condom on my finger. "I slide this down on your dick, baby. No hands. You don't even know it's there."

I shook my hand and the condom flew out into the street, then I searched my pockets for a tissue, finally settling on a dollar bill, which I also tossed into the street. She started laughing, pointing at my face. "You got to get out more often, baby."

Gregory walked over to the T-bird, checking his watch. The laughing hooker called to the big girl in the fur coat.

"Yo, Wanda. Yo, Wanda."

Before she got a chance to pass the joke along, a blue-and-white radio car from the precinct came through the block. Customers drove off quickly, the women clattered down alleys.

"What say we ride up to the Bronx," Gregory said as I got in the car. "Drop in on Tina Marquez."

"Neville Drumm reinterviewed her and ruled her out again."

"I'm dying to see what she looks like," Gregory said. "Don't tell me you're not curious."

"It's almost midnight."

"She's a dancer, right? Probably just getting home. She'll be glad to see a couple of good-looking guys like us."

"Oh, yeah," I said. "Maybe she'll cook us breakfast." I searched the glove compartment for napkins.

"Just tell her the same funny story you told the hookers," Gregory said.

13

The Bronx is the only borough of New York City connected to the mainland of North America. We arrived twenty minutes after leaving the laughing hookers of Manhattan. Gregory parked the T-bird next to the playground opposite 719 Crotona Park North. The playground had been swept clean, not a shard of glass or empty crack vial in sight. The street, in contrast, was lined with carcasses of cars in the process of being cannibalized. Trash collected under wheelless frames.

"My car going to be safe here?" Gregory said.

"Nothing is safe here," I said.

I had no idea what Tina Marquez looked like. She was twenty-five years old, and her only arrest had been for holding drugs for her husband, Hector Marquez. She'd shoved several eighth-ounce bags of cocaine into her mouth and stood there denying everything to cops, probably sounding like Brando in *The Godfather*. Apparently someone convinced her that a broken bag would send her into massive cardiac arrest, and her two children would grow up without a mother. Tina cooperated and was granted probation. Hector pled down to five years.

The street seemed hillier and much quieter than I remembered from my days in the precinct. The moon peeped through the treetops of the park. As I got out of the car I saw a silhouette against the playground fence. A large, moving silhouette. Gregory saw it, too.

"Ryan," the silhouette growled. "Brother Ryan."

I unsnapped the clasp on the hammer strap of my holster and loosened my gun. Joe moved to the trunk of the car, a better shooting angle, so he wouldn't blow off the top of my head from across the roof of the car. Wind blew, leaves rustled. Something smelled like the horse shit Sanitation swept up after parades. Gregory leaned across the trunk, elbows propped, his gun pointed at the silhouette.

"Who the hell are you?" I yelled.

The silhouette backed up toward the swings, and I saw the Civil War cap and the huge wooden cross swinging across his chest. It was Francis X. Hanlon, the old cop fighter. He backpedaled, slithered through a hole in the fence, and disappeared into the blackness of Crotona Park.

"You got friends everywhere," Gregory said.

"Because I leave them laughing."

An unconscious guy in overalls sprawled across the alcove of 719 Crotona Park North. We walked slowly up three flights. All the metal doors looked as if they'd been beaten with hammers. Gregory knocked on the door with the hand-painted 3C. The hallway had the bitter almond smell of heroin being smoked.

Gregory said, "Package for Tina Marquez from Polo."

"For Chrissakes, Joe. Polo?"

"What, pally? I said 'police,' didn't I?"

I checked the alley from the landing window, watching the fire escape. Then we heard the voice of a child from behind the door. We listened to the clumsy attempt to turn the latch. Then the knob turned slowly and a little girl peeked out, maybe four or five years old. The look on her face said that she hadn't expected us; she began to cry. The chain lock tapped against the frame. Then footsteps coming down the hall, adult bare feet on bare wood. A woman's voice, excited, talking in Spanish. I saw a flash of white shirt, bare leg, as she tried to close the door, but Gregory had wedged a wingtip in the doorway.

"Police," I yelled.

Gregory leaned into the door, just upper-body weight. The woman was strong, she pushed back hard. Gregory's left arm was caught in the door. It was too late to back away. We'd only wanted to see what Tina looked like. Now we were in it. I straight-armed the door just over Gregory's shoulder, and the chain lock burst from the rotted wood. The woman stumbled backward. Gregory reached around the corner, looking for a light switch. The little girl screamed. I tried to calm her, then I saw the gun pointing at Gregory's head.

I lunged and grabbed the top of the gun, squeezed the cylinder to try to keep it from turning. The body of the child was trapped between us, clutching my pants and tiny handfuls of leg hair. The woman managed to cock the gun, and I wedged the fat of my hand under the hammer. My elbow banged across her face as she pulled the trigger. The firing pin dug into the web of my hand. I yanked the gun out of her hands and shoved her. She fell to the floor as the lights came on.

"Irish bastards!" she screamed.

The gun was a silver-plated .32 revolver. With my free hand I eased back the hammer, removed my hand, and very gently, very slowly, lowered the hammer back down the rest of the way onto a live round. The gun was fully loaded. Gregory kicked the door closed.

"You got a warrant?" the woman said. I had to look twice. She was the pale blond groupie we'd seen with Sonny at the Ross homicide and in the Sawmill bar. The one with the white eyebrows. "Let me see your fucking warrant. Anybody could say they were cops."

Gregory pivoted smoothly through doorways of other rooms. I walked the blonde back until she plopped down on a sofa. A boy in a Spider-Man shirt held the little girl in his arms.

"Just the three of you," I said. "Anyone else here?"

"You see anybody else?" she said. "I don't see no warrant."

"Where's Tina Marquez?" I said.

"For what?" she said. "Who wants to know?"

She was thin but sinewy. Her legs and arms showed long, ropy muscles.

"Her probation officer said she'd be here," I said.

"She didn't mark me down, right? I saw that bitch Tuesday. I can prove it."

"You're Tina Marquez?"

"I said hello to Mrs. Marshall, okay?" she said. "Ask her, she used to be my PO. I never miss my appointments. Ask her."

On the floor was a huge console TV and a stacked stereo system complete with CD player. The apartment was nice, generally clean, furniture new. Not bad at all.

"She is dying to violate my probation," she said. "Three years, I never fucked up once. Ask Mrs. Marshall, okay?"

The green eyes of the boy in the Spider-Man shirt were riveted on me, as if he wanted to burn my face in his memory. His hair stuck up in points like a homemade cardboard crown.

"You don't look Hispanic, Tina," I said.

"Perfect," Tina said. "Cops, right? All you worry about is what nationality you are. Like it's still the 1900s or something."

"It's the name *Marquez*," I said. "You don't expect someone quite so Nordic."

"That's what's wrong with you guys. You got to *understand* everything. Figure the angle. I'm German-Irish, for your fucking information. My married name is Marquez, okay? My name used to be Christina Stohlmeyer. My father is Whitey Stohlmeyer."

"Whitey from the Marina del Rey?" Gregory said.

Every Bronx cop knew Whitey Stohlmeyer. Whitey was the manager at the Marina del Rey, a banquet hall that had hosted a thousand cop parties. Gregory turned on the table lamp and holstered his gun.

"How is Whitey?" Gregory said.

"We don't have a relationship anymore," she said, moving her jaw rapidly as if to yawn. I could see that the spots on her face were freckles and the scars on her arm were old track marks. Old needle marks, nothing fresh.

"You guys ain't from Probation, that's bullshit, right?"

Tina's eyes, like her hair, were as light as her complexion, a stonelike, pale gray. Difficult to look at, like the eyes of someone blind.

"We're from Homicide," I said. "We need to ask you about the murder of Police Officer Marc Ross."

"The squad already talked to me," she said. The squad, I thought, very familiar with cop lingo.

"This is a follow-up," I said.

"Ever hear of business hours?" she said. She was wearing a white Budweiser T-shirt and red panties. Her feet were bare, toenails painted the same deep red as her fingernails. She had a small stone imbedded in the nail on the pinkie of her left hand.

"What did you tell them?" I said. "We could always check it out."

"I was with someone." She shrugged.

"All night?" I asked.

"Matter of fact, yeah," she said. She looked at me closely, and it clicked. She finally recognized us. "You're the guys from the Sawmill the other night. Sonny can't stand your fucking ass."

"What about you?" I said. "I'd think you wouldn't be able to stand those guys. They arrested you, sent your husband to prison. Now you're hanging around with them."

"Those guys saved my ass," she said. "Sonny got me into detox, helped me straighten my life out." She lit a cigarette and rearranged the kids on her lap. "I was doing four dime bags a day when they collared me. Now I'm off the shit completely. Call my PO. She tests me once a week. Go ahead."

"Are you working anywhere?" I asked. I noticed the CD collection, several brand-new titles in the rack.

"Dancing at Gato's Lounge on Westchester Avenue," she said. "Three nights a week."

"Topless?" Gregory said.

"What else, fucking ballet?" she said. "Why? You don't think I got the equipment for topless?"

"I wouldn't know," Gregory said.

"Who were you with the night Marc Ross was killed?" I said.

"They know that shit. I already told them," she said.

I'd read Drumm's report, but it wasn't specific. Only to say she was with a male, a known member of the community. The kids continued to stare at us.

"I want to hear you say it," I said.

"Sure, fine. I was with Sonny."

"Sonny Guidice?" I said.

"You *didn't* fucking know, did you?" she said.

"What's your relationship with Sonny?" I said.

"Ask him."

Before we left I went into the bathroom to wash my hands. I knew it was my imagination, but I could still feel the saliva from the hooker and her condom trick. I searched around in more makeup than I'd ever seen in my life, stacked on the toilet tank, in boxes on the floor. I found a bottle of alcohol, poured it over my hands, and scrubbed.

We took Tina's gun. Told her we'd voucher it into the precinct as found property after we'd checked it through ballistics. The little boy in the Spider-Man shirt continued to stare at me as we walked down the hallway. It was as if he recognized me from somewhere.

"Just remember my name is Marquez," she said as she closed the door. "Tina Marquez. Don't call me Stohlmeyer. I'll never use that name again."

14

"Big Sonny's a regular ladies' man," Gregory said.

"Always was," I said.

After we left Tina's we cruised the perimeter of Crotona Park. Even in the cold night, men lurked around the gates of the park, walking toward the T-bird as we drove by, trying to make eye contact. Trying to see if we were buying, then quickly ducking back into the park.

"I don't trust Sonny," I said.

"I'm beginning to see why you can't stand the prick," Gregory said. "A real barracuda."

The ghetto is filled with poor young women, incredibly powerless and vulnerable. Most are struggling to be the good mother, counting kids after every loud bang from the street, trembling at each deep, angry voice in the hallway. They're frightened, and they're fair game for every pariah wandering the streets, from drunken boyfriends to barracudas in blue. The precinct cop can easily ride in as the white knight, because these women see him, if not as the way out, at least as one night of safety. No wonder they welcome them into their beds. Some guys take advantage, the sportfishermen, they reel them in, throw them back. Some even believe it's because of their looks or charm. Guys like Sonny.

"What do you make of the rebar murders?" I asked.

"Two scumbag drug dealers?" he said. "I think the guy who did them should get a medal."

"It happened right across from Tina's apartment."

"What's that supposed to mean?" he said.

"Don't you think it's a coincidence that two of Santana's drug dealers died just a few hours after Marc Ross? Directly across the street from a place where Sonny Guidice spent the night?"

"Drug dealers get killed all the time. Season's always open."

"Remember what Paul Verdi said in the Sawmill the other night?" I said. "That he suspected Santana of having something to do with the murder of Marc Ross. Think about how adamant Sonny was that it couldn't possibly have been Santana."

"What are you driving at?"

"Maybe Sonny was bullshitting us. He's capable of revenge, of killing those dealers to get back at Santana. Something is going on. Some war, some psycho ego thing is going on between Sonny and Tito Santana."

"Jesus Christ, pally. Don't repeat that to anyone else. That's freaking crazy."

"Assholes like Sonny think an eye for an eye is mandatory."

"You got something on Sonny? Something you're not telling me?"

"I only worked with him three times," I said.

"And never again after he shot that kid, right?"

"Right."

"That still bugs you, don't it?"

"Wouldn't it bother you?" I said.

"Yeah, but I'd get over it."

Gregory drove west on Tremont. I knew exactly where he was going. It would be my first time down that street in over twenty years; I'd avoided it the rest of my time in the precinct. He parked at the corner. The address had been 1645 Bathgate. The building was gone. The entire area had become the Bathgate Industrial Park, three blocks of sleek, modern concrete buildings behind security fences.

"Tell me the story," he said.

It was the first time I'd talked to anyone about it since the grand jury. Except for Leigh, who'd heard it a thousand times. All the physical traces of that day were gone, but the memory was clear in my mind.

Sonny Guidice was filling in, an unknown quantity, less than a year in the precinct. It was just after six P.M: 1805 hours. The call was an assault in progress. When we got there we heard the woman screaming in apartment 4C. A man, inside the apartment with her, told us to go fuck ourselves. A neighbor said he'd been beating her for hours. The door and door frame were solid metal. The woman kept screaming.

We went up to the roof and down the fire escape. The night was warm but windy; the fire escape rattled as we climbed down. When we passed the bathroom I saw the woman, naked from the waist up, washing blood from her face. I went to the bedroom window and pulled it up. It was dusk, and shadows striped the wall as I pushed aside the curtains and quietly stepped down into the room. I held the curtains for

Sonny, then began moving toward the door. I could hear the man's voice, he was right around the corner, in the bathroom with her. As I moved past the bed, I caught a sudden movement rising up from the floor. A striped polo shirt. Then the sound of Sonny's gun, a deafening, wind-sucking blast, and I felt myself jump into the air as the kid flew back against the wall.

"The kid did have a gun, right?" Gregory said. "Looked like a real gun, anyway. In that light."

"He was seven years old, and it was a water pistol. A lime-green water pistol. I think he was coming to help us arrest his mother's ex-boyfriend, who'd beaten her half to death before."

"But Sonny saw *a* gun," he said. "Isn't it possible from his angle he thought it was a real gun? Bottom line: Was it a justified shooting in your mind?"

"That's what I told the grand jury."

"You did the right thing," he said.

"He was seven years old, Joe," I said. "His blood splattered all over my face. When I got back to the locker room I could still hear the mother screaming."

"It was an accident, pally," he said softly. "Don't mean that Sonny ain't a prick. But it was an accident. Forget it."

I won't forget it, I thought. It's wrong to forget, because we'd abused that woman more than any boyfriend ever did. But I didn't say that to Gregory. He thinks I dwell on things.

"I'll tell you the truth," he said. "I think you're looking to nail him now for something that happened twenty years ago."

A "burglary in progress" call came over the Seventh

Division radio Gregory had installed in the T-bird. Tremont and Third Avenue, four blocks away.

"Your problem," Gregory said, "is you think he should be grieving about Marc Ross the way you did about that kid. Some people don't grieve, pally. That don't make 'em criminals."

A blast of siren came from behind us, and a radio car passed by, red light flashing.

"Look at that shit," Gregory said. He meant that we'd been taught not to use the lights and siren or turn them off when you were so close to a location that the noise could warn off the criminal.

We followed the flashing lights. It was a slow night; every car responded, the street awash in swirling red. Gregory stopped up the hill, looking down toward Third Avenue. A woman walked by with a pit bull on a leash. Pit bulls seemed to be the local dog of choice. The dog was wearing a muscle shirt.

"Look at all the ponytails," Gregory said. "What happens if they get in trouble out here?"

There were several female officers at the scene. Gregory called all the young female cops "ponytails."

"They have radios," I said. "They'll do fine."

A male voice over the radio announced itself as five one Adam and declared the burglary unfounded. Cars began leaving the scene. Doors slammed, red lights extinguished. One of the female cops was the tall redhead, Caprice Antonucci, who'd called me "Mr. Ryan" the night of the Ross homicide. She was agitated about something; we could hear the echo of her angry voice. She was pointing her finger, getting in the face of a male cop. The male cop was Sonny Guidice.

"Tell you what," Gregory said. "We've been working

our asses off. Tomorrow night is the racket for Chief Shammy O'Brien at the Marina del Rey. Let's put a twenty-eight in, take the night off, and go. It'll give me a chance to campaign."

"It'll give me a chance to talk to Whitey Stohlmeyer."

"Oh, shit," he said. "I'll lay odds this ain't something Whitey wants to talk about."

"Don't worry about it. I'll go easy on Whitey. But Sonny Guidice gets no slack whatsoever. Absolutely none."

It was four A.M. when I got home. The front light was on, as was the hall light. I went upstairs to check on Leigh. She was on my side of the bed, the green light of the clock radio reflecting on her face.

"I heard you come in," she said.

"Take your insulin shot?" I asked.

"Yes, yes," she said impatiently. "There's a casserole in the refrigerator. I left a note."

I kissed her, patted her hip, then went down to find my note. It was usually on the table, but the table was covered with old photographs. I found the note taped to the refrigerator: broccoli and chicken casserole, in the green bowl. And microwave instructions; she wrote out the microwave instructions every time.

While I ate, I looked through the pictures on the table. The mess surprised me. It was not like Leigh to leave things around. Anything left out, the newspapers, the mail, a note on a scrap of paper, went one of two places: away or out.

Leigh had been in the process of framing a picture. It was an old black-and-white of Margaret, the day we took the training wheels off her bike. Margaret was pedaling toward the camera, her face full of excitement and bravery. I was running behind her, hand extended, looking as if I were trying to pull her back. I took Leigh's note from the refrigerator, attached it to the photo, and wrote: "I get the picture."

15

The next morning Gregory called from the blessing of the horses in midtown. He said he'd pick me up at home and we'd go to the Marina del Rey in one car. After Leigh went to work, I drove to the Five One Precinct.

The old precinct was one of only a few buildings left on the block. During its heyday it was always under siege, two cops stationed at the front door to turn away psychos and drunks. On weekends, welfare check days, and nights when the moon was full, they mopped blood off the floor.

But the Bronx changed. Complete blocks of apartment buildings burned down, thousands moved away. The Five One Precinct was now surrounded by rubble-strewn empty lots. The station house once called Fort Apache was now called the Little House on the Prairie. I parked next to a demolished radio car, the driver's side door tied on by clothesline rope.

Inside, the place was eerily quiet and had the feel of an abandoned seaside home, the furniture covered with sheets. A uniformed cop was at the desk with a young gold-toothed black kid in handcuffs. The gold teeth were "rap caps," a rap music fashion statement. They weren't real dental caps, but gold-plate facades the kids bought in jewelry stores for $25 and put on themselves with pliers and Krazy Glue.

The desk officer handed the cop an appearance ticket, which was given for minor offenses. The prisoner, if he could prove minimal ties in the community, got a date to show up in court and was released. The cops called them "disappearance tickets," because the majority never showed.

A sign with a picture of a finger pointing up said, "Detectives *arriba*." I climbed the metal-tipped stairs. Sergeant Drumm was in his office, a room barely big enough for a desk and a file cabinet. The walls were painted tan on top, dark brown below. An air conditioner jutted from the window.

"Where's your bodyguard?" Drumm said.

"On the campaign trail."

I leaned against the wall; there wasn't enough space in the room for another chair. A row of fluorescent lights ran down the middle of the ceiling. On the wall was a map dotted with colored pins: red for homicide with firearms, yellow for homicide without firearms. The color red was dominant. Two yellow pins stood together in Crotona Park. I knew they were murder by rebar.

"Your boss call you?" he said.

"No, why?"

"I spoke to her this morning," he said. "I'm turning the Ross case completely over to you. Can't afford that many cops working off the chart. Too much other shit going on."

"I don't blame you."

"Hate to do it, a cop killing. I just don't have the people."

The Five One squad was down in man power from the old days, but crime had dipped with the exodus of people. Assaults and robberies were way down, homicides were only one-third of what they were in the seventies.

"I'd like to look at the case folders on the two drug dealers killed in Crotona Park," I said.

"The rebar murders. Don't you have enough to do? I could give you all my cases."

"No thanks," I said. "I'm just curious."

He pulled two large manila folders from a stack. "Knock yourself out," he said.

I sat at the table in the lunch room. Ivy League was the only detective on duty; it was his turn to "catch." In other words, whatever walked through the door for the next two hours, from purse snatch to triple homicide, was his to investigate. Ivy League gave me a nod and went back to reading the *Times*. The TV was on, a daytime talk show. Regis and Kathie Lee. A picture of Marc Ross on the bulletin board was encircled in black crepe.

I dumped out the first envelope onto the table and picked up the crime scene photos. Everybody looked at the photos first. Junior Nieves had thick black hair, shiny and wet with blood. His nose was swollen across his face, and his hands remained up, his body curled and frozen in the fetal position. Photos from the morgue, in better light, showed the extent of the trauma. Bruised and broken fingers appeared to have been attempting to ward off frontal blows.

"You know he went to Cardinal Hayes?" Ivy League said, pointing at the TV.

"Who?"

"Regis Philbin. That's where my dad went. Hayes."

"Good school," I said.

According to the report, the damaging blows to both rebar victims came from the front. In blunt instrument cases the ME could trace the direction of cracks or fractures to the skull to determine the direction of force. Not a professional job, I thought. Injuries to the brain were more likely to be fatal when delivered to the back of the skull, not the front. Professional hit men knew this, which was why Mob execution victims were shot in the back of the head. Sonny would know it, too.

I looked through the Colon file. From the pictures it was apparent that the ME was trying to ascertain the markings of the weapon. The pattern of the wound often matched the shape of the weapon. The ME had laid a piece of rebar alongside the face of Jesus Colon. The imprint matched like a rubber stamp.

Whoever killed Junior Nieves and Jesus Colon walked right up to them. It was somebody powerful, somebody they both knew. In my mind I could see Sonny, in a fit of rage at the death of his partner, charging into the park. Tina Marquez, when questioned in the Ross murder, said she had spent that entire night with Sonny Guidice. Neither one, in my opinion, had a credible alibi witness.

As I stood up, a small plastic Baggies fell out of the file. Inside was a religious card. On the front was a picture of the Virgin Mary ascending into the clouds. On the back of the card was stamped "Hernandez Funeral Home," with a printed prayer that began, "Lord, make me the instrument of your peace."

I asked Sergeant Drumm about the card as he dropped coins into the candy machine.

"Oh, shit," he said. "That was supposed to go back to the property clerk."

Drumm bought a Snickers and looked at the card.

"Out of Mallomars?" I said.

"Got some home in the freezer."

There were three candy machines in the Five One. The precinct clubs owned the machines. The profits went to finance the annual precinct picnic and for flowers sent to the families of deceased cops. Junkies kept the machines going. Junkies loaded up on sweets before going downtown, well aware of the long hours ahead in the pens at central booking.

"We found this card about ten yards away from Nieves's body," Drumm said. "No prints on it. Hernandez said they keep stacks of these cards in the back of all their funeral homes. Seven locations in the Bronx. Anyone could walk in and pick them up."

"So that's it?"

"That's it," he said.

The main office of the Hernandez Funeral Home was on the Grand Concourse, near Fordham Road, where Leigh and I bought our first furniture thirty years ago. It was on my way home, so I stopped. Outside the funeral home, workmen were installing a new awning. It was my first daytime ride through the Bronx in years, and I was surprised at all the new construction.

I pulled into the bus stop, then remembered that Gregory had our only PD parking plate. We'd had two plates until Delia checked the books. I backed up into the meter as the Bx2 bus swung around me and pulled to the curb with the hiss and pop of air brakes. Women shoppers got off, women shoppers boarded, and the door closed. I shoved my notebook into my jacket pocket and dug coins out of the console tray. Then, as the bus started to pull away, I saw Tina Marquez run from the bank, carrying a huge shopping bag that said "Caldor."

Tina ran alongside the bus, slapping the side of it with her free hand until the driver stopped. She hand-fluffed her blond, spiky hair as the door opened, gave the driver a big smile, and climbed in.

I fed the meter and went into the funeral home. A menu board in the foyer announced that visiting hours started at seven. Under that were three names listed in white plastic letters: Lourdes Mejias in room A, Anita Sanchez in B, and Darnell Robinson in C. The air was stale with flowers. I walked down a long hallway, looking for anyone in black. My shoes creaked on the bare wooden floor. The place was empty except for Anita, Darnell, and a small girl in a pink dress: Lourdes. I opened a door that said "Staff Only" and found a young woman with a face trained for bad news.

"May I help you," she said somberly. She said she was Marta Hernandez. In her late twenties, dressed in a white silk blouse and jeans. Long black hair, piled on top of her head, cascaded down in the long tubelike curls my mother called kielbasa curls.

"I'm Detective Ryan," I said.

I asked her about the prayer card. She said she'd already talked to the detective about it. Her voice had just a faint trace of an accent, more Bronx than Hispanic.

"I don't know what else I can tell you. We give out prayer cards by the thousands, usually with the name of the deceased printed on the back."

"This card had nothing stamped on the back except Hernandez Funeral Home."

"Blank cards we leave on a table near the entrance."

"How many different types of cards are there?" I said.

"Oh, God, dozens. At least."

Marta wore a ring on each finger. She opened the top drawer of a green file cabinet and pulled out an album of religious cards. I pointed out the one, the Blessed Virgin ascending, pink roses falling around her.

"Any significance to this card?" I said.

"I cannot speak for all the other directors. But this is a card I would give in the death of a child."

I hadn't noticed it before, but the card depicted angels, infant angels, floating above the Virgin Mary.

"Could I see a list of children you've recently buried?"

"I'll have to ask my father," she said. "He's downstairs."

I followed Marta Hernandez down a wide metal staircase, ready for the worst. But as we pushed down the bar and opened double steel doors, I heard the sound of leather slapping and the scraping of shoes shuffling across canvas.

In the center of a large room with a low ceiling was a boxing ring built only inches above the cement floor. Two slim brown-skinned boys jabbed at each other under the watchful gaze of an old man holding a stopwatch. The room was warm and smelled of sweat.

"My father," Marta said as we approached the man standing on the ring apron. "It's all he does anymore. Work with these boys. We have five Golden Glove champions from here."

We weaved our way between young boys skipping rope, punching heavy bags, speed bags. Some were grunting, some breathing rhythmically, some blasting air through their noses. The walls were covered with fight posters: Boom-Boom Mancini, Hector Camacho. Purple satin robes blaring "Hernandez Funeral Homes" in iridescent script hung from hooks. I stood back as she spoke to her father, expecting to be introduced. But he didn't want to know me.

Marta and I went alone into a back room filled with empty coffins. Different colors, different sizes. Some large, some the size of a beer cooler you'd bring to the beach. She sat at an old wooden desk crammed into a corner, turned on the computer, and hit a series of keys.

"This printer is faster than the one upstairs," she said. "I can go back two years with this. Otherwise we have to look through files by hand."

"One year is fine."

"What age group?"

"Twelve and under," I said. "No. Make it sixteen."

Marta punched keys and the computer clicked and whirred, then a list popped up, filling the screen. She paged down and down. There was always more death than you thought. Tragedies that didn't touch you personally evaporated in the buzz and babble of daily life.

"I can separate them by age and gender," she said. "But they're still listed chronologically. By date of death."

I knew that. I could see the name on the top of the list. It was Lourdes Mejias. I knew where she was. Upstairs, in a pink dress.

"How many names are there?" I said.

"Sixty-seven," she said.

"In a year?" I heard the surprise in my own voice.

"You kidding?" she said. "We're way down. In the seventies we got two or three a week in this office alone."

"What happens if we stop at age fourteen?" I said.

Forty-one names came up.

"Should I cut it down further?" Marta said. "Stop at the twelve-year-olds?"

"No," I said. "That's enough."

Marta printed the list, then walked me to the front door. For the second time I turned my back on Lourdes Mejias in her pink dress.

16

The Marina del Rey is a catering hall at the far southeastern tip of the Bronx, at the end of Tremont Avenue. It overlooks the East River near the point where it meets the Long Island Sound. Over the years I'd made dozens of cop rackets at the Marina. Gregory had attended hundreds. But this time I was sober, and Gregory, who used to park outside the gate and walk in, drove the T-bird right up to the front door and waited for the valet.

"You're talking to Whitey Stohlmeyer on your own," he said. "I want no part of that."

"Understood," I said.

He tipped the valet a deuce from his thick roll of singles. At affairs like this, Joe Gregory tossed dollar bills like grass seed into the wind. We stepped into the lobby and lined up to get our tickets. The secretaries to the chiefs, a clique of their own, sat behind a folding table, checking off the paid list, scrutinizing new checks. They all wore corsages and ran the financial end of the rackets the way they ran the PD, without giving an inch. Everybody paid: no special contracts, no exceptions.

Chief Seamus O'Brien and wife, whom few had seen before in his forty years in the department, were greeting guests in a reception line. Mrs. O'Brien wore the same corsage as the secretaries.

"Tell you a story about Shammy O'Brien," Gregory said. "True story. This one night he gets bombed making the rounds in Manhattan. Totally shit-faced. A couple of hours later he wakes up on the subway, his pockets are slit, his wallet, gun, and shield are gone. What he does, the sly bastard, is he goes down under the Brooklyn Bridge and pushes an old bum into the East River. Then he jumps in after him. Not only does he avoid the fine for losing his gun and shield, which he claimed he lost in the water, but he gets a medal as the *Journal American* hero of the month."

Whitey Stohlmeyer was behind the table, checking last minute arrangements. Whitey walked with a limp, the result of challenging an el pillar with his Impala. El pillars always won.

"Might as well do it now," I said.

"I'll find the cocktail line," Gregory said.

Whitey stood in front of the fountain, the centerpiece of the lobby. A white grand piano floated on a Plexiglas lily pad in the center of the fountain. Behind the piano was a wall of mirrors reflecting the scene. After Whitey finished his conversation with a uniformed waiter, I moved in.

"Whitey," I said, "my name is Anthony Ryan, from the chief of detectives office. We met a few years ago."

He said, "Oh, yeah," but he didn't know me. He'd met armies of cops.

"I'm the Great Gregory's partner," I said. The buzz of voices was getting louder as the lobby filled up.

"Joe Gregory, that crazy bastard," he said, smiling. "Is he here?"

"He went to get a drink."

"That bastard didn't stop to say hello."

"He was very thirsty," I said. "He said he'd see you later."

"I could tell you some stories about that guy," he said.

Whitey was bald, just a rim of chalky hair, but he had the same gray eyes as his daughter. I could see where Tina got her coloring.

"Whitey, I want to talk to you about Tina."

Whatever blood contributed to Whitey's complexion evaporated, and he blended in with the piano behind him.

"Christina," he said. "When I knew her she was Christina."

"I saw her the other day."

Whitey raised his hands to stop me. "You got kids, Ryan?" he said. "Am I coming up and telling you about your kids? No, I'm not. 'Cause you'd say it's none of my business. And you'd be right. See my point?"

"She's doing good, Whitey. She looks good, her kids look well taken care of."

"That's great. It's real noble of you to deliver that message. I wish her the best. Now excuse me, I got a racket to run."

"Do you know this cop she's going with?" I said.

"Excuse me," he said again, and limped toward the banquet room.

I wandered around until I found a roving bar and

ordered a club soda. Lines of guys in wrinkled suits were circling the hors d'oeuvres table. A few more women were showing up at the affairs, but the ratio still had to be thirty to one. I saw dozens of faces I recognized, it just took an extra second to factor in the aging process. Retired cops attended in larger numbers than active ones. The room was filled with guys telling the same old stories, trying to pretend they didn't miss the job terribly. Gregory stood in a circle of old detective commanders, each one wearing one of Gregory's shamrock detective badges. I squeezed in and stood next to Neville Drumm.

"Twenty-five years ago this summer I took over the Five One squad," Neville said. "Remember that summer, '69? Antiwar demonstrations all over New York."

"The amazing Mets," I said.

"The Black Panthers," Gregory said.

"Yeah," Neville said, "and Neil Armstrong walked on the moon, we had Woodstock, the Manson murders out west, Chappaquiddick."

"Chappaquiddick never should have been a big deal," Gregory said. "Who the hell was advising Teddy Kennedy, anyway? All these Harvard eggheads, they had all night to come up with a story, and that was the best they could do? I'll tell you this, if Teddy Kennedy had driven off the Fifty-ninth Street Bridge and I was the squad commander, I would have dived into the water and handcuffed that broad myself."

"What crime did she commit?" I said.

"Grand larceny auto," Gregory said. "I would have said, 'Listen, Teddy, this is what happened: you got out to take a piss, she jumped behind the steering wheel and took off. You ran after her and saw the car plunge into the water. You dove in, tried to save her, but it was too late.' Teddy would have been the president. I would have been the goddamn attorney general."

The decibel level escalated as the room filled and the booze flowed. It sounded like a hive of giant bees with the amps turned all the way up. Whitey Stohlmeyer finally limped in and called everybody into the main dining room. I filed by him on the way down the corridor. He never looked at me.

"Struck out with Whitey, right, pally?" Gregory said. "Told you, didn't I?"

"You did."

"You expect him to welcome you with open arms?"

"He's still her father."

"And I suppose you're going to remind him of his parental duties."

"Maybe I will."

Gregory and I stopped by the men's room on the way, knowing some dinner speeches got out of control. A greasy-looking kid in a waiter's uniform handed out paper towels at the sink. Gregory tipped him a buck. The kid sneaked a sip from a plastic cup he'd hidden behind the towels. His eyes watered when he put it down.

"Delia's here," Gregory said. "Should we sit with her?"

"No," I said.

"Good. She's sitting with the power crew from the Guardians. We might get in her way when she tries to get her nose up the chief's ass."

We grabbed a table with Neville Drumm and a crew from Missing Persons. Two wine carafes filled with draft beer were on each table. People on the dais were already eating. Everybody at our table picked the prime rib. I ordered shrimp scampi.

Above the center of the dance floor was a huge glass chandelier that looked like a million icicles. I thought about the icicles that formed the Blessed Virgin Mary the bitter cold night we found the body of Marc Ross. I thought about where the killer went. How far did she walk in that weather, covered with blood?

A former chief, a usual toastmaster, read one-liners from a stack of index cards. He'd already gotten O'Brien's wife's name wrong twice. The disc jockey tried to match drumrolls and canned laughter with the punch lines. Then Shammy got up to speak and was either drunk or too emotional; his speech was disjointed and rambling. I felt sorry for him but wished he hadn't spoken so bitterly about the new PC. Shammy'd been asked to retire. He should have done it with grace. When he started to sing "Four Green Fields," they helped him to his seat.

"Shammy has Irish Alzheimer's," Gregory said. "He's forgotten everything but his grudges."

When the speeches ended, the guys who didn't rush to the men's room rushed to the floating bars. I'd been watching Whitey, and I saw him sneak outside onto the deck.

I stepped out into the cool night air. Whitey was at the wall, at the end of the flagstone patio. I walked toward the red glow of his cigarette and stood a few feet away, looking out at the river. The river was wide at this point, where it joined the Long Island Sound. The night was quiet and serene, not a car horn, not a voice. The outline of trees and the moon reflected in the still water. It could have been the lakes of Sligo.

"I don't know anything about any cop she's living with," Whitey said. "Couldn't be worse than what she's had."

I could tell Whitey had been drinking.

"She was first in her class at St. Luke's," he said. "Nuns loved her. Could have had a full boat scholarship to Fordham. Full boat. She was so smart. I know everybody bullshits about their kids, but this is the truth. You could look it up at St. Luke's."

A burst of laughter came from inside. The wind blew off the water. It wasn't a bitter wind. It had the smell of mud and a hint of the brackish water of the sound. A barge sat in the middle of the river, straddling the line between the Bronx and Queens.

"I wanted her to be a lawyer or a doctor," Whitey said. "She wanted to be an actress. Always in dance lessons, some kind of lessons. Plays at school, and everything like that. I talked to her a million times. What can you say? Kids today. They know everything. Can't tell them shit, right?"

"They have those years, Whitey. But they get past them."

We were in between bridges. To the right was the Bronx Whitestone Bridge, to the left the Throgs Neck Bridge. Two long strands of silvery beads reflected in the black water. The beads of an incandescent rosary.

"No college for her," Whitey said. "No sir. Enrolled in that acting school downtown. An apartment in the Village, the whole shmear. Then she called me, needed a part-time job. I know people in this business. No problem. Got her waiting tables in a nice place. Windup is that's where she meets this creep Hector Marquez. He was a busboy. She never came home again."

Whitey sucked on his cigarette desperately, as if trying to draw the life out of it.

"She might want to come home now, Whitey," I said.

"Don't patronize me," he said.

"I'm not. I think she'd appreciate your help."

Joe Gregory whistled from the patio door. He had his coat on, and he was waving his arms for me to come quickly. It was way too early for him to be ready to leave. I knew it had to be important. I turned to walk away.

"Hey, Ryan," Whitey said. "Tell her to call me."

17

Rebar man had struck again. Gregory's T-bird brought up the rear of a small convoy of sirens and lights racing from the Marina del Rey to Crotona Park.

"This police work shit is cutting into my campaign time," Gregory said. "This ain't even our case."

"There has to be a connection here," I said.

"What connection, what?"

Light filtered through the thickening foliage of the park. Gregory bounced the T-bird over the curb and squeezed through the old iron gate. The path was barely wide enough for a car. We passed within inches of a broken drinking fountain and green benches bolted into concrete. Gregory parked on the grass at the end of a line of NYPD vehicles.

"Lot of blue in here," he said. "Must be expecting the crowd to turn ugly."

People had drifted over from the buildings that ringed the park. They weren't there to watch us work; death was the drawing card. They'd disappear as soon as the body was carried away. We put on our shields and kept to a straight line, a path to the body we knew the others had walked. Yellow crime scene tape was tied through the trees, funneling everyone up to the scene.

"What's this shit?" Gregory said. "Like the teller line they got in Citibank."

Behind the ten-foot wall of the handball court, Emergency Service floodlights focused on a bloody figure spread-eagle on a grungy mattress. The body was curled, but you could see the face was mashed and bloody. Blood had sprayed a halo around his head. Several small, yellow-capped vials lay near his knee. A crack pipe and a cheap blue cigarette lighter lay on the grass against the wall. In the darkness at the edge of the path, uniformed cops bantered with the crowd.

"He's over there, pally," Gregory said. "I know you're looking for Sonny Guidice."

Gregory pointed to the Crime Scene Unit van. Paul Verdi and Sonny Guidice carried flat boxes filled with containers of coffee. They were handing them out to the cops working the scene.

"You think Sonny killed this guy," Gregory whispered, "then went out and bought coffee for everyone?"

"I always buy when I kill someone."

"Whoever did this had to get blood all over them," Gregory said. "The guy is standing right there. No blood." He moved close to me, and I could smell the booze. I was becoming more uncomfortable with him when he drank. "You best keep theories like that to yourself. We don't have a lot of friends here as it is."

Gregory moved off to work the crowd. Emergency Service wheeled another searchlight closer to the body. The perimeter search had ended, and they were lighting the body for pictures. I asked Neville Drumm if the victim had been ID'd. I called him "Sarge," because young cops were listening.

"Jorge Colon, the brother of the first vic," Drumm said. "And the weapon was rebar, again. No doubt about it."

"He work for Santana?"

"Took his older brother's spot."

"Looks like a user."

"Yeah. Some of them are. But they come back here away from the street. They say Santana would kill them if he found out."

"Maybe he found out," I said.

"If Santana killed this guy, he killed all three."

The crowd beyond the path was getting bigger and louder. A boom box blasted a rap song. Someone turned the volume to max every time a certain line played. I couldn't understand the words, but I was sure the message was "Fuck the police." I walked over to Gregory. He was talking to a guy in a Yankees jacket.

"Tell my partner what you told me, Chico," Gregory said. "And his name really is Chico, pally."

"That's my mattress," Chico said, pointing. "That *maricón* is bleeding on my mattress. I don't want it back, shit. Fuck that shit."

"How'd they get your mattress?" I said.

"Stole it."

"Why?"

"They steal everything," he said.

"Tell him how," Gregory said. "He loves these stories. He collects them."

Chico said that several months ago he and his wife had been arguing. He told her he was going to sleep on the roof landing. Chico took the mattress and walked out the door. His wife ran into the hallway and begged him to stop. They talked and started making up in the doorway, and the making up became passionate, so he closed the door to his apartment. Less than a minute later he decided he needed the mattress, but when he opened the door it was gone.

"Give me a badge and gun," Chico said. "I'll kill all these motherfuckers."

It was less windy than it had been at the Marina. The air was damp, and the grass smelled strong. It occurred to me that spring had finally arrived. Over a month late.

I started walking back toward the car. The crowd was still coming down the path. It was just after nine P.M. I heard Gregory running to catch me.

"C'mon, we'll stop back at the racket," Gregory said. "Have a quick one and I'll drive you home."

"Give me a minute," I said. "I'm going to see if Tina's home. I'll meet you on the corner."

I crossed through the playground, which smelled of fresh paint. They took great care of this playground, even painting lines for games on the blacktop.

At the corner, I surprised a skinny kid with vacant brown eyes selling subway tokens. His nose and lips were dotted with flecks of silver paint. Paint sniffers were notorious token suckers. They'd hang around subway stations and suck tokens right out of the turnstile slot. They sold them on the street for whatever they could get, but all they needed was enough money to buy the next aerosol can. In the angle of light the silver spots on his face looked like black holes.

A blue Chrysler from Metro Cabs idled at the curb in front of Tina's building. I went up and knocked on her door. I heard her kids calling, then the sound of high heels clicking down the hallway.

"Oh, man," Tina said. "What do you want now?"

"I have something to tell you."

"Shit," I heard her say as she unlocked the door.

"Make it fast," she said. "I got to get to work."

She looked different dressed for work, eyes heavily made up. Dark red, almost black lipstick. The kids stood in the middle of the floor, all holding things, pillows, books, dolls.

"We'll give you a ride," I said.

"I got a cab downstairs," she said. "Emily, you got your medicine? Get your medicine. Tell Lita to give it to you before you go to bed."

"Are they going to their grandmother's?" I said. I knew *Lita* was a term used for "grandmother." Tina walked into the bathroom and ran water on a washcloth.

"They call my neighbor *Lita*," she said. "She baby-sits for them. Now say what you got to say that's so important."

Tina knelt in front of the kids and scrubbed their faces and hands roughly with the washcloth.

"I spoke to your father. He wants you to call him."

She looked at me, a fast glance out of the corner of her eye, then finished washing the boy, who this night wore a Superman shirt.

"C'mon, kids," she said. "C'mon, c'mon. Kevin, watch your sister." She herded the kids down the hallway. I followed.

"He said he wanted you to call him, Tina," I said.

"What did you tell him about me?"

"I said you could use some help with the kids."

"I'm doing just fine with the kids."

"Whitey is their grandfather."

Tina knocked on the door of the apartment across the hall. The kids looked up at the door in anticipation. Kevin's hair stuck up, still wet from the cloth.

"He should have thought of that years ago," she said. "I don't need his help now."

"It's better than taking shit from Sonny Guidice."

"Is it?" she said. "You don't know anything, do you."

The door to 3A, across the hall, was opened by a boy with a T-shirt tied in a knot at his waist, his hair pulled straight back in a ponytail. A striking boy. Beautiful. His face was so smooth and finely textured, it looked woven to perfection. But he was older than my first impression. The kids ran past him, down a long hallway to an older woman with salt-and-pepper hair piled up on her head.

Tina slapped the boy across the abdomen and looked past him. "I'll be home by two, Lita," she yelled to the old woman.

"Let them stay," the boy said. "Don't get them up in the middle of the night." Then he smiled, an immense white smile, and stepped back behind the door, but not before I saw his right forearm, the blistery scar of a severe burn. I could hear the wheel spinning on *Wheel of Fortune*.

"Thanks, Lita," Tina said. "Take care, Angel."

Angel. Angel closed the door. Tina clacked down the stairs ahead of me. The Metro Cabs driver was a black man with a message in red marker written across his shaved head: "Our fate is in the hands of the Lord." Tina opened the door and climbed in. After they left I tried to describe the boy's beauty to Gregory.

"Let's not get carried away here, pally," he said.

I knew I'd seen him before. In a magazine. Maybe a

model or an actor. The eyebrows slightly arched, too smooth and even, as if plucked. The big brown eyes, the whites so clean and perfect, they looked blue. But it was the skin; I'd never seen skin like that before.

And then I knew where I'd seen that face before, that smile. It was framed in a big, black gypsy hairdo. And running. Running to a cab in Chelsea.

"That's who it is," I said. "From the Sweet Life. That's who we followed. That's who I lost in the park that night."

18

The following night we were back to get a closer look at Angel. At seven P.M. we parked next to the playground, opposite 719 Crotona Park North. The weather was getting warmer; kids played in sweatshirts and light jackets.

"This is like having a date for the prom," Gregory said. "Wondering how she'll look in her new gown."

"I could be wrong about this," I said.

"You ain't wrong, pally."

The phone currently installed in apartment 3A was unlisted. We'd officially requested the number, plus records of outgoing calls. Con Ed told us the electric was in the name of Lupe Aponte, but bills were paid with checks signed by Angel Aponte.

"What's our story here?" Gregory said. "We don't want this he-she to disappear into the wind on us."

"I'll ask them if they know anything about the murders in the park. Their window faces right into the park."

Sonny Guidice and Paul Verdi passed us twice in the radio car, swooping into the park from different angles, circling their prey: the hand-to-hand crack sellers who appeared from the bushes every time a car cruised slowly down the block.

The park was full of dealers. Anybody with a hundred bucks and a hot plate could go into the crack business. Some just sold "dummies," placebos like soap chips, in a crack vial. One guy sold his asthma medicine cut up to look like beige crystals.

"I heard Sonny keeps a fresh supply of rebar in the trunk," Gregory said. "So whenever the mood strikes him he's ready."

"Knock it off," I said.

Francis X. Hanlon, the old cop fighter, was out in the street, raising his hand, playing traffic cop, whenever a kid crossed the street. When a carload of teenagers made the turn into the block, stereo thumping, Francis X. stood there, arms folded, until they passed. Tina's angry little boy, Kevin, was among those crossing earlier. All the kids said good night to Francis X., calling him "Padre."

"Look at that psycho," Gregory said.

A small Hispanic woman in a flowered house dress came out of 711 Crotona Park North from under a pink plastic awning with hearts that said "Juanita's Beauty Salon." She scuffed across the street on the backs of her slippers and handed a paper bag to Francis X. He blessed her, a big swooping sign of the cross in the air. Then he ripped open the bag and began to eat. It looked like a plate of rice and beans.

"Now they're feeding him," Gregory said.

"They're taking care of him, for taking care of the kids."

"He ever take a punch at you when you worked here?"

"Never."

The first time I saw Francis X. he was hanging in the Five One squad room. Literally hanging. I had only been out of the Police Academy a few weeks. I was getting dressed in the locker room when some older cop told me to go to the squad room. "They got that cop fighter again," he said, "jumped Tommy Kiley." Francis X. was hanging from the cage, handcuffed above his head, his feet tied with a sheet. A few cops were lined up, waiting their turn, while Tommy Kiley thumped punches into his rib cage. Most of us walked away. I never saw it happen again. Beatings like that ended long before the 1972 Knapp Commission on Police Corruption.

"Let's go," I said. "Get this over with."

We shoved everything under the car seat: radio, flashlight, and files. I got a whiff of fresh paint when I got out. Someone had painted the monkey bars red. It looked like the same red they used to paint the hydrants. Francis X. sat on a swing, eating yellow rice with a white plastic spoon and singing one of those hymns you hear coming from a Bowery mission.

"Your buddy's calling you," Gregory said.

"He's singing," I said.

"No, he's calling you."

"Brother Ryan," Francis X. said. "I had a dream."

"Now he's thinks he's freaking Martin Luther King," Gregory said.

"You and me," Francis X. said. His beard was full of rice.

"Probably dreaming about the night I hit him," I said.

"I blame the state," Gregory said. "Letting people

like him out on the street. Find the damn money in the budget."

"That's nice, Francis," I said.

We walked up three flights, staying away from the open rail and an aimed brick from above. I wondered how many thousands of flights of stairs a ghetto cop climbed in his lifetime. Dozens of times a day, every day. And all the buildings were five stories, because if builders went any higher, they'd need to install elevators and expensive water pumps.

Gregory banged on apartment 3A for several minutes. When the old woman finally answered she swung the door wide open and walked back into the apartment.

"Policía," Gregory said as we hesitated, looking down the long hallway.

It was the same railroad apartment as Tina's, the mirror image: all the rooms on the right, windows to the park on the left. I closed the door and we walked down the hallway, passing a bathroom, a kitchen, and a closed black door with a hand-painted moon and stars.

In the living room Tina's kids sat on the floor, watching *The Cosby Show*. A sheer curtain separated the living room from a back bedroom. A crucifix was centered above the bed, a double bed neatly made, covered with a faded quilt. On the dresser, candles burned around a statue of the Blessed Virgin. I assumed that Angel's bedroom was behind the closed door with the moon and stars.

"We'd like to ask you some questions," I said. I found myself talking loud, as I did to my father. The old woman, on a worn pea-green recliner, watched *Cosby*, didn't pay any attention to us. "Last night there was a murder across the street."

We stood there. She continued to stare at the TV. A

wall tapestry behind her depicted the faces of JFK, RFK, and Martin Luther King Jr. On top of the television was a plastic palm tree, "Puerto Rico" painted in white across the base.

"Do you live here alone?" I said, getting louder.

"She don't speak English," Tina's boy, Kevin, said.

The apartment was warm and smelled of something fried. The window that faced on the park was coated with a greasy film. A Roach Motel sat directly behind the TV.

"Señora," I said.

"She can't hear, either," the boy said, pointing to his ears.

When the commercial came on the old woman got up and opened the door with the moon and stars. She slammed it behind her, but it didn't lock and Gregory pushed it open.

The old woman had her back to us, going through a black satin jewelry box on a red lacquer dresser. Four white Styrofoam heads lined the dresser. Each bore a fancy woman's wig: two blacks, one each blond and red. Dominating the room were two metal clothes racks on wheels, the kind you see being pushed around the garment district. Both overflowed with skirts, dresses, and blouses. An unmade single bed lined the opposite wall.

The old woman saw us and came out quickly, closing the door behind her. She handed me a business card. It said, "Sally's II the best TV bar in the theater district."

TV did not mean television. Television was what the old woman was staring at when we left.

We parked on West Forty-third Street next to the *New York Times* building. Three-card monte was the game on the corner. Grimy black ice hid in corners where the sun never shined. The smell of burning chestnuts came from a cart outside a *Times* loading bay. The theater crowd, dressed to the hilt, was hustling in all directions. The three blocks directly north of where we parked still contained the best live theater in the world. A sign outside Sally's II advertised a nightly "drag doll revue."

Inside Sally's, a red canopy covered a circular wooden bar in the front room. A few little cliques gathered around the bar. Microskirts and stiletto heels seemed to be the rage. I wondered how drunk you had to be to pretend any of them were women. But maybe that wasn't the game.

We grabbed a spot at the bar. Gregory stood next to a person in a short leather skirt who sat cross-legged on a stool, showing off the thighs of a linebacker. On the opposite side of the bar a drunken businessman was in a deep discussion with the barmaid. The barmaid leaned over within inches of his face. She wore a sheer black dress. Her panty line indicated a preference for high-cut French bikinis.

"Ask her," I said, motioning to the linebacker.

"You mean him," Gregory said. "That's a guy."

"Tell her that," I said.

Sinatra sang "My Way." That fact alone put Gregory in a bad mood. I leaned around him and faced the linebacker.

"Is Angel around?" I asked.

"We're all angels, sweetie," she said. Her leather jacket unzipped to the navel to expose breasts and nipples. The barmaid turned around and looked at me.

The barmaid was Angel. She moved toward me slowly, wiping the bar. It was Angel, no doubt about it. Dressed in basic black, the neckline showing modest cleavage, black fishnet stockings, and blood-red high heels.

"Angel," I said.

"My name is Lucinda," Angel said, "but I could be an angel."

"Be an angel now," I said. "And meet us in that back booth."

"Why would I want to do that?" Angel said.

I showed my shield. The businessman gulped his drink and scooped his money off the bar.

"Melody, will you . . . ?" Angel said.

The linebacker named Melody swung off the stool and stepped behind the bar. A small white Buddha sat in the center of the canopy, bathed in a blue spotlight. "Would you guys like a drink?" Melody asked.

"Not me," I said.

"On the house," Melody said.

"Bud. In the bottle," Gregory said.

In the age of AIDS, Gregory ordered bottles in places where he didn't trust the glasses. If he had to get a glass, he'd ask for a mug, then he'd pick it up with his left hand, figuring fewer left-handers, less chance of diseased lips. Play the percentages, he said.

Angel grabbed her purse, and I followed her to the back booth as she overswiveled her hips like Monroe. She was thin but had a waist and hips.

"No one here calls me Angel," she said, sliding into the booth.

Above her head the wall was filled with signed black-and-white studio photos of begowned creatures, all tacky fashion and glamour. Heavy on outfits with feathers.

"For the record, Angel," Gregory said, banging his beer down on the table, "are you male or female?"

"What record?" she said.

Even up close her skin was incredible. The fine texture didn't need makeup. The smell of her perfume was soft and delicate, not overpowering, as was that of the line-backer.

"I'll tell you this for your record," she said. "If I win the lottery tomorrow, I'll be on the next plane to Trinidad. When I come back I'll tell you very proudly that I'm a woman."

"Why Trinidad?" I said.

"Actually, Trinidad, Colorado," she said. "It's a small town near the New Mexico border. There's a clinic there. It's where everybody goes."

"Ever go to a club called the Sweet Life?" I said.

"Who doesn't?" Angel said. "Third Tuesday of the month. It's a blast. You ought to go."

Angel's voice was husky and deep. But if she called you on the phone and said she was Lucinda, you'd buy it.

"Did you go there Tuesday the nineteenth?" I said.

She flaked a piece of lipstick from the corner of her mouth and put a cigarette in. I picked up her lighter and lit it for her. She stared at me across the flame. Gregory was watching the bathrooms, trying to figure the etiquette.

"You chased me though the park," she said, blowing smoke through her nose. "When I saw you with Tina last night, I knew I'd seen you before. I thought maybe in a past life."

"Did you spot us following you?" Gregory said.

"The cabbie did."

"Why did you run?" I said.

"Are you kidding?" she said. "You want to know how many nights guys have followed me home?"

"Not really," Gregory said.

I started with the sketch of the killer. It didn't look like Angel to me, but I wanted to see a reaction. It was a smile, a big white-toothed smile. And that complexion, so smooth, reddish brown. Like your skin after the best beach day of your life.

"I hope that's not supposed to be me?" she said. "Jesus, look at those eyes."

"Do you think it's supposed to be you?" I said.

"If it is, I'm suing."

"Where were you on the night of April tenth, 1994?"

"What night of the week was that?"

"Sunday."

"I work Sundays from seven until close. I haven't missed a night since I started six months ago. Ask Melody, she's the manager."

Gregory got up and walked toward the bar. Melody was sitting alone. Obviously we were bad for business.

"What time do they close this place?" I said.

"If it's slow," Angel said, "like during the week, we get out of here at one. Doesn't happen often. We have late regulars, and a second show at midnight. Some theater crowd drifts in. Lost tourists, mostly. We advertise in *Playbill*, and we always get a few who think a TV bar is someplace they might run into Oprah. It's hilarious watching them figure it out."

She opened her small black leather purse and pulled out a gold tube of lipstick. Her fingernails were dark red; the color matched her shoes. Lou Reed sang about colored girls.

"You like Lou Reed?" she said. "He's a bad boy."

"Are you a bad girl?" I said.

"How bad do you mean?"

She sat back and worked the lipstick around her full lips. "Is anyone going to tell me what this is about?" she said.

"It's about a murder," I said.

"Oh, I confess," she said. "I'll gladly cop to that. But I'd cut their balls off first. That neighborhood would be great without those bastards."

"You're talking about the drug dealers in Crotona Park."

"They killed a little girl my mother was baby-sitting for," she said. "Maria. Sweetest little thing. Rode by in a car, shooting out the window. That's real men for you, right? Big tough men."

"I'm not talking about them."

"Who are you talking about?"

"A cop," I said.

"Chalk that one up to me, too. What the hell?"

Gregory sat back down, next to me. He hadn't let go of his beer.

"Manager backs her story," he said. "For what that's worth."

"Will you be willing to stand in a lineup?" I said. "Dressed as you are now?"

"Just give me a day's notice," she said. "I can look better."

I handed her the sketch of the dress. The fine-grained skin wrinkled in her brow as she studied it. The dress Angel was wearing was long sleeved. She kept tugging the sleeve to cover the burn on her arm.

"How did you get the burn?" I said.

"Flame thrower," she said. "Jerking around in the park when I was a kid. Spray stuck to my skin."

"Hairspray?" I said.

"WD-forty," she said.

Homemade handheld mini–flame throwers were in the arsenals of many street kids. They'd tape a butane lighter to the top of an aerosol can of hairspray or cleaning fluid. Then they'd flick the lighter and push down the top of the can, and the spray would shoot out in a streak of fire.

"I have a friend who has a burn like that," I said. "She always wears long gloves."

"I've got more gloves than Imelda has shoes," Angel said.

"Jesus Christ!" Joe Gregory yelled, and jumped about two feet in the air, banging his knees against the table. He stood and jammed his hand down into his pocket, as if his shorts were on fire. He pulled out the beeper and threw it on the table.

"A vibrator, how kinky," Angel said. The beeper rattled across the table.

"You had it set to the vibrating function," I said. "Call the night desk."

Gregory went to look for a phone. Angel blew smoke through her nose and looked at the sketch again. She pushed it back to me.

"It's a lovely dress," she said. "But I've never seen it before in my life."

"Not even at the Sweet Life."

"My tastes are more simple than this dress," she said. "Life is complicated enough."

She whisked her hair back off her face. She wasn't wearing a wig. Her hair was thin but shiny.

"Do you know Sonny Guidice?" I said.

"He a friend of yours? No, don't tell me, I don't care. He's a jerk."

When Gregory returned his face was still pale, and he was sweating. He picked up the beeper and shoved it into his coat pocket, then grabbed me by the arm.

"C'mon, pally," he said.

I stood and handed my card to Angel. Told her I'd call her when I'd arranged the lineup. Gregory pulled me again, toward the door.

"Are you okay?" I said.

"It ain't this one," he whispered.

"You know that for a fact."

"I know that for a fact," he said. "The real one just killed another cop in the Bronx. She just killed Paul Verdi."

19

Cop killings always come as a surprise to cops. That's because we operate in an aura of personal immortality. Gregory and I left Angel and rode north, toward the Bronx, in silence. We didn't have all the facts. We needed more facts to distinguish this occurrence as rare, like being hit twice by lightning. No matter how many times we've heard the funeral bagpipes, the next dirge always begins with an icy shriek.

"Why do we say *the* Bronx, anyway?" Gregory finally said. "Nobody says *the* Brooklyn, or *the* Manhattan."

The lights of the city burned with stunning clarity. Soot-covered tenements displayed unique architecture: parapets, cornices, arches I'd never noticed. Graffiti suddenly seemed important.

"A man named Jonas Bronck," I said, "was the first settler north of the Harlem River. Bronck had a big farm, lived there with his family. People going there would refer to the family, as if it were a personal visit. They'd say, 'We're going to the Broncks.' "

"Bullshit. Where'd you read that?"

"I didn't. I heard it on the Circle Line tour."

The radio was quiet. Every few seconds someone would push a transmit button just to hear the static. I was sure the upper echelon, concerned about the instant reaction, hoped the word of Verdi's murder wouldn't leak until after the change of tours. More than half of the cops working the trenches had under five years on the job. Street cops thrive on adrenaline and emotion. Throw a huge dose of youth into the mix and the pot boils over.

But before we reached the Willis Avenue Bridge, the news began to spread.

"Cop killed," a voice over the radio said quickly and with a nervous anonymity. A blast of static, then an eerie silence.

"Where?" a voice said.

"No unauthorized transmissions, please," the dispatcher said. "Units must identify themselves and wait to be acknowledged by Central."

"The Bronx," the first voice said. "The Five One."

"Motherfuckers," someone said.

"Cocksuckers," another voice.

"No unauthorized transmissions," the dispatcher said firmly. "By order of Chief of Patrol Donald P. Walsh. This is KEA841. The time is twenty-three forty-five hours."

"Get the motherfuckers before they get you," someone growled. Then a chorus of profanity and static. An armed, angry mob in blue-and-white cars, all holding down the transmit button, shouting over one another in a frenzied babble of wrath and fear. The dispatcher, helpless, let it play out.

"I've never been on the Circle Line tour," Joe Gregory said as we entered the Bronx. "Never been to the Statue of Liberty, top of the Empire State, roof of the World Trade. Lived here all my freaking life. Lotta shit I never did."

Carter Avenue was clogged with police cars. Cop murders usually drew the biggest crowds, the most blue uniforms, a small fortune in brass. We parked half a block from the scene. Directly opposite 1809 Carter Avenue a handful of print reporters and freelance cameramen surrounded a tiny silver-haired man in a well-tailored black suit. Lenny Marino, the PBA president, looked tan and freshly shaven as he jabbed his finger angrily.

I followed Gregory down a narrow alley behind an abandoned pickle factory. At the end of the alley a Crime Scene tech man dusted the padlock of a ten-foot iron gate. Behind the gate was a walled-in courtyard filled with cops and floodlights. Toward the rear of the courtyard stood a blue-and-white car.

Joe Gregory walked straight to the radio car. He shoved his tie inside his pants so it wouldn't dangle in the pool of blood just below the driver's side door. Then he squatted and looked into the eyes of the dead cop.

Officer Paul Verdi had been shot in the left temple. The entrance wound, an inch behind the left eye, was smudged, but it was small and round. The exit wound on the right side of his neck was typically larger and jagged. The smudge of soot on his face indicated the gun was held close, but not against the skin. I could see the outline of a comb in his right chest pocket.

"He was shot from outside the car," Sergeant Neville Drumm said. "Check the door. Blood on both sides."

Blood, still wet enough for the tech man to use an eyedropper, pooled in a ledge on the top of the door and ran down the light blue paint of car number 3402. The driver's window was open, but the upper door interior frame and roof liner were splattered with blood. Verdi, on his back, was stretched across the front seat, his nose against the bottom of the steering wheel. It appeared he'd been shot sitting up, then he'd slumped or had been pulled across the seat. Like Ross, his pants were down. His thighs and white Jockey shorts were stained with dark tan streaks. Small scarlet blots randomly marked his underwear and skin. Not blood, lipstick. At least six separate smears.

"This scene is bullshit," Gregory said. "Look at all the lipstick and makeup. Who the hell gets that much lipstick on a guy's underwear, unless it's intentional?"

"Any witnesses?" I asked. The floodlights gave off the smell of burning metal.

"We got a bus driver," Drumm said. "Says he saw a black-haired woman get in the radio car on the north side of the park. Long white gloves, fancy dress. Same basic description as the Ross case."

Joe Gregory jammed his hands into a pair of surgical gloves and began working the upper body. I knew he was looking for another button. It wasn't there this time. He marched around to the other side of the car and leaned in, close enough to examine the lipstick marks.

"I figure she got out to take a piss, or something," Drumm said. "Then she came around the side, the window was down. Blam. One shot. Look at this on the ground."

A trail of blood spots on the concrete led a few steps away from the car and stopped well before the alley. It didn't look like the blood of someone injured, fleeing the scene. Blood that fell from a moving body landed in erratic patterns and in a teardrop shape, the pointy end indicating the direction of flight. These were horseshoe shaped and too evenly spaced. Stride length. The heel of a high heel. She'd stepped in her victim's blood and tracked it toward the gate.

"Did you find a shell casing?" I said. If the killer had used an automatic, the shell casing would have ejected. I was thinking about Marc Ross's missing Glock 19, perhaps matching clip markings. If it was the murder weapon.

"Nada," he said. "Nothing's easy."

I looked around at the courtyard, thinking, Why here? It was a completely isolated spot in the center of abandoned factories. The alley was the only way in or out. A Dumpster in the corner overflowed with folded pizza boxes. Beer cans littered the ground. I knew exactly what the place was.

"This is a coop," I said.

"Like you've never been in one before," Drumm said.

A coop is a hiding place cops use to take a break, away from the eyes of bosses or civilians. It's a sanctuary where they go to find a few moments' peace. Some guys sleep, read, or eat; some guys party. When I was in uniform, every street cop held the key to something. I had the camera shop on my foot post. The shop's owner kept four cots in the back closet. He said it was the cheapest security investment in town. The courtyard had all the requirements. I was sure that, in this place, Paul Verdi would have locked the gate behind him when he drove in, in uniform, with a woman.

"How did she get out?" I asked.

Drumm shrugged. "The first cops on the scene found

the gate locked. Verdi's keys are still in his pocket. She either climbed over the fence or had her own key."

"Where was his partner when all this was going on?" I said.

"Sonny was in the station house, writing up a drug collar they'd just made in Crotona Park. Verdi went back to the scene alone, scouting for evidence."

"He was definitely scouting for something."

"Maybe he was scouting for pussy," Drumm said. "I'm telling you what I know."

"Verdi had to know her to bring her here," I said. "What does Sonny say?"

"Has no idea who it could be."

"Maybe he hasn't thought hard enough. I'll talk to him."

"Waste of time," he said. "Already went through it with him."

"So I'll do it again."

Sonny Guidice was in the center of a group of uniformed cops. I pushed my way into the protected circle. Sonny's nose was red, as if he'd been crying. He looked sick, straining to breathe.

"Fucking Ryan," he said.

"Sorry about your partner," I said.

"Nature of the beast," he said. He took three deep breaths.

"What beast?" I said.

"The job. Nature of the fucking job. You know the risks when you raise your hand for the oath. Every fucking body hates you. Everybody wants to see you dead."

His eyes were black but glassy, pupils dilated. After twenty years of darkness the animal adapts, becomes nocturnal.

"If I was with him, man," Sonny said, "never would've happened. No fucking way."

A uniformed cop with a shaved head, whom I'd seen with Sonny's crew in the Sawmill bar, murmured his agreement.

"Did he do this often?" I said. "Patrol alone?"

"Nah," Sonny said. "He said he saw the perp throw something into the bushes. He dropped me off at the house and went back. I'm booking the prisoner, next thing I know all hell breaks loose. Timmy comes running in, says Paulie got shot."

"Paulie have enemies?" I said.

"You shitting me? This fucking jungle? A cop here ain't doing his job if he ain't making enemies."

"Any particular enemy you can think of?"

"Hey," he said. "We made a ton a collars. Half the time we don't even recognize the mutts ourselves. They come up and say, 'Hey, remember me?' We look at each other, don't know the guy from Joe Shit the Ragman."

"What about Tito Santana?" I said.

"I don't know, man."

Sonny's face trembled, and he kept kicking at the dirt. After every sentence he looked away into the air, leaving me to talk to his profile. I didn't think Sonny Guidice had the subtlety to put on this good an act. He was frightened.

"I was fucking with him, man. . . ."

Joe Gregory had borrowed a four-battery flashlight and joined the Crime Scene Unit, checking the ground in the corner behind the Dumpster. Sonny's nose was running in the cold air; he kept rubbing it with his sleeve.

"Think hard, Sonny," I said. "A woman was seen getting in this car with your partner, near Crotona Park. He must have trusted her to allow that."

"Maybe she said she was a witness," he said.

"Why would he bring a witness into the coop?"

"I don't know that. I don't. Really."

"What do you know?"

"I know a good fucking guy is dead over there. A better cop than you ever were."

The ESS captain called for more light behind the Dumpster. A mound of old snow behind the car had been blackened by exhaust fumes.

"Was Paulie a ladies' man?" I said. "Did he have a girlfriend?"

"My partner was married, Ryan. Is this the time for this shit? Really?"

"The clock is ticking. The more it ticks, the better chance the killer will walk."

"Don't ask me that shit," he said. He started shifting his weight from foot to foot, blowing on his hands. "It's like a fucking IAD question."

"You don't have a choice here," I said.

"We'll see about that," he said. "Hey, Timmy, go find Lenny Marino for me. Bring him back here."

"The PBA can't help you, Sonny," I said. "You're not the subject of this investigation. Neither is your partner."

"But this ain't kosher, what you're doing. A guy's reputation is at stake here. Next thing I know, Margie reads some headline in the *Post* saying Paulie's the biggest cocksman in the city."

"Margie is his wife?"

"Yeah," he said. "And he's got two kids out on the Island. Little girls."

I could smell something on Sonny, something slightly sour. He was still dancing from foot to foot.

"Hey, Ryan," he said. "I know you're doing your

job, and all. But I already gave my statement to Sergeant Drumm over there. So fuck you and your bullshit." Then he pushed past me, banging hard into my shoulder. I watched him disappear down the alley.

Joe Gregory always said "Trust your instincts." When the hair on the back of your neck stands up, something is definitely wrong. Sonny Guidice might have been emotional over the death of his partner. Maybe he had other things on his mind. Different people react in different ways. I didn't know. But the hair on my neck was at attention.

"My money says this is a setup," Gregory said as he yanked off the surgical gloves.

"Find anything in the car?" I said.

"Like what?"

"Like evidence."

"Makeup on his shorts," he said. "A gallon of lipstick."

"What was so interesting behind the Dumpster?"

"Fresh cigarette butt."

"Lipstick on it?"

"Not that I could see. Some cop could've flipped it back there."

It took Crime Scene two more hours to finish. The PC never showed. Somebody had warned him the incident was tainted. What they refer to downtown as "moral turpitude."

I walked down the alley, looking for Sonny Guidice. A few freelance photographers milled around the street, hoping for a shot of the body. The same grubby faces every night. Freelancers rode the city until dawn, monitoring all police bands, looking for bloody scenes to sell to tomorrow's papers. Hoping for the one-in-a-million shot, make the front page of the *Times* and put their careers over the top.

Sonny was nowhere to be found. Gregory came down the alley behind me, hands in his pockets, his head down.

"Where'd everybody go?" he said.

Less than a dozen cops were left. An overweight sergeant sat in the radio car, his hat down over his eyes, a black mourning band covering his shield. I found Shaved Head on Webster Avenue.

"Lenny sent him home," Shaved Head said.

"The PBA president sent Guidice home?" I said, my voice getting higher.

"Don't quote me on that," he said. He knew he'd screwed up as soon as he said it. "Might have been Inspector Brosnan, the CO. They were all talking. Shit, I don't know who the fuck gave the order."

He knew who sent Sonny home. I kept looking at him, not quite believing it.

Radio cars drove by in silent procession, up and down Webster Avenue. Cops from different precincts. A curious, impromptu honor guard drawn by the cold reality of our life. At the last second they avert their eyes, deciding they'd rather not know.

"Sonny was under a lot of emotional stress," Shaved Head said. "His nerves are gone."

"So are two cops," I said.

20

On the way to One Police Plaza I wrote down everything while the scene was still fresh in my mind. Although later reports would spell out the facts, there were always nuances, moods, impressions of the moment that wouldn't be captured in stunted copspeak. Sonny, goddamn Sonny. I couldn't understand why he wasn't outraged.

Maybe it was me, maybe I'd been away from the streets too long. Maybe Gregory was right; I was on a witch-hunt, and Sonny wore the black pointy hat. I tried to remember what it took to work around the clock in those precincts. The defenses you had to build around yourself to live so far from the mainstream. But I wasn't ready to deal with the kind of man I was then.

"See the entrance wound?" Gregory asked me. "Nine-millimeter, sure as shit. My money says the bullet came from Ross's gun."

"Everybody in the Bronx has a nine."

"We'll see what Ballistics says."

"Yeah, right," I said.

Ballistics matches are far from a sure thing. Bullets fragment or become damaged banging around bones. Matching becomes difficult. Even if a bullet can be matched to a gun, guns are traceable to owners less than half of the time.

"Both of these homicides were setups," Gregory said. "She's trying to make it look like a sex thing. Heat of passion, bullshit. We got a cop killer out there, pally."

"A very selective cop killer. Picking Sonny Guidice's team."

"And who has the most to gain from that scenario?" Gregory said. "My money says Tito Santana. They been destroying his street operation. The collar they made tonight . . . that was Santana's man. Need I say more?"

"I think we should look at him."

"What?"

"I said I think we should look at him."

"Sorry, I'm always surprised when you agree with me."

We drove through the empty Bronx streets, waiting for lights to turn, listening to them click through the cycle. We passed the board of elections and I remembered a night spent in that building, guarding election machines after a recount had been ordered. At midnight we locked ourselves in and slept in front of our assigned machines. During the night the heat went off automatically, and the building quickly became cold. We rummaged through the election supplies for the only blankets we could find. Later I awoke disoriented, half dreaming. I saw a dozen cops on the floor, each one wrapped in an American flag.

"Why did she cut Marc Ross, but shoot Verdi?" I said. "If she works for Santana, she could easily have gotten a gun the first time, to use on Ross."

"Women and knives, the old story. Weapon of choice. She did Ross and found out cutting is too bloody. Too messy. Ruined her dress."

I'd never bought the reasons for the old theory that stabbing was a woman's crime because it's a less violent, therefore less masculine, crime. Stabbing is not less violent. It demands the strength to slam a knife through skin, fat, muscle, cartilage, ligament, and bone. Shooters are the cowardly killers, remote, unconnected to the bullet. The knife wielder must be willing to get blood on his hands, to stand within the victim's reach, to inhale the stink of his dying breath. It demands the purest hate. It demands balls. Gender has nothing to do with it.

"Why didn't she steal Verdi's gun, too?" I said.

"One gun is enough," he said with a shrug.

At the courthouse on East 161st Street, a uniformed cop carrying a cardboard tray, probably coffee and doughnuts, rang the bell near a solid metal door. He was an old hairbag cop, his uniform faded and frayed, worn white around the pockets. During graveyard tours they dig out their oldest uniforms. After midnight everyone wears their old blues.

From the hill near the courthouse you could see into Yankee Stadium. We rode down toward it. The view was from center field, looking toward the empty blue seats of the upper deck, so vast in the starlit night.

I could remember, as a kid, waiting in the shade of the el on hot summer afternoons for the metal gate to go up and seventy-five-cent bleacher seats to go on sale. We'd take the train from the neighborhood, a dozen kids strong, and sit on the warm wooden benches and yell to Mantle in center, and to Yogi, a speck in the distance. We'd stay in the bleachers until the fifth inning, then go underneath, past the bathrooms and snack stand, race across the bullpen, hoping no one was warming up. We'd sneak into the right field seats, then we'd chase foul balls and work our way toward the Yankee dugout. The ninth inning was usually ours. The Yanks way ahead, crowd gone, the ushers sneaking home. For one inning we lived like rich people, in season boxes a few yards from our heroes. Then we'd all ride home in time for dinner, pitying anyone who didn't live in New York.

"I say we roust Santana," Gregory said. "See what he has to say."

"You think he's going to talk to us?"

"He freaking better talk to us."

"Why, Joe? Because we're cops? He doesn't give a shit who we are."

In the nights without baseball, River Avenue was a city of empty parking lots, boarded-up vendor stalls, and packs of wild dogs. But a few blocks below the stadium there is a line that always forms, in season or out.

"Go slowly," I said.

We drove by women and children, carrying bags and soda bottles, just like the line the night Marc Ross was killed. But these madonnas were not waiting to see the Mother of God. They were standing in single file outside the Bronx House of Detention, waiting for buses and vans to take them to see the fathers of their children in the prisons of upstate New York. In their bags they carried a change of clothes for the long trip, hairspray, and rolls of quarters for the vending machines in the lobby of each prison. Dressed in their sexiest clothes, they raced to the machines to bring candy and potato chips to their men, who rubbed their legs under the table and told them that they loved them.

But they knew it was bullshit. Because the men came back with big arms, all bulked up, looking good. Too good for them, they'd think, and after a week home they'd find something better, something easier. The kids never got to the stadium, only a few blocks away.

"You ain't still pissed off at Lenny Marino?" Gregory said. "Are you?"

"No," I said.

"He's just doing his job. The PBA president looks out for the cops, that's his job."

"I know."

"You got something bothering you, pally," Gregory said. "You're too agreeable. Spill it."

"You don't want to hear it."

The lights of Manhattan lacked the crystal clarity they had on the trip uptown. I felt a dull sadness. The reality of the courtyard had diminished the intensity of focus.

"Sonny Guidice stinks," I said.

"You mean like BO?"

"That's part of it."

"That's the shit sweats," he said. "Something your body excretes when you're scared shitless. Smells like your skin when you drink beer and eat Limburger cheese, right?"

"Not exactly."

"Well, what exactly?"

"It's more than that," I said. "He's too wired. Paranoid as hell. Like a guy who's stoned on drugs."

Gregory pulled onto the FDR Drive, and Manhattan felt like a different country. He stared straight ahead at the traffic, still moving at a predawn pace. Then his right hand appeared in front of my eyes. Pinched between his thumb and forefinger was a small purple-capped vial with a beige crystalline rock stuck in the middle.

"On the seat of the radio car," he said. "Under Verdi's legs."

I didn't need a lab analysis to tell me it was crack cocaine.

21

Clerks and cops arrived early at One Police Plaza with grim expressions and copies of the *Daily News*. The banner said COP KILLED. Under it, the poker face of Paul Verdi. They tell you not to smile in these official photos; in case you kill someone, they don't want the picture of a grinning cop on page three.

I'd been immersed in folders in the quiet of our darkened office, but when the sun came up elevator bells dinged, cables *whoosh*ed hurriedly, phones rang, lights came on. Shortly before ten A.M. Delia and Gregory walked in; they'd attended the autopsy. Gregory disappeared into the coffee room.

"You look like hell," Delia said. She sat on top of Gregory's desk, facing me. Joe's desktop stayed completely bare, except for his telephone and picture of G. Gordon Liddy, his all-time favorite stand-up guy. "I just spoke to the chief, Anthony. The PC is going to announce the formation of a task force. We're going to run it out of this office. We'll have to make some room."

She looked around the room, checking the available space. Delia wouldn't go to the funeral. She'd attended only one cop funeral in her life, that of her father, as a twelve-year-old girl. She waved a copy of the *Daily News* in front of me.

"The papers are saying it's the same perp as the Ross case," she said. "The chief wants to know how they came to that conclusion."

"Lot of people at the scene, lot of brass, some bigmouths."

The paper she'd waved was the New Jersey issue of the *News*, not a good idea for her. Since her divorce she'd been living with her sister in Hoboken and using her mother's Kew Gardens apartment as her official address. It was very hush-hush. New York City cops weren't allowed to live in Jersey.

"Let me make this clear," she said. "I want to avoid even the slightest appearance of leaks coming from this office. And I'll dump anyone who feels the need to cozy up to the press. Anyone."

I turned around fully to Delia. This wasn't a chat; she had an agenda. She was alluding to Gregory's reputation for being friendly with reporters. She was looking for one good reason to get rid of Gregory, because she saw him as a clear danger to her career. But she'd made her point and gone back to mentally planning the arrangement of desks.

"I didn't tell Gregory," she said. "But Ballistics says the slug is from Marc Ross's Glock 19. Publicly they admit the slug was only in fair shape. Privately they're very sure. They tested the gun last year."

"Gregory already predicted it would be from Ross's gun."

"Maybe he's psychic," she said. "I don't care what he conjures up as long as the Glock story doesn't appear in the papers."

"Was there evidence of sexual activity on the body?"

"Lipstick, makeup . . ."

"Semen?"

"Not from the external exam. Maybe the lab might find something."

"It was a staged scene, Delia."

"Maybe," she said. "You think we should concentrate on Santana?"

"He has motive."

"I see you're signing out personnel folders," she said.

"I have your signature down pat. I'm going through every collar Ross and Verdi ever made."

"I already had that done," she said. "You just spent your night accomplishing nothing. If you'd talk to me more, you wouldn't be wasting this time."

"Doesn't hurt to do it twice."

"What other steps do you plan to duplicate?"

Johnny McGuire, the tech man, was at a front desk, soldering wires on an electronic bugging device that looked like a miniature floating harbor mine. The smell of burning plastic filled the office.

"Okay, Lieutenant," I said. "You can help me. Let's use your contacts in IAD to get me whatever files they have on Officer Alphonse Guidice."

As soon as I said that I regretted it. Delia's ex-husband was a captain in IAD. Her divorce had just been finalized. It was a lousy way to put it. I didn't have to say "your contacts."

"First, follow through on Tina Marquez," Delia said

as she stood. "I want to eliminate her as a suspect before I change the focus to Santana. There's a lineup folder in my office, stop by and get it. Show it to that ex-cop, the marina guard, what's his name?"

"Larry Stanky," I said.

She walked a few steps, then turned.

"I'll consider your IAD request," she said. "In the meantime, no secrets. I want to know everything."

No, you don't, I thought as she walked away. You really don't want to know about the coke found under Verdi's body. The purple-capped vial in Gregory's top desk drawer, right under the spot your ass just vacated. And you don't want to know that we decided to sit on the evidence ourselves, to wait until the toxicology report on Verdi comes back. Definitely you do not want to know that our plan, if it becomes necessary, is to "find" the cocaine later.

I photocopied the arrest folders, then headed for the coffee room. Gregory and Albie Myers were holding a political strategy session as I walked in. Detective Albie Myers was Joe's boyhood friend and campaign manager. His title was chief crime analyst, but he ran the coffee club, the picnics, the 50/50 raffles, the entire office. The membership roll of the Emerald Society was taped to the wall. Next to most names were checkmarks, green for Gregory supporters, red for Kivelahan, who had the audacity to think he could win. Uncommitted were unmarked.

"I went over those Bronx arrest stats, Anthony," Albie said. "Those guys were really hammering away at Santana. They made a ton of collars. From his bio, from what I can see, Santana's a legit suspect."

"Told you, pally," Gregory said.

"I didn't say he wasn't."

I checked the refrigerator for fresh milk. Albie Myers had requisitioned the refrigerator from the department after it was accidentally discovered that the last, unlabeled, section of our Coke machine held beer. Albie's justification was that we needed the refrigerator to store film. It held more *cerveza* than celluloid.

"Were they good collars?" I asked.

"What do you mean, 'good'?" Albie said.

"Were they seizing good weight? Did it come back as drugs, not soap or lactose? Was there anything at all funny about anything?"

"Nothing funny I could see. Good weight, very solid cases for uniformed street cops."

"I'll look them over myself," I said.

"I figured you would," Albie said.

Albie's street cop career consisted of a week on the street and thirty-five years behind a desk. Gregory searched for the teabags while Albie squeezed me for late coffee club and Emerald Society dues. A cup of coffee cost me twenty-five bucks, and the milk smelled sour.

"Tell me about Santana," I said.

"Volume dealer, mostly crack," Albie said. "Controls the north end of Crotona Park from Third Avenue to Southern Boulevard. His dealers hang around the park, but don't hold anything but misdemeanor weight on their person. Big stashes are stored in secret apartments in the area."

Albie Myers and Gregory had been Rockaway lifeguards for several summers as kids. Ironically, Albie had hated paperwork so much then that he would "save" oxygen rather than fill out forms for a new canister.

He'd clamp the mask over the face of a clearly dead floater they'd pulled out of the surf and go, *"Whoosh, whoosh,"* out of the side of his mouth. The crowds hovering around their tanned hero never realized he'd faked turning on the valve. One canister a summer was his goal.

"Is Santana a Puerto Rican?" I said. "Dominican, Colombian, Panamanian . . . ?"

"He's from Belize," Albie said. "According to the Juvenile presentence report, he was raised in a Jesuit orphanage. Ran away at eleven, came here, lived in basements. The old story."

"Where the hell is Belize?" Gregory said.

"Just off the southern tip of Mexico," Albie said. "That's his problem, he isn't aligned with any of the local Hispanic families. He likes being a renegade, though. When he was thirteen he blew away two PRs, a gang thing. A month after he got out of Warwick he was hanging on the back of a bus on Third Avenue, the bus sideswiped an el pillar. Crushed his right side. He lost an arm and leg, but gained a quarter of a mil out of court."

"I'm sure he invested it well," I said.

"Wine, women, fast cars. He backed a nightclub on Tremont and Boston Road called the Toucan Club. Lost his ass. Used to have live birds in cages. They'd always die in a few days from the smoke."

"And his friends sucked the rest of the money from him," I said.

"When he was down to his last fifty grand," Albie said, "he bought a kilo of heroin from the Colombians. He started with the coke later."

"Heroin?"

"Colombians have gone big into heroin. They get it from the Far East, then use the smuggling lanes already set up for coke."

"Is there enough of a market?"

"Heroin is big again. Lot of older junkies moving away from crack. The shit Santana sells on the street is eighty percent pure, so they can smoke it, snort it. He's starting to cut the purity back, but he's already worked up a whole new clientele."

Eighty percent heroin would have killed most of the junkies in the Bronx when I worked there. The average was four to five percent pure, the rest was milk sugar, lactose, sometimes Cremora.

"Are purple caps his trademark?"

"No, yellow. Santana always uses yellow caps on all his vials."

"Who uses purple caps?"

"Purple is the Highbridge Boys, a Manhattan gang, Puerto Ricans, young guys. Been trying to take over the Bronx for years."

"No shit," Gregory said. He looked at me over his half glasses. "Interesting. Purple is the Highbridge Boys."

The vial that Gregory found under the body of Paul Verdi had a purple cap.

"Is Santana crazy enough to kill cops?" I said.

"He's definitely psycho," Albie said. "He's been warring with all the other drug operators, including the Highbridge Boys, since he's been in business."

"Where can we find him?"

"If you are of a mind to do that," Albie said, "he stays at the Toucan Club."

"My partner here is of a mind," I said.

"A mind like that is a terrible thing," Albie said.

I left them discussing a fax campaign and waited outside Delia's office until she put down the phone.

"I'm sorry about that line about your contacts in IAD," I said. "I could have phrased that better."

On her desk was a sketch of the office. Oblong boxes were penciled in at various angles.

"I don't even remember what you said."

Delia's office smelled of flowers and glue. A new chart, on the wall behind her, had a map of the Five One affixed to it. Several pins stuck in the area around Crotona Park.

"What are you getting me into here, Ryan?"

"I'm trying to figure out if there's some connection between the deaths of the cops and the deaths of Santana's drug dealers."

"By looking through IAD files?" she said. "Do you have solid information on Officer Guidice?"

"Are bad vibes solid?"

"Don't play me like that, Anthony. I don't want to hear that you're holding out corruption information."

"Never," I said. "You have that Tina Marquez lineup folder?"

She handed me a manila folder with the case number written across the top in Magic Marker. I knew it would contain four lines of booking photos of pale blondes, one of which would be Tina Marquez.

"After you do that," she said, "I want you to sit on this Santana. Don't approach him just yet, we may use a different strategy with him. Stay at a distance." A small radio behind her was tuned to a jazz station, the sound turned way down. "And by the way, that IAD file you wanted will be in the building Tuesday afternoon. In the department advocate's office. Don't ask me how."

22

"Did Paul Verdi have a family?" Leigh said. It was the same first question she always asked.

"Wife and two little girls," I said.

"Jesus," she said. "Is there anything I can do?"

"Write her," I said. "Let her know someone's thinking of her. I don't know what else."

Leigh had been upstairs when I walked in the door. I heard her in our bedroom. I'd never noticed the house creaking when the kids were home. But since they'd left I could hear every groan. I knew exactly where Leigh was walking above me: from the bed to the dresser. The noise communicated our every move, connecting us in the present.

When I went up I saw that dresser drawers were pulled out. Clothes were stacked on the bed, suitcases open on the floor. Years ago I would have panicked at a scene like this: the clothes, the suitcases. I would have been positive that she'd had enough of being a cop's wife.

Of being my wife. We'd weathered some difficult years, but you never knew the depth of the scars. It seemed to me that the families of cops were always in the process of healing.

"Packing early, aren't you?" I said.

"Just some things," she said. "Sweaters, things like that. You can't leave everything to the last minute."

"True," I said.

When I was a younger married man I would have tried to argue the logic of packing so early. And especially so many sweaters for a few days. But I've learned to go with the flow. I know it's her way of keeping busy.

"Will you be involved in this homicide, too?" she said.

"The PC is forming a task force. We're putting the Ross and Verdi cases together."

"I suppose I don't have to pack for you, then."

"Don't say that, Leigh. I'm going to the wedding."

"We'll see," she said. "We'll see what happens two weeks from today."

"Two weeks from today we'll be at the wedding," I said. "I'm not going to miss the wedding. I promise you that."

"I'm sorry, Anthony," she said softly. She walked to the window, the east window, which faced Sacred Heart Church. "I don't know what's wrong. I'm mad at you because it seems like you don't want to go to Margaret's wedding. Then I hear about this cop's wife, and two little girls, and it seems like such a goddamn stupid thing to be upset about."

"It's not stupid."

"I want you to be close with Margaret again," she said. "If it was up to you two, you'd just drift apart."

"It's not all my fault. I think she picks these guys—"

"Stop, Anthony," she said, and put her arms around my neck. "She doesn't pick guys just to get on your nerves. Stop analyzing everything."

I pulled her to me, and she pressed her face to my chest.

"I'm sorry," I said.

"I don't know why Margaret is marrying this damn surfer, either," she said. "But I know she's still our daughter. We can't turn our back on her."

"I know," I said.

"Don't work on the case tonight," she said. "Give it a rest."

The next morning, after Leigh went shopping, I went upstairs to the den. The sun came through sheer blue curtains. I put my watch on the table so I'd know enough to quit before Leigh came home for lunch.

I finished typing in the names of the children from the Hernandez Funeral Home. I'd started it before but had never been able to finish. Then I entered the arrest activity of Sonny's team. I had to admit, Sonny's team was extremely active. They concentrated on specific blocks, making dozens of arrests, then moving on to another part of the precinct. They covered the whole precinct, not favoring anyone. Arrest reports were thorough, particularly those of Marc Ross.

The only weakness I could see was that amounts seized as evidence were relatively small. But that wasn't unusual. Uniformed cops didn't have the resources to cultivate and build cases on high-level dealers. The low-level street people they *did* target, the hand-to-hand dealers in the drug trade, were rarely trusted to hold large quantities of product.

Then, in late 1993, Sonny's team went to work on Tito Santana's operation on the northern edge of Crotona Park. They were relentless; not a week went by between arrests. Sonny started making more arrests himself, and the weight went up, the arrests were higher quality. Perhaps he was showing them the right way to do it. Maybe Sonny was a better cop than I thought.

"Caprice Antonucci called me again," Leigh said as she sliced a tomato. "She wants to talk to you about something. She sounded upset."

Leigh liked to take her blouse off for lunch, to avoid food accidents. She'd wear a short bib-type apron over her bra.

"She say what she wanted to talk about?"

"She sounded serious, and she was never a serious girl."

"Tell her to call me," I said.

"I did, again," Leigh said. "She says she sees you in her precinct all the time. I don't know why she doesn't talk to you then."

After lunch, I showered and got ready to meet Gregory. I thought about Caprice Antonucci telling Leigh she sees me in the precinct. I had always kept my two worlds separate. Now Leigh seemed to know something about me from a source other than me. It made me uneasy.

23

The NYPD Advocate's Office was on the fourth floor of One Police Plaza. Accordion music greeted us as the elevator door opened. We followed a trail of dripping ice into the trial room.

"The NYPD is an Irish institution," Gregory said. "That's why the lights outside the precincts are green."

"I like that," I said. "That would make a nice opening statement for your victory speech."

"Barney Savage used it last year."

"They won't remember," I said.

The trial room was a miniature courtroom with five rows of spectator benches. It was part of the advocate's office, which handled all interdepartmental trials, prosecuting cops for violations ranging from off-post to murder. Delia told me that Sonny's IAD file would be in the trial room, "accidentally" stuck between two active files. The commanding officer, Captain Joe McDarby, used the room for parties, and McDarby lit the cocktail lamp every time somebody passed a bar.

The celebration, in full swing, was for the end of the Fort Hump trials. Fort Hump was the name cops gave to an experimental Queens precinct where 50 percent of all ranks were female. The issue on trial had not been corruption, but hormones. Sex was the scandal of Fort Hump: sex in the radio cars, sex in the holding pens, sex in the captain's office. In the end, numerous participants were found guilty of conduct unbecoming an officer. But crime in the precinct actually decreased during the experiment, as did civilian complaints. For better or worse, seven teams married, while thirty-one male cops were divorced by civilian wives. And despite dire predictions by the PBA, injuries to officers did not increase, and not one team parted due to death.

Captain Joe McDarby stood behind the raised judge's bench, playing "La Femina" on the accordion. Delia leaned over the clerk's table, cracking nuts with the gavel. We worked our way toward the prosecution table. In regular courtrooms the prosecution was on the side nearest the jury box, but there was no jury here, only a judge appointed by the PC. In this courtroom the booze was on the prosecution table, food on the defense.

"Smell it, pally?" Gregory said. "The pungent aroma of ethical standards. Or is that lawyer bullshit?"

In this setting, hundreds of New York City cops were fined and fired every year. A lot was at stake, a small fortune in pension and benefits. Some cops brought the PBA lawyer, some hired their own attorneys. But they could bring Perry Mason: if the PC wanted them out, they were gone, and that was the way it should be. No appeals, no tears, please.

"You have less than an hour," Delia said, pointing at the clock. "After you finish I want you to find Larry Stanky and have him look at the Tina Marquez lineup folder. Put an end to that angle once and for all. I hate loose ends."

"Absolutely," I said. "So do I."

"Just do it," she said.

Delia went back to talk to Inspector Bruce Browne from IAD. He had carried Sonny's file over from Hudson Street. Browne kept slicking back his silver hair and eyeing the crowd. He probably knew what was going on, but he was an icy piece of work, and we had to play his game.

"We see Santana next," Gregory said. "Forget about Sonny. No more bullshit ideas, pally."

"Soon as I finish here."

Besides Browne, a few other heavy hitters were in attendance: two deputy commissioners, the chief of Organized Crime Control, the trial commissioner, and a contingent from the PBA. Gregory scanned the room, looking for Macs or Mics or O'Somethings; election time was drawing near. He checked his pockets for his shamrock detective badges and drifted toward the defense table and the Swedish meatballs. For the first time I realized how much a courtroom resembled a church.

McDarby had his eyes closed, into his music. He'd been a foot patrolman when he was admitted to Fordham Law School. Gregory had arranged to have him transferred to our office as a clerk, so he could work steady days and go to school nights. We'd collected on this debt many times since he became CO of the advocate's office. Cops like McDarby honored their contracts. When he stopped playing I walked behind the bench. His face was flushed, his curly hair damp with sweat.

"I don't see you much since you stopped drinking," he said, glancing over at Inspector Browne. "Only when you need a favor."

"So I'll drop by more."

McDarby took a big swig of Heineken and set the bottle back down on the Bible. His shirt was wrinkled from the accordion. A drumbeat came from the stenographer's table. McDarby glared at Delphine Seldman, secretary to the chief of Organized Crime Control. Delphine, gift-wrapped in a kelly green dress, pumped up the volume on the tape deck. She was one of the debutantes in the building, always received a personal invite. McDarby whispered only into the ears of the best-looking women. During Christmas or on promotion days, Gregory and McDarby, two old Joes, wandered the floors, glasses in hand, sniffing out festivity.

"It's in my office," McDarby whispered. He poked idly at the accordion, a note here, a note there, trying to look casual, as he slipped me a key. Gregory said McDarby would stay a cop for forty years; he wasn't devious enough to make it as a lawyer on the outside. Bob Marley sang, "I fought the law and the law won."

"Lock the door," McDarby said. "If Browne catches you in there, say you're using the phone. You got maybe twenty minutes. He never stays more than an hour, so he can claim it was his lunch hour."

"Last contract, I swear," I said.

"Just turn off the goddamn tape deck," McDarby said. "I'm doing 'Lady of Spain' whether they like it or not."

McDarby's office was on the opposite side of the building, overlooking the East River. A Bostonian shoe catalog was on his desk, open to the wingtips. Sonny Guidice's IAD file was under the catalog. It was thinner than I expected. Complaints went back to the mid-seventies, most of them for rudeness, some brutality. All had been investigated, no serious punishment meted out. But in the nineties something changed.

I heard somebody talking loud in the outer office and covered the file with the shoe catalog. I put the phone to my ear and circled a pair of cordovan cap toes, size nine and a half. On the wall was a framed picture of Spencer Tracy in a movie courtroom scene. The noise subsided, and I went back to the file. A series of entries started three years ago:

10/05/91 1045 hours, anonymous M/C alleges P.O. Guidice removed numerous bags of heroin from unidentified youths near Clinton Avenue and Jefferson Place.
5/29/92 1320 hours, anonymous M/C alleges P.O. Guidice stole cash and vials of crack from Willy on Bathgate.
6/2/93 0315 hours, anonymous F/C alleges that P.O. Guidice and two unidentified male P.O.s beat and robbed Sky, a drug dealer in Crotona Park.
8/14/93 0350 hours, anonymous F/C alleges P.O. Guidice and partners stole a kilo of coke from Dejuan and sold it for $16,000.
3/21/94 0320 hours, anonymous F/C alleges P.O. Guidice protects drug dealers on Southern Boulevard.

The last three complaints, made by an anonymous female caller, all occurred in the early hours of the morning. Someone else losing sleep over Sonny Guidice.

All complaints were closed out as unsubstantiated. It was obvious they had not been given serious effort. I couldn't believe that IAD had not been all over Sonny Guidice.

Laughter came from the trial room; the party was heating up. Bob Marley had taken over the musical chores again. I copied all the information and never touched Sonny's file with anything but a pencil. After I locked the office I began the process of pulling Gregory away from a party.

24

Gregory parked on Boston Road, directly in front of the Toucan Club. I finished rewriting all the hurried scrawling I'd started in McDarby's office.

"Active cops get a lot of complaints," Gregory said. "All the scumbags, first thing they do when they get arrested is make a complaint of brutality or corruption. Hoping they can use it as a bargaining chip. It's a documented fact."

Across the street a slender man was up to his elbows in the engine of an orange Chevy Malibu. Tools were laid out on a greasy sheet on the sidewalk. Nailed to a telephone pole was a plywood sign that read "Benito's Auto Repair." Benito didn't have a shop, but he'd staked out a section of public street to begin chasing the American dream. His radio blared a Latin version of "Under the Boardwalk." It was an area where it was easy to understand why there were more Rodriguezes than Smiths in the New York City phone books.

"Say good-bye to the battery," Gregory said as we approached the Toucan. We were less than three blocks from the spot where we'd found the body of Marc Ross.

The front door of the Toucan Club was locked, but we'd seen Santana's Mercedes in the back. Gregory banged on the door, and it brought a pissed-off, snarling dog, who bounced off the frame so violently, the entire front entrance rattled.

"We got a plan here?" Gregory said.

"This is your baby," I reminded him.

Two guys in a white van stopped at the light and eyeballed us warily. The van was covered with a sprayed-painted message, big, swirling curlicue letters over and over: "Jaime-Ecuador."

"We closed," a woman said, yelling through the door of the Toucan. The dog's growl got deeper, angrier.

We identified ourselves and bullied her until she started to open the door. The dog pressed his nose through the crack, saliva dripping.

"Put that mutt somewhere," Gregory said, holding the doorknob so only the dog's ugly snout protruded. "Put him away."

A few seconds later Gregory opened the door slightly and peeked in. The woman dragged the immense rottweiler across the floor. Only when she shoved it into a side room did we step inside.

"Where's Santana?" Gregory said.

The woman washed dog hair off her hands, then dried them with a small white bar towel. The Toucan Club was stifling, airless, and smelled so overwhelmingly of dog shit my eyes started to tear.

"I'm the manager here," she said.

"Our business is with Santana," Gregory said. I could hear the dog crashing against the door.

"Mr. Santana is not part of the management of this establishment," she said.

"His car is in the back," Gregory said. "Tell him to get his ass out here. We want to talk about a homicide."

It was four-thirty P.M. Business hours were five P.M. to three A.M. Happy hour prices, live music Fri. and Sat. Lap dancing, dirty dancing, and more. The decor was deep purple, purple mirrors, purple lights and walls. The booths and stools were purple velour, badly stained and torn. Rainbow-colored toucans glowed in iridescent paint in the purple sky.

"If you officers leave your cards, I—"

"Nilda," said a woman who'd come from the back. She was dark skinned, extremely attractive, but looked as though she'd been sleeping. "It's okay."

"Fuck it, then," Nilda said, and went back to rinsing glasses, banging them onto the rack.

The sleepy woman led us into the back room, past the dog who tried desperately to crash through a closed metal door.

I remembered being in this bar when I was in the Five One Precinct, long before it was the Toucan. I'd been working a foot post nearby, but I was bouncing around, drinking my way through a four-to-twelve tour. I was in full uniform, at the bar, when the Seventh Division shoofly, Captain Jesse Katz, blasted through the door. I ran into the ladies' room, locked the door, and climbed out the bathroom window in my thirty-pound woolen horse blanket of an overcoat.

At midnight, when the tour ended, Captain Katz was waiting behind the sign-out book, glaring at every face, trying to identify the cop he'd seen running through the dimly lit bar. He suspected me, but I'd been schooled by the old-timers: "Even if they have pictures, deny it was you." Katz swore to get me, but I was transferred before he had the chance.

Gregory and I followed Sleepy Woman into a cave of a room, all purple couches and drapes. Except for a small barred window, the only light came from the flicker of the TV hanging from the ceiling. In the corner directly under the television, a man with a greasy, pock-marked face sat on a bar stool. A large round mattress stood on its side against a back wall. Sleepy Woman collapsed onto a purple overstuffed chair and looked up at cartoons.

"Detectives," a voice said. I hadn't seen the tiny figure in black sitting on the couch. "I'm Tito Santana. Sit down." He pointed to a couch opposite him. "Boricua scared you. My baby. She's tough."

"She didn't scare us," Gregory said.

I knew *boricua* was slang for a Puerto Rican girl. Mr. Santana, from Belize, had an attitude where Puerto Ricans were concerned.

"Hey buddy," Gregory said, pointing at the greasy-faced man in the corner. "Why don't you sit over here where you can see the TV better? Wile E. Coyote on the tube. You don't want to miss this."

We waited a beat. Greasy Face didn't move. Gregory started walking toward him; he wasn't going to allow anybody to sit outside of our vision, and never behind us. Santana said something in Spanish, and Greasy Face took a spot against the wall next to him.

"You're going to like this episode," Gregory said. "My favorite, but I won't spoil it for you."

Santana wore dark glasses and was extremely small. He had short, black, close-cropped hair, black pants, and a black shirt that appeared to be silk. The right sleeve and pant leg were pinned back neatly. A single aluminum crutch lay against the arm of the couch. He offered his left hand flatly, palm down, as the cardinal offered his ring to be kissed. We ignored it and sat.

"I hear you say something about homicide," Santana said.

"Yeah, two cops," Gregory said. "Didn't you hear about that?"

"I hear," Santana said. "But that's all." He turned to look at Sleepy Woman, called her Lupe, and told her to turn the TV down. Two dark blue tears hung below Santana's right eye. Tattoo tears. A Hispanic prison thing, one tear for each person you've killed. Santana had killed two teenagers when he was only twelve.

"We figure you do more than hear," Gregory said. "We figure you know things."

"Why you say that?"

"Because we know things, too," Gregory said.

"You ever kill anybody, Officers?" Santana said. He looked at me, then at Gregory, and we both shook our heads no. "It's not like in the movies," he said.

"No shit," Gregory said.

"I kill two men," Santana said. "The first, Victor Reyes. I kill him in a garage on Third. First shot, I shoot him in the back of his leg. He grabs his leg and he says, 'What the fuck you doing, man?' I say, 'I'm killing you, you dumb fuck.' Then I shoot him again and it goes in his side and he starts to run, kicking his legs like a wild deer. I chase him to the door and have to knock him down and hold him and shoot three more times into his head before he close his eyes for good."

"Do we look like we give a shit?" Gregory said. "We ain't got time to play games with you. We know that two cops were banging away at your operation. Working on you almost exclusively. And now they're both dead."

Santana turned again to the woman, who appeared to be nodding off. He spoke angrily in Spanish. She scratched her arms, then looked through the folds of her dress for the remote control.

"I read the papers," Santana says. "That's all I know. I am a legitimate businessman."

"This is a business problem, isn't it?" Gregory said. "It's about business."

Santana again glared at the woman. Gregory got up, snatched the remote from the woman's hand, and snapped off the TV. She sat there still staring and scratching her arms.

"You got a problem with business, right?" Gregory said, gesturing with the remote as if it were a gun. "The cops gave you a business problem. You know how to take care of problems, right?"

"I got no problem," he said.

The room had gotten much darker with the TV off. Besides the barred window, a small glow came from a Budweiser electric wall clock. A string of Clydesdales pranced across the purple wall, pulling a wagon filled with Christmas cheer. I wondered how Santana could see with those dark glasses.

"The cops in this precinct are giving you a problem," Gregory said. "All those arrests, the hassles, lost product, lost man-hours, legal expenses."

"I don't know what you're talking about," Santana said.

"I'm here to tell you your problems are going to get worse," Gregory said. "We're going to be all over you, like flies on shit."

Santana smiled and nodded his head, as if he finally got an inside joke. The dog in the office had calmed down. About every thirty seconds he'd bark, then quit.

"You people . . . ," Santana said, shaking his head. "Go back and tell your friend I don't pay tithe."

"What friend?" Gregory said.

"Who's asking you to pay tithe?" I said.

"I bust my ass to get where I am," he said. "Nobody pushing me out."

"What are you talking about?" Gregory said.

"Everybody wants something," he said. "You want something, he wants something, she wants something."

"Do you think this is a shakedown?" I said.

He laughed and waved his hand. My eyes had begun to adjust to the dark. Santana didn't answer; he looked up at the black screen of the TV.

"I salute nobody's flag," Santana said. "Not the Italian's flag, the Colombian's flag, the Puerto Rican's, not the police flag."

"Is Sonny Guidice shaking you down?" I said.

I saw him reach for a crutch, the leather wraps stained black in the center. He pulled it to him and rose easily to his feet. He couldn't have weighed ninety pounds, but his left forearm was muscular, with large blue veins.

"You people don't understand respect," he said.

"Respect what, Tito?" Gregory said. "Your right to sell drugs to kids?"

"I got work to do in my office," he said. "Sometimes my dog gets past me. I can't hold her back."

He limped ahead. The dog growled and slammed against the other side of the door as Santana leaned against the wall and held his hand on the doorknob. Gregory followed Santana. I watched Greasy Face.

"I can't hold this dog back," Santana said.

"So let her out," Gregory said. "If you got the balls."

It was the wrong thing to say to a guy like Santana. The door flew open and Boricua came right at Gregory, sliding on the tile floor, nails clicking like a typewriter. The dog bounced awkwardly off a wall, then clamped her jaws on the barrel of Gregory's gun.

Boricua's massive head acted as a silencer, muffling the sound, as blood and hair and bits of bone and brain flew back against the wall and onto Tito Santana's expensive clothes. Boricua fell heavily to the floor, a staccato thud like a sack of potatoes.

"That wasn't like the movies," Gregory said.

25

We left the Bronx, Gregory driving like a fugitive. The battery hadn't been stolen, but a gouge ran down the entire left side of the T-bird. It looked like a knife or maybe a box cutter.

"What is tithe, anyway?" Gregory said.

"It's a tax, or levy," I said. "He means graft. He doesn't pay graft. Probably the only word he remembers from the Jesuits."

We were on our way to Larry Stanky's in Queens, so he could view the photo lineup Delia had prepared.

"You believe that shit?" he said.

"I think there's something there."

"Why'd you ask him if Sonny is shaking him down?"

"Some questions have to be asked."

"Like what? Oh, I get it. It fits in with your private war theory. Sonny Guidice is shaking Santana down, so Santana gets pissed off and has Ross killed. Then Sonny gets revenge, or goes one up, by whacking the shit out of two of Santana's dealers. Then Santana kills Verdi. Stay tuned, fans, to the battle of the psycho Bronx assholes."

"Don't ask me what I think if you're going to be sarcastic."

"Before you start weaving these big webs, pally, I want you to think that sometimes things happen, they just ain't connected."

"Questions have to be asked."

"Like what?" he said.

"Like what is it with you and dogs?"

Larry Stanky lived in Long Island City, Queens. We drove over the Triborough Bridge, down Vernon Boulevard, then ate gyros at a stand across from an auto scrap yard under the Fifty-ninth Street Bridge. The car was filled with the scorched-metal smell of cordite from Gregory's gun. Gregory used extra napkins to clean the blood and saliva off the barrel. Then he opened his notebook and began writing.

"That little bastard is a few ounces short of a kilo," Gregory said.

"Grams," I said. "A few grams short."

"Grams, right," Gregory said. "I couldn't believe he let that dog out. Freaking psycho. I say fuck him if he can't take a joke."

Gregory had used the same cracked-leather notebook since I'd known him. It was stuffed with loose notes, business cards, and cocktail napkins, all bound with two heavy-duty rubber bands. I wondered what he was writing. I'd never looked at his notes in the twenty years we'd worked together. Maybe: May 3, '94. Partly cloudy, warm, 64 degrees. Worked Ross/Verdi case with Ryan. Shot rottweiler.

"You saw that woman Santana called Lupe," he said. "She fits our description. I'll bet he's got a whole stable of women that'll do his bidding."

"She's a stone heroin junkie. She was nodding off in front of us. I doubt she'd have had the strength to drag the body of Marc Ross across the console of his car."

"Aren't you the guy always preaching 'Never underestimate the women'?"

Larry Stanky was asleep when we got there, resting up for his graveyard shift at the Manhattan Marina. While he dressed, we waited with his wife, a round, pale woman, and watched a home shopping show. The apartment smelled of cat piss, but I asked her if she owned a dog.

"No, why?" she said.

"My partner is allergic," I said.

Larry came out of the bedroom dressed in his guard's uniform, still rubbing sleep from his eyes. Mrs. Stanky boiled water for tea and called us to the kitchen table, six feet away. I pulled the lineup folder from my briefcase as she sliced an Entenmann's crumb cake. It was the first time I'd looked at the pictures, and it took me several minutes to find the photo of Tina Marquez. Whoever had selected the pictures had done a very good job of finding women with similar features. Maybe too good.

"It was a little while ago," Larry said.

"Do your best," I said.

I turned the folder around and opened it in front of him. Larry's eyes darted nervously over the photos. I sipped tea in heavy white cups with saucers, trimmed in rose, the kind you could buy from the diner supply houses on Bowery. On the floor in the corner were two round plastic bowls, one water, the other dried cat food. Little red nuggets had spilled onto the beige tile floor.

"Not even close," Larry said, closing the folder. "It's none of them."

"You're sure," I said. "Look again."

"Okay," he said. "But they're all too light skinned."

I knew he'd made up his mind. He breathed heavily, a faint whistling from his nose. The kitchen clock was in the shape of a cat; the tail twitched back and forth. It was almost nine P.M.

"I got a good look at her," he said. "But in person it's easier. A real lineup is different. This camera washes them out; they all look dead here. Live is different. People got motions and body language, shit like that."

"You saw her sitting down in a car," I said.

"Yeah, but . . . you know," Stanky said.

"He's right," Gregory said, checking his watch. "Let's do it live."

Thirty minutes later Larry and I sat in the T-bird in front of Gato's Lounge in the Bronx. Gregory had gone inside to find Tina and enough similar females to constitute a reasonable lineup. I didn't ask how he was going to get them to stand for a lineup. It didn't matter. I thought it was more important to try to get the cat hair off my pants. I'd already decided Larry Stanky was useless.

"I don't want to be late for work," Larry Stanky said. He was still in his guard's uniform but had brought a raincoat to throw over it.

Gregory knocked on the car window. I had to open the door because he'd taken the keys, no way to open power windows.

"All arranged," Gregory said. "They got a back room. We'll do it back there."

As we got out I whispered, "What the hell did you tell them?"

"I shelled out a few bucks," he said. "That's legit."

"Do they know what's going on?" I said.

"Yes and no," he said.

We followed Gregory through the bar. The stools were filled by sullen, dark-skinned men and one big Irish drunk in a green sanitation department uniform. Virtually all of them sat alone, elbows on the bar, twisting drinks in their hands. There was no one behind the bar, no one dancing. An empty pedestal inside a round cage of nylon rope was bathed in pulsating scarlet light. The jukebox was silent.

We walked through a beaded curtain into a back room with four round tables. The room was empty, but I could hear voices from the manager's office. A mop and bucket sat in the middle of the floor.

Gregory set us up in the corner. *El Diario* lay open on the table. He reached up and unscrewed the bulb in the overhanging light. I took the newspaper and swatted the table and chair, hoping to scatter whatever cockroaches were hidden. Stanky and I sat down in darkness, surrounded by stacked cases of empty beer bottles.

"What the fuck is he doing?" Stanky said.

"Creating," I said.

Gregory moved the mop and bucket and arranged a small spotlight that the cleaners used to see in the dark bar. The light shone on a wet ring where the bucket had been. Next comes Emmett Kelly with a broom, I thought.

I assumed he'd convinced the women to cooperate by paying them, but it seemed more theater than lineup.

Why were they sequestered in the manager's office? Why the lights?

Tina poked her head out of the manager's office. She said, "Play C nine."

Gregory went to the jukebox and punched buttons. The laser found the disc, and it was theater, it was lineup, it was pure Joe Gregory. Tina led the way with a smile, silver bikini bottoms, and silver platform shoes. She ran to a spot on the floor and began rolling her shoulders, her feet rooted to the floor, gyrating like a belly dancer with total body control. Her breasts were larger than I'd thought, her nipples a pale pink. She wore little makeup. Her muscles rippled as she moved.

The second girl was as professional: leopard-skin bikini bottoms, black shoes with bulky Cuban heels. Taller than Tina, but not as ripped, she had dark hair and straight, shapeless legs.

The last three women came in their underwear, two in red panties, one in black. Larry Stanky ran his hand through his hair, then knocked a half-filled beer bottle to the floor.

"Your partner is fucking crazy," he said. "And I mean that sincerely."

The thinner woman in red rubbed her stomach like a hungry child and swayed with the lethargy of a junkie. The one in black panties was barefoot, at least forty, with deep stretch marks and a swooping abdominal scar. She tried to hide a rip in the seam of her panties by angling her hip away from us. But she was the most enthusiastic dancer, enjoying her special show, putting her heart into her dancing, holding her bouncing breasts, one in each hand.

It was a long three minutes, a tough round of boxing for the three amateurs, poor conditioning more obvious with each chorus. Black Panties was breathing hard when the music ended. A triangle of sweat darkened the back of her ripped underwear as she ran back to the manager's office. Gregory stood up and reached into his pocket. I knew he'd made a half-now, half-later arrangement. I wondered where he'd gotten the other three dancers. I assumed one was the barmaid, the other two probably customers.

"So now you've seen them in the flesh, Larry," I said.

"Sorry," he said. "I didn't recognize any of those broads."

"Maybe you didn't get as good a look at her as you thought."

"Hey, I got a good look," he said. "These ones here: one's too light, one's too dark; one's too fat, one's too skinny."

"Sounds like 'Goldilocks,' Larry. A fairy tale."

"That night was no fairy tale," he said. "She was scary. I'll know her. You just ain't got the right broad."

26

The next morning Delia called me at home. I told her we'd eliminated Tina Marquez as a suspect. She said to meet her after lunch outside Elaine's restaurant on Second Avenue; it was important. I called Joe and we hooked up in Ruppert Towers. Gregory knew somebody in security.

"I know why she's hanging around Elaine's," Gregory said. "She's hoping to run into the PC, or somebody that can help her holy freaking career."

"She's looking for an apartment in the area, Joe. She grew up on Ninety-sixth."

Delia was at the newsstand next to Elaine's. She had a Gap shopping bag on her wrist and was reading the latest *Post* headline about police corruption.

"What were you doing in the Toucan Club?" she said. "I told you to tail him, not to approach him."

"What club?" Gregory said.

"We have you on video," she said. "Going in, and

coming out. If you'd come to the task force meetings, you'd have known we put a camera across the street."

"Nobody notified us about any meeting," Gregory said.

"Bullshit," Delia said. "Albie Myers said he told you personally."

I could smell chocolate-chip cookies from a designer cookie shop three stores away. They blew the smell out into the street. The weather was brisk, the sun showing some strength. People were out shopping and strolling.

"I didn't bring you here to chew you out," Delia said. "That's in the past. I don't want to argue about it. I want to know if you spoke to Santana."

"Of course," Gregory said.

"In the back room?" she said. We both nodded.

"Good," she said. "Draw me a sketch of the place, and the best spot to place a bug in that room. We're getting a court order tomorrow. Undercover has been in the bar area, but never in the back."

On the corner, a scraggly kid handed out pink pamphlets hawking a topless-bottomless bar. I took one and squatted next to a stack of newspapers and diagrammed the bar as best I could. The headline of the newspaper announced the preliminary findings of a commission to investigate corruption in the NYPD. It wasn't a proud day.

"What about this vicious dog?" Delia said. "The wire team is worried, they're planning to tranquilize it."

"Dog's not a problem," Gregory said.

"Why the hell is that?" she said.

"Passed away," he said.

A young couple stood next to me on tiptoes, peeking into Elaine's. I knew they were tourists; they smelled of chlorine from the hotel pool.

"The job never should have lowered the standards,"

Gregory said, pointing at the newspaper headlines. "We got criminals, junkies, on the job. People can't read, women can't do one push-up."

"What you're saying is they shouldn't have recruited minorities," Delia said.

A group of little girls from a Catholic grade school walked past in high blue socks and plaid jumpers. All carried crayon drawings, little figures and hearts that said "Happy Mother's Day." I handed my drawing to Delia.

"I don't give a shit what color a cop is," Gregory said. "As long as he doesn't have a yellow sheet longer than my arm. I'm saying we don't need to be a social agency. We need to get the best possible people we can recruit. See what I'm saying?"

"I see exactly what you're saying," she said.

We left Delia and returned to the Bronx. Gregory wanted to start on a list of female associates of Santana, but Delia had told us to stay out of the Toucan until they had the bug in. We drove past the place, but Santana's car was gone.

Gregory cruised the South Bronx, looking for Santana's silver Mercedes, through areas I hadn't been to in twenty years. In the daylight I was able to see all the new construction. It was a far different Bronx from what I remembered. The streets no longer seemed teeming, claustrophobic, and dangerous. Blocks that once looked like bombed-out WW II Berlin now looked like quiet, tropical resorts. There was still decay, but virtually every area showed signs of improvement. Some places were visually stunning, the experience almost surreal. Hundreds of new condos with neat green lawns, pastel facades, balconies, aqua-and-salmon-colored awnings.

We found the Mercedes parked in front of a pet store on Bathgate Avenue. Santana was not in the car, only the driver, Greasy Face.

Gregory stopped up the block, next to a bodega with the sign "Loose Cigarettes" in the window. Loose cigarettes were a ghetto thing. Stores sold one or two cigarettes at a time, twenty cents apiece, three for fifty. People up here bought one can of beer, a small bag of chips; they hung on the stoop, had a smoke, put some coins on the number. It was a pocket change life.

"Whatever happened to that cigarette they found behind the Dumpster at the Verdi scene?" I said.

"Camel, unfiltered," he said. "Had enough saliva for serology to get a blood type."

"Maybe there was a second perp. It's worth a thought. Someone hiding behind the Dumpster. I've never been comfortable with the one-woman-show theory."

"You mean someone waiting in there?" Gregory said. "How'd he get in that place? It's like a fortress."

"Using the same key she let herself out with."

The pet store was north of the new Bathgate Industrial Park, which was once the old Spanish *marqueta*, a place I'd always enjoyed. I could remember warm Saturday afternoons in my new blue uniform, walking past the stalls of merchants. Frilly lace dresses and flowered rayon shirts hung on racks overhead. Young girls flirted. Botanicas with pictures of Jesus in the window, his eyes following you down the street; ceramic saints and tapestries of the Blessed Virgin. And the infectious music, the blood-pumping Latin beat blasting from rusting speakers on top of a frayed awning. Old girls flirted. Bins filled with records and tapes: Celia Cruz, Willie Colon, Tito Puente. The air filled with the smell of garlic and fried pork, *cuchifritos*, bins of plaintains. And in metal tubs under crushed ice, *cerveza, mucho frío*.

"Here he comes," Gregory said. "Empty-handed."

Santana leaned his crutch against the Mercedes, opened the door, grabbed the roof, and swung his body in. We followed them down Webster Avenue behind an old Ford station wagon with six mattresses tied on the roof. Another pet store; this one was closed. Santana didn't get out of the car.

They drove slowly back up Third Avenue. Santana went back to the Toucan Club. Gregory kept on going, and we made a tour of Crotona Park. Another new housing project overlooked the southwest corner of the park, neat ranch-style houses behind ornate fences. The street was called Suburban Place, and it looked like suburban Pennsylvania. The leaves were starting to fill out the trees. A dozen men in baseball uniforms crossed the street into the park. "Danube Azul" was printed across their shirts.

"Where the hell did they get that name?" I said. "The Blue Danube."

"Blue Danube used to be a bar on Morris Avenue," Gregory said. "A lot of Polack types hung in there. My Polack aunt lived across the street. Some PRs bought it and kept the name."

"Your aunt still live here?" I said.

"No. Moved to Arizona."

I saw Sonny Guidice's old car parked in front of Tina's house, on the playground side of the street. I talked Gregory into picking up coffee and a tea, then parking at the west side of the playground. Kids were eating shaved ice from a cart and comparing the color the syrup left their tongues, electric blue, neon red.

Sonny's car was a beat-up old Ford Granada, but that didn't fool me. It was a trick of the old corrupt plainclothesmen: the guys making the most money drove the worst cars. I could see both the car and the entrance to 719 Crotona Park North through the bars surrounding the playground.

"I remember the Blue Danube bar well," Gregory said. "My old man and me painted every apartment within two blocks of that bar. My aunt moved constantly, always looking for a better apartment, or ten dollars cheaper rent. Many a time we carried her old furniture up and down Morris Avenue. Never needed a truck because she wouldn't move far from the Blue Danube."

"She should see the Bronx now. She might move back."

"Too late, the dry heat killed her," he said. "I remember laying in bed in her house at night. Looking across the street into the bar. Watching those women polka. Big zaftig women, laughing, faces all sweaty."

Francis X. patrolled the playground. The playground had been the center of drug activity up until two years ago. Neville Drumm told me that when Francis X. took over, the gangs moved to the other end of the park. The playground was full of kids, the swings in use, a line for the slide. Francis X. stood at the gate like the doorman at a trendy nightspot. A woman in a white hospital outfit dug in her purse until she pulled out a handful of change. She dropped the coins in his hand.

"If I had kids," Gregory said, "I wouldn't let that psycho stay in the same time zone as them."

"You've never had kids," I said. "Francis X. is the lesser of many evils. Look at the playground. It's clean, safe."

"But what's his motive here?"

"People feed him, give him money."

"He's doing this for money?"

"It's not just the money," I said. "It makes him feel important, useful."

I told him how in Salinger's *The Catcher in the Rye* Holden Caulfield tells his sister how he'd like to live the rest of his life guarding children at play. He'd stand in the tall grass, the rye, near the edge of a cliff and catch the playing kids before they got too close to the edge.

"You don't belong in this job, Ryan," Gregory said. "You should be somewhere reading poetry to school kids. I'd be goddamned if I'd trust that crazy bastard out there to catch my kids."

The girls had taken over the swings. The oldest was no more than nine. Their high, sweet squeals of laughter were like mint on the tongue. Out of the corner of my eye I saw Sonny on the stoop of 719.

"Sonny's moving," I said. "Let's tail him. C'mon, c'mon. Let's go." I took the tea out of his hand and snapped the lid on. Sonny skipped down the steps, flipping his keys, Tina right behind him. Sonny opened his car door, then leaned over to let her in. I held the two hot containers between my feet.

"I hate this shit," Gregory said.

Sonny pulled out almost as soon as the car started. We waited a beat, then got into traffic. I noted the time on an index card: fourteen-thirty hours. I didn't want the tail of a cop in my notebook, yet.

Tailing on one-way streets is delicate. Not much traffic, so you have to maintain an extra distance between cars. We tried to stay one light back, but Sonny jumped traffic lights when he felt like it. But who was going to stop him in his precinct? We stayed a block behind; traffic was light and blocks were short.

We tailed them up Webster Avenue to Fordham Road. I remembered I'd once seen Tina coming out of a bank on Fordham and the Concourse, near the Hernandez Funeral Home. But they turned at the Golden Arches and into McDonald's.

"Mickey D's," Gregory said. "Maybe he's dealing in counterfeit Big Macs."

"Just hang in there for a minute," I said. "Just wait. Let's see where they go."

I noticed that the new-car smell was gone from the T-bird. It was starting to smell like all the old department cars we'd had in the past: coffee, wool, beer, smoke, pizza, Old Spice.

We waited until the Granada cleared the drive-through. Then they drove back to Tina's house and carried their bag upstairs. Gregory said he could smell the fries. Francis X. was still on guard at the playground.

"That's the last time I tail this guy for you," Gregory said.

27

Monday night the precinct radio waves were filled with Indian war whoops. One whoop, then a few seconds later a return war whoop. Then another.

"Sounds like a meet," I said.

"We used to whistle," Gregory said. "Two for yes, one for no."

We were sitting opposite the Toucan, watching two old men play dominoes in front of a bodega. We'd spent Mother's Day weekend sitting on Tito Santana, waiting for the mistake that would trigger the toppling of his empire. We'd photographed dozens of women entering and leaving the bar. The bug the tech team had installed in the Budweiser clock on Tito's wall was working well. All we needed was the right conversation. We'd noted times, plate numbers, taxi medallions.

More war whoops came over the radio. Cops used creative signals to communicate a secret meet at some prearranged spot. When I was a rookie the Five One

Precinct old-timers used barnyard animals. There'd be moos, clucks, gobbles, and neighs over the radio. Morning always arrived with a crowing rooster. Gregory pulled into traffic to ride the precinct, see what we were missing.

It was the first warm night of the year. People were out on stoops, leaning against cars, squatting on fire escapes. Rap music competed with Latin music from boom boxes. A man in a ripped shirt darted across the street and disappeared into an alley. The police radio was busy. Good weather was bad news for cops.

A Five One Precinct radio car was parked in front of a pizza parlor. The cop we'd nicknamed Shaved Head, one of Sonny's crew, came out carrying two large pizza boxes in the air, one hand, over his head, like a fancy waiter. He put them in the trunk of the car. As soon as he was back behind the wheel, he picked up the radio mike and put it to his mouth. We heard his war whoop loud and clear.

"Pizza party," Gregory said.

"See where it is," I said.

"No," he said. "Absolutely not. I will not do that. I already tailed a cop for French fries, I'm not doing it for pizza."

Shaved Head took off. Gregory turned the opposite way on Tremont. I rolled down the window, stuck my hand out to feel the warm breath of my city. At the light at Marmion Avenue, opposite the One Price $7 Clothing Store, two men in a black Pontiac pulled alongside. The passenger started to roll down the window, as if he had something to say or sell. When he got a good look at us, he rolled it back up and the Pontiac made the next right. Gregory turned down a narrow side street and got stuck behind a sanitation truck. Cans clanked and banged, the trash compactor ground and crushed. It rumbled a few yards farther and stopped again.

Soul music came from the open door of a storefront social club. An immense black woman in a tight blue dress filled the doorway with her hips. She was laughing and drinking as she glanced up and down the block. When she saw us she went back inside, closed the door.

"Let's call it a night," I said. "Enough cops out here as it is."

Since the death of Paul Verdi, the Five One Precinct had been overrun with uniformed cops, borrowed from other precincts. The NYPD always reacted by "throwing blue."

"Let's take one more pass at Santana," he said.

We drove past the Toucan; still no Mercedes, so we made a circle around Crotona Park. The dealers were hiding, too many cops spoiled the fun. Nervous crackheads eyed us from both sides of the street. Most wore caps backward and huge pants that barely hung on their asses.

Crackheads were dangerous junkies, frantic thieves who drove up the crime rate. Crack created paranoid, desperately wired users. It was cheap, three dollars a vial, but it was a short-lived high. Twenty minutes, then they were out to steal again. A heroin junkie with a dime bag could be out of circulation for eight hours before he'd need to score.

"Jesus," Gregory yelled, and slammed on the brakes. A loud thud, then we swerved to the right. Francis X. Hanlon slid off the right front fender and crumpled to the pavement. He rolled over in the street as I searched for the button to unlock my door.

"Crazy bastard," Gregory said.

I jumped out, but Francis X. was already up and moving, limping like a wounded deer. I followed him to the park gate, but he cut through bushes and I lost him instantly.

"Get in," Gregory said.

Gregory mounted the sidewalk and drove down the dark narrow path. Francis X. wore old running shoes. We spotted the reflective heel tape bouncing in the darkness as he cut off the paths. Gregory followed him across the grass, up a hill, but we lost him at the crest.

Clusters of heavy old trees lined the crest of the hill. Gregory said he remembered a cop who ran over a pair of lovers in the grass in Central Park. We stopped. Below us was a small clearing completely surrounded by the treed hills. Lights glowed in the center of the clearing. Gregory doused our car lights and turned off the T-bird's engine. In the center of the clearing below us were three radio cars in a circle, one with its headlights on. A woman danced in the smoky spotlight.

"Oh, shit," he said. "They had to see our lights."

"They're not watching us," I said. "Where did Francis X. go?"

"Swinging through the vines. Who gives a shit?"

A fourth radio car sat off in the edge of darkness. I could see Shaved Head in the circle of radio cars, but not Sonny. Pizza boxes and beer cans were scattered around on the hoods of the cars. I counted six uniformed cops and three women. The one who was dancing was unbuttoning her blouse.

"Let's get out of here," I said.

"Maybe I can roll back without starting the car."

He slipped the car into neutral and rocked his body on the seat. We didn't move, but it was too late anyway. Shaved Head had walked over to the fourth car parked in the darkness. A naked woman came out of the backseat, followed by Sonny, pulling up his pants. Shaved Head pointed up toward us as the woman squeezed between them and retrieved her clothes from the front seat. She was a heavyset woman with dark hair. It wasn't Tina.

Gregory started the car and put it in reverse as Sonny and Shaved Head charged up the hill.

"Don't run, Joe," I said. "It's too late to run."

Gregory murmured, "Shit," as Sonny circled around and approached us like a carjacker, trying to get the element of surprise by attacking on an angle from the rear, in the blind spot in the mirror. He came to my side of the T-bird, breathing hard. He put his gun against my cheek. I could smell gun oil.

"Get that out of my face," I said.

"You following me, you bastard?" he said. "Are you fucking following me?"

"If I wanted to follow you, you'd never know it," I said.

"I believe you, Ryan. I really believe you. Get out of the fucking car."

"Step back," I said.

"Careful, pally," Gregory said.

I started to open the door, then turned to Gregory. "Promise me you'll kill this prick."

"Count on it," he said.

I got out of the car, slammed the door, and stepped to my right so Gregory could have a clear shot through the window. Then Sonny handed his gun to Shaved Head and lumbered toward me, rocking his shoulders. His face was white with rage as he threw a big roundhouse right, turning the punch as we'd been taught in the academy. But he was so slow and I was so focused, I watched the punch in the air and ducked it easily.

Sonny stumbled forward with the force of the miss. I kept my head down and stepped in, delivering a short hook to his gut. At the same moment his face slammed into the top of my skull. I felt the crunch. I grabbed him by the shirt, spun, and flipped him down on his ass.

Sonny's lip swelled up immediately. The skin split when it could stretch no farther. Blood ran down over his chin. He saw the blood, scrambled to his feet, and charged, pinning me against the T-bird. He hit me once in the face, but I caught most of the blow with a forearm. He was too close to get leverage and too heavy for me to push away.

Then I felt an arm between us, in front of my face. An arm covered in wool. Wool that smelled like dried horse shit. It was Francis X. His forearm wrapped tight around Sonny's throat, choking him. Sonny tried to pull the arm loose as they staggered backward.

"No, Francis," I said.

I heard the click of a hammer cocking. Shaved Head was dancing, circling to get a shot at Francis X.

"Don't kill him, Francis," I said. I stepped in front of Shaved Head. I could hear Gregory saying, "Pally, pally."

Francis X. dropped Sonny to the ground and came over and put his arms around me. He smelled of sickening-sweet wine and tobacco and days of a madman's sweat.

Francis whispered in my ear, his voice guttural as if the worst disease had struck his throat. So raspy I could barely make it out. "She's talking to me," he said.

"Who?" I said.

"Shoot the motherfucker," Sonny yelled.

"Mary," Francis X. said.

I stepped toward the back of the car and maneuvered Francis X. out of the line of fire.

"Mary who?" I said.

He put his face against mine. "Maria," he said, so raw, it hurt to hear it. "Maria is Mary."

"I know that," I said. "I know."

He smiled and held my face in his hands as if I were a favorite grandchild. Bits of food were stuck in his matted beard. His hands were hot and rough on my face.

"Bless you," he said. And with a few quick steps disappeared into the trees and the night.

28

In bed that night I kept replaying the scene with Francis X. I was angry at myself for not seeing how sick he was, for trying to romanticize his guarding the children. I should have seen the danger, but I saw only what I wanted to see. My wife says it's the quality that keeps me human. Gregory says I do it too often, and once is too often for a cop.

"She's talking to me," Francis X. had said. "Maria. Maria is Mary."

I'd always been a poor sleeper. Leigh thought she could teach me. She pushed herself tightly against my back, her legs bent up behind mine. Leigh said I didn't understand the rhythm of letting go. She pressed her body against mine so I could feel the cadence of her untroubled breathing. Her breasts were warm and full against my back. I stroked her hip, the tips of my fingers tracing fine, silky streaks of stretch marks. When her breathing became deep, I pulled away gently, knowing

I was a poor student, a lost cause. I dressed and walked outside.

My neighborhood in Yonkers was mostly working people my age whose kids had married and moved away. Many of us had originally moved from the city, only to have our kids move back to Manhattan. I walked downhill toward Sacred Heart Church. It was quiet enough to hear the sound of crickets as I crossed the wet lawn in front of the convent. The statue of the Blessed Virgin Mary stood with her hands outstretched. A holly bush blocked the spotlight, so I moved closer and touched the dew-wet stone. Mary was barefoot, the paint chipping on her toes, the snake under her feet.

There was something about Sonny's shooting of little Martin Luther Hopkins that I'd never told anyone, not even Leigh. A few days afterward I was at home alone and the phone rang. I was groggy, half asleep, half hung over. A young child mumbled something I couldn't understand. I sat up and asked who it was, and the child mumbled again. The same words. I asked over and over until I was almost crying, begging the child to say it again, say it clearly. Then I prayed he would hang up, because I couldn't. It sounded like "I'm Martin now."

Although I have no idea what it's like to have a breakdown, I know that's as close as I've ever come.

Back home, I started the computer and went to the list of names that I'd gotten from the Hernandez Funeral Home. I paged down, looking for Mary or Maria. Thirty years ago there would have been dozens of Marys on any list in the Bronx, but no more. Then I found Maria. Maria Torres, age seven, of 719 Crotona Park North.

I remembered that Angel had told me that her mother had been baby-sitting for a girl named Maria. A girl who was killed in a drive-by shooting. Maria Torres lived above Angel. She was buried on April 9, 1994, the same day the Blessed Virgin Mary appeared in ice. The day before the rebar murders began.

I called the Five One squad to find out what time Sergeant Drumm was due in. "He's on his way," the cop said. "Rebar man is alive and well in Crotona Park. And another scumbag has bit the dust."

Gregory was sitting on the passenger side of the T-bird when I arrived, watching the playground. It was a surveillance trick, to make it appear as if you were waiting for someone. Four radio cars were parked in the grass, just beyond the playground. The body of a chubby, dark-skinned man lay sprawled on the blacktop path next to a broken water fountain. His face was so black and swollen, it looked like a basket of rotted plums.

"You see the chalk?" Sergeant Drumm said. "Where the hell do they get the chalk?"

Except for splattered blood, nothing else was around the body, no weapons, no drug paraphernalia, no holy cards. Nothing except a chalk outline, drawn by some chalk fairy, some rookie cop who'd seen too many movies and felt the need to draw a chalk outline around the body. No detective ever outlined a body in chalk until it was ready to be removed. A good defense lawyer could have crime scene pictures thrown out of court because the scene was contaminated, not as originally found.

Gregory said, "Who we got here this time, Sarge?"

"Elidio Duncan, a Santana crew chief," Drumm said. "Radio car found him at oh five hundred."

A Crime Scene Unit tech man squatted over the body,

holding tweezers and a small white envelope within inches of the deceased's legs. He picked at the ground and saturated clothing for fibers, hairs, whatever he could come up with. It was not quite ten A.M., but a small crowd had formed, mostly little kids, out to get some safe playing time before the scumbags woke up.

"I think I know who did this, Neville," I said. "I think it's Francis X. Hanlon."

Drumm pulled his head back and looked at me. "You're shitting me," he said.

I'd seen Tina's son, Kevin, in the crowd. He was wearing a Spider-Man sweatshirt, bouncing a red-striped golf ball on the blacktop.

"Where's your mom?" I said.

"At the launder-mat," he said. "Sonny gave me this ball."

"He's a real sport," I said. "Kevin, do you know where the Padre stays? Will you help me find him?"

"My dad told me to stay away from the Padre."

"You mean Sonny?"

"Sonny's not my dad," he said. "Is the Padre in trouble?"

"The Padre is sick, Kevin. He needs to see a doctor."

"Maybe he's sick in his house," Kevin said.

"Let's go to his house and see."

Gregory and I followed Kevin down a dirt path into an area thick with heavy trees and bushes. In a small clearing littered with beer cans, potato-chip bags, and condoms, several cardboard boxes were stretched flat into beds, one end greasy with the oil from someone's hair. Kevin said it wasn't the Padre's house, it belonged to someone else.

We crossed the footpath as a boxer, his face hidden in a hooded sweatshirt, jogged backward and threw jabs and hooks into the air. A skater breezed by him, startling him into a quick, violent flurry.

Kevin led us up a hill toward the tennis courts, to a thick clump of bushes behind a brick administration building. Beyond that, the squeal of sneakers, the slap of a tennis ball. Kevin pointed to the bushes.

I pulled away loose clumps of branches. They weren't rooted, merely placed there to enhance the thickness. Something Francis X. probably learned in Vietnam. Gregory took out his gun as I looked in.

It was a small clear area, the grass worn down to a smooth dirt floor. A large piece of canvas was tied to stakes in the ground, pots and pans piled in an orange plastic crate. A hose sat in the fork of a stick and ran back through the bushes toward the tennis house. Another brown plastic milk crate held a hammer, a roll of toilet paper, and a paintbrush dried fire-engine red. Sticking out of another crate was a slightly bent piece of rebar, about two feet long, covered with blood and bits of hair.

"I can see the murder weapon," I said. "We need a search warrant."

"Not for bushes we don't," Gregory said. "It's a public park."

"Don't argue with me about this, Joe. Go get Sergeant Drumm, and read the legal bulletins once in a while."

"That's what I got you for," he said.

Kevin sat in the grass next to me while I waited for Gregory to come back. The grass smelled strong and had the coarse seediness of early spring. A group of teenagers strolled down the path, carrying blankets and paper bags.

"You better go home, Kevin," I said.

"Nobody's home."

"Go to see Angel."

"Angel's up there," Kevin said, and pointed up into the top of the trees. I remembered we were due to have an eclipse of the sun around noon.

"In the sky?" I said.

"In the sky in an airplane."

"What's he doing in an airplane?"

"Going to get an operation to be a girl."

"When did that happen?"

"It didn't happen yet. When he gets there he'll get an operation and be a girl."

"But he's already gone?" I said.

"Yeah, he's gone. In a plane."

Kevin looked back up at the sky. I wondered where Angel suddenly got all that money, but I was more concerned about why the park was filling up with young Hispanics. I noticed larger groups coming from both sides of the park, heading toward the big open meadow.

"They got a meeting," Kevin said. "The Latin Kings."

"What's the meeting about?"

"About respects."

"What does that mean, Kev?"

"Nobody fucks with them."

I knew about the Kings; I'd written an intelligence report years ago. They'd grown tremendously and no longer wanted to be called a gang; now they were a family.

Small clusters of gang members came from all directions. A surprising amount of women. I knew there was a Puerto Rican girls' gang, the BICs, the Boricuas in Charge. I wondered what was taking Gregory so long. The eclipse was due to start at around noon. I didn't want to be in the park during it.

The gang members all wore colored beads around their ankles, wrists, and neck, multicolored strands that identified their allegiance. The Latin Kings and Queens wore yellow and black, three yellow, then three black, and some strands reached past their waists.

It seemed to be getting colder. I checked my watch; I thought Gregory should be back. Kids continued to arrive. Other groups. The Netas, an old Puerto Rican Indian folkloric term for the rejoicing of a new arrival. Their beads were white, red, and black, with a small cross, like a rosary.

A sudden darkness startled me. I squinted up at the blue sky, not to look for Angel, but because I was worried about the eclipse. But a man was blocking the sun. A man wearing a large wooden cross.

"Brother Ryan," Francis X. said.

He looked battered, his arms skinned as if he'd been dragged by a truck. A huge welt covered the right side of his head.

"You need a doctor," I said.

A radio car came up the hill toward us. Two young cops jumped out and took cover behind open car doors. I snatched up Kevin and turned my back to the cops.

"I'm on the job!" I yelled, and fumbled in my pocket for my shield. "Don't shoot. I'm on the job."

"We're taking the Padre into custody," a cop said. "It's all over the radio. Citywide order."

"He's in my custody," I said.

"Then fucking cuff him," the cop said.

I held up my hand to Francis X., telling him, "Stay there, don't move." I tried to unhook my handcuffs from the back of my belt, but it was awkward holding Kevin. Then I heard Gregory's voice telling everyone to relax. I turned around and saw Gregory and Drumm.

Behind them, the Latin Kings were moving up the hill toward us. Francis X. started singing, a low moan, the same words I'd heard him sing in the playground: "Make me an instrument of your peace." His mouth was so dry, I could hear his tongue sticking. The wind picked up, the leaves rustled above us.

"We got phone warrants," Gregory said.

Francis X. glanced up at the sun and moved toward me. I heard the guns cock. More radio cars moved across the grass.

"Brother Ryan," Francis said.

One of the Latin Kings yelled, "Hey, man, why you hassling the Padre?"

"Wait, godammit, everybody wait," I yelled.

I put Kevin down and pushed him toward Joe Gregory. Francis X. had his mouth open, his blank eyes focused on my face. I put my hand on his shoulder; his arms felt limp.

"Your work is not done, Brother Francis," I said softly. "Mary isn't finished with you."

Francis X. looked up at the sky again. I couldn't tell if the eclipse had started or not. The sun didn't look different to me. But I didn't know what he was seeing.

"It's another sign," I said. "Mary has a new flock for you, a ministry that needs you, Brother Francis. She wants me to take you to it."

He held his hands out toward me. Arms together. I heard the sound of my handcuffs, the teeth clicking through the ratchet.

29

When Caprice Antonucci knocked on the door the next morning, Leigh was standing over me on the bed, naked, swatting at a fly with a rolled-up magazine. The bed shook, miniblinds jumped from the window, dust flew with each swat.

"What the hell is going on?" I said.

"It's a fly," she said, peeking down at the front step.

"No, I mean is somebody at the door?"

"Yes, Caprice Antonucci," she said, but she kept on swatting.

"You want me to get it?" I said. "I mean the door."

"No. I do everything else," she said. She threw on a robe and ran downstairs. The miniblinds were still swinging.

Leigh had taken a few extra vacation days to get ready for the wedding, and she was getting antsy. She got up early to call our son in Los Angeles. I was sure he was glad to hear his mother's voice at four A.M. PST. After that I heard her banging the vacuum cleaner around downstairs. I assumed she was getting ready to jump in the shower when she spotted the fly. I heard her coming up the stairs.

"Caprice Antonucci is downstairs," Leigh said, removing the robe and searching the bedroom floor for her panties. "She wants to talk to you."

"She say what it's about?" I said.

"I didn't ask. She's in the kitchen. Comb your hair before you go down."

I pulled on a pair of jeans I'd thrown across a chair. Leigh had the magazine in her hand and was scanning the windows for the fly.

"What did Tony say?" I asked.

"He said: Mom, do you know it's four o'clock in the morning?"

"I mean about the wedding?"

"He'll be there. He said he goes to all her weddings. He talked to Margaret yesterday, the ceremony is still on the beach, weather permitting."

"How come I didn't know that?"

"I told you. You don't listen. Now come on, put something decent on and come downstairs. You have company."

Company, I thought. I haven't had company in ten years. I grabbed a sweatshirt and went down. Caprice Antonucci was sitting at my kitchen table.

"Sorry for getting you up," Caprice said.

"You didn't," I said. "We were on the phone."

Caprice wore tight jeans and a Knicks sweatshirt. She appeared younger out of uniform and thinner without all that leather gear around her. And she sounded nervous.

"I heard about how you locked up the Padre yesterday," she said. "All the cops were talking about it. That was cool. The way you did it."

"Thanks," I said.

Leigh had gotten dressed, put on one of my flannel shirts. "I'm going out in the back and dig the big suitcase out of the shed," she said.

"You guys going on vacation?" Caprice said.

"Margaret is getting married Saturday," Leigh said.

"Oh, cool," Caprice said.

"I'll let you two talk shop," Leigh said. "The coffee is fresh. Sorry, I don't have any doughnuts. I know how you cops like doughnuts."

"Very funny," I said.

When the door closed, Caprice said, "Mrs. Ryan is a really cool lady. All the kids at school really like her."

Caprice's hair was cut short and blunt. It was a dark, coppery red, the color of an Irish setter. She had angular features, a small square jaw, a sprinkling of freckles around her nose, and a pronounced overbite.

"You used to work with Sonny Guidice, right?" she said. "When you were in the Five One. He's a character, isn't he?"

In the bright sunlight of my own kitchen, I could see that Caprice Antonucci had red eyebrows, and dark brown eyes that were locked on my face.

"Among other things," I said.

"I figured maybe you were old friends," she said. "Until I heard you had a fight with him."

"I can't stand Sonny," I said. "Never could."

She laughed and looked around at the coffeepot. I took the hint, got up, and poured two cups.

"I graduated from Sacred Heart with your son," she said. "Tony used to tell stories about things you did. It kind of made me want to be a cop."

"Oh, don't blame this on me," I said.

She laughed again, a bit too loud. I wondered if she made that up just to be friendly. I was surprised to hear that my son had talked about me and my job. I couldn't remember telling him any stories myself. Maybe Leigh had.

"Could I talk to you about something?" she said.

I could tell it was heavy, the way she looked at me, eyes wide, mouth slightly open.

"You're not wired, are you?" I said.

"Oh, shit, no," she said. "You can search me." She stood and picked up her sweatshirt to her neck, exposing a lacy beige bra and small freckled breasts.

"Good, good," I said as she turned to show her back. "I was only kidding."

Caprice sat down and stared into a space above my head. Her perfume smelled like vanilla, more confection than mystery.

"I went to the academy with Paul Verdi," she said. "Good guy. Really. He was crazy then. Well, not mental, but crazy in a funny way. Fun to be around. Know what I mean?"

"I know exactly. I have a partner who's mental, but he's a lot of fun."

She turned the cup in her hands and sighed heavily. Her teeth had made deep marks on her lower lip.

"I don't know if I'm doing the right thing, Mr. Ryan. I don't want anyone to think I'm a rat, but I hate what's going on in the Five One."

"Like what?" I said.

Caprice had big hands for a woman. Her nails were short, with clear polish.

"Most of the cops I know are good people," she said. "They do their jobs, stick their necks out every day."

"But," I said.

"Paulie told me things," she said. "I'm not looking to be the female Serpico, or anything like that. But he told me about money they made, things they did."

"Who's 'they'?"

"Sonny's crew. At first it was just Paulie and Marc Ross; now he's got Timmy."

"The guy with the shaved head."

"Yeah. And he's trying to pick up somebody else. Sonny's got the guys who work six-to-twos wrapped around his little finger. Paulie wanted out. He wanted out in the worst way. Sonny said it was too late."

"In for a penny, in for a pound."

"What?" she said.

"It's just an old saying," I said. "What kinds of things did Paulie tell you?"

Caprice told me that Sonny had some kind of deal with the Highbridge Boys, the Manhattan drug gang. He was being paid to put all their competition out of business, so the Highbridge Boys could take over the entire Bronx. Sonny had a go-between who dealt directly with them; Sonny was never involved. But he'd skim cash and drugs, then sell confiscated drugs to the Highbridge Boys.

A perfect scheme, Paulie had said. Because they still made arrests of some Highbridge dealers. Sonny arranged their arrests by telling them to go to a certain spot where they'd meet a guy who was waiting for them. The guy would get into their car with drugs on him. All they had to do was drive to the station house and book him for sale and possession of narcotics.

"It's called an accommodation arrest," I said.

The old division plainclothesmen used to arrange arrests with the mob gambling bosses. The bosses would pay some poor schmuck to take the arrest. The schmuck would wait on a corner with numbers in his pocket, usually just enough to make it a crime. The plainclothesman would book him, but the case would get reduced or thrown out of court. But the cops would chalk up an arrest on the sheet, cover the quota, and look as though they were doing their jobs.

"What about Santana's operation?" I said.

"Same as the rest. Put him out of business. Paulie said he's a stubborn bastard, so they broke his chops something fierce."

"You know that for a fact?"

"I know what Paulie told me," she said, shrugging. "That's why I came to you for advice. I don't know what else to do."

I could hear Leigh banging around in the shed outside. She was always threatening to clean it out. This could be the day.

"What did you see with your own eyes, Caprice? Anything illegal at all?"

"Drugs. They all had drugs. I saw money, a wad Paulie had. Sonny told them not to be showy with money. No fancy cars, or nothing. He held the money for the three of them. He only gave them so much at a time."

"Did you ever see Sonny, or any of them, talking to one of the dealers?"

She shook her head slowly and looked as if she were having second thoughts. She was treading on dangerous ground. Cops who worked in ghetto precincts saw themselves as belonging to a remote outpost. That's why so many precincts were nicknamed Forts: Fort Apache, Fort Surrender. They were foreign legionnaires, who depended on each other for survival. In times of siege they hid behind the wall of the fort. The wall was blue and silent. I knew that for a fact, because I'd spent enough time behind that wall.

"Did you ever make calls to IAD?" I said. "Late at night?"

"A couple of times," she said. "I was hoping they'd nail Sonny, before Paulie screwed up for good. Nothing ever happened."

"Do you think Paulie's involvement in corruption got him killed?" I said.

"I don't believe he'd bring some strange woman into the coop like that. Not the Paulie I knew."

"He wouldn't bring a woman in there."

"No way."

"Did he have a girlfriend?"

She got up and walked to the sink. She rinsed her cup and set it in the drain. I could see the answer to my next question in her face.

"Were you and Paulie lovers?" I said.

"Hey, Mr. Ryan," she said. "I know his wife, his kids, and all that. She's been hurt enough. Know what I mean?" She reached for her jacket. "I think I screwed up, too. Just now."

"No, you didn't," I said.

After Caprice left I called Delia. She was at another function. A law enforcement executives meeting and barbecue on the roof of John Jay College.

I went to the computer to pull up the arrests made by Sonny's team to see if I could see the pattern Caprice was talking about. The problem with analyzing arrest information was that dispositions were rarely available. It often took months to get a final disposition on a case, and no one went back to enter it on the record.

I paged through the arrests, stopping at Marc Ross's

grab of Hector and Tina Marquez. Not because there was anything major; the collar, like all of them, looked good on paper. One word caught my eye: Camels. Ross was very thorough. He listed all the personal property taken from Hector Marquez: forty-seven dollars and thirty-five cents in U.S. currency, a tube of Chap Stick, a pack of Camels. We'd recovered the stub of an unfiltered Camel at the Verdi crime scene. Ross's report didn't say whether Hector smoked filtered or unfiltered.

On my way to John Jay I drove down Columbus Avenue. On the corner of West Seventy-eighth, an infant, bundled in a nylon snow suit and a wool hat, sat on a live pony against the brick apartment building. The parents danced around, trying to make the child smile for the photographer. The photographer was smoking a pipe.

The John Jay College of Criminal Justice was a new, modern structure built behind the classic facade of DeWitt Clinton High School on Tenth Avenue and Fifty-eighth Street. I ran up the old stairs, then took the new elevator to the top. I walked across the tennis court and the track that ringed the roof. Smoke rose from charcoal grills. I pulled Delia from the burger line and told her Caprice Antonucci's story.

"Call IAD," she said, shrugging.

"I know this girl, Delia. She went to school with my kids. I'm not going to throw her to the wolves."

"You don't have a choice. Besides, what justification do we have to avoid IAD?"

"I thought we could cover it under our major case number on the Verdi-Ross homicides. I thought we could walk it into the DA's office ourselves."

"You thought wrong," she said.

The Met Life blimp flew overhead, hugging the east side of the Hudson. I looked down the line of ex-cops and ex–FBI agents, many of whom I'd worked with in the past. They looked like the businessmen they'd become.

"What's it going to look like?" she said. "My ex-husband is in IAD, and I keep avoiding them. I'll tell you what they're going to say: that I'm some bitter scorned woman who lets her emotions cloud her judgment. I won't have that. Uh-uh. No way."

In the time I'd worked with Delia, the thing I liked least about her was that she hid behind the rules when it was safer for her to do so. I didn't mind all the schmoozing she did to advance her career; I knew a lot of guys who'd make her look like a shy recluse. But don't hide behind the rules.

"IAD is already in there," Delia whispered. "They've set up a sting apartment on Crotona Park East."

"Thanks for telling me now," I said.

"I couldn't tell you, and you know it. I shouldn't be telling you at all."

"I'd hoped you wouldn't put me in this position."

"You put yourself in this position."

Sid Kaye moved to the mike and asked everyone to take a seat so the meeting could begin. I sat next to Delia on a wooden picnic bench. Delia ate her hamburger with a knife and fork while Sid Kaye butchered *Robert's Rules of Order*.

"All she has is hearsay," Delia whispered. "We can't do anything with hearsay. Someone will have to wire her and send her up against Guidice. See if she can get any admissions on tape."

I thought about Caprice Antonucci going against Sonny. I thought about what it would do to the rest of her young life in the job. I knew what it would do to the wife of Paul Verdi, because Sonny's lawyer would surely use her relationship with Paul to discredit her.

"Call IAD," I said. "Let's set something up."

"You really think she'll do it?" Delia said.

"No," I said. "I'll do it."

30

The next day Gregory drove me over to Hudson Street, where an IAD technician used white adhesive tape to secure a body mike to my chest. It consisted of a transmitter, half the size of a deck of cards, taped to the small of my back. A single wire curled around and upward at midchest. They insisted on instructing me in proper procedures, even made me sign a form saying I'd been so instructed.

After they finished Gregory and I rode to the Market Diner and picked up a coffee, a tea, and two fried-egg sandwiches. It was noon, and instead of returning to One Police Plaza he parked facing the East River just north of the Fulton Fish Market. I had two hours to kill before meeting Sonny Guidice.

"Call your friend in State Corrections," I said. "Have him check on the status of Hector Marquez."

"Why?"

"Because he smokes Camels," I said.

"He's smoking them in prison."

"Just do me a favor. Make sure he's still there."

We parked looking down at the dark water, under the East Side Drive. The front end of the T-bird pointed toward the Watchtower building across the river in Brooklyn. Adhesive tape was wrapped completely around my rib cage and seemed to be getting tighter with each breath. Gregory opened the bag and put the sandwiches on the newspaper between us. I handed him the ketchup packets from the glove compartment.

"IAD got the apartment all set up?" he said.

"Delia said it's good, looks like a drug stash. More hidden cameras and mikes than a TV soundstage."

"How you going to get Sonny to bite?" he said. "You ain't exactly his asshole buddy."

"Greedy guys are easy," I said.

Out in the river, a tug moved quickly downriver toward Governors Island. Behind us a few trucks idled, stragglers from the overnight chaos of business in the fish market. Exhaust fumes floated up toward the highway above us.

"You think this is going to cure anything?" he said. "Cops like Sonny are always going to find a way to steal."

"So we make it a little harder on them."

"Things ain't going to change, pally. Read the papers. Kids we got coming on the job today weren't brought up like we were."

"Please don't tell me the job was better in the old days. I remember the old days. They weren't glory days."

The fish market was deserted, all the stalls closed. Still, even the lingering diesel fuel couldn't smother the overpowering smell of fish.

"Remember last time we were here?" he said.

The last time Joe and I were parked in this spot was before the South Street Seaport was built in 1983. It was a cool day in late March. Joe's father, Liam, was with us then, and we discussed his involvement in an old investigation. That day I threw a piece of evidence into the river, only because Liam asked me to.

"When we left here that day," Gregory said, "my old man said that he just did the worst thing a cop can do. He was sick because he had to bring you into it."

"I understood. That was a different situation, a different era."

"I swore that day that I'd back you up no matter what, pally. That still holds. It ain't my cup of tea, but I'm with you on this. A hundred percent."

I could hear the clock running in the quiet of the car. Huge, grimy seagulls worked on clams dumped against a chain-link fence. They picked them up and dropped them on the pavement repeatedly until the shell broke enough to expose meat.

"Some of these young cops ain't too bad," he said.

"They need time. And the right teachers. Not guys like Sonny Guidice."

Police work is an experience-heavy occupation. It takes years on the street in a busy precinct to develop calluses on your nerves. Four years minimum. Six is better. It takes a thousand nights to tame the yips that attack your hands and eyes on burglary runs in cold, dark warehouses; to find the balance of compassion and vigilance to handle unpredictable domestic fights; or to learn to maintain your cool on wild, full-siren, lights-flashing, all-out runs: man with a gun, shots fired, ten thirteen. It takes years to fine-tune the process of control. To learn when to act, when to back out; when to shoot, when to take cover. It takes time and guidance, and some kids don't get enough of either.

"IAD don't want me along today," Gregory said.

"You don't want any part of this," I said. "You're only a couple of days away from being the president of the Emerald Society."

"Election is Saturday. It's here already."

"Good luck," I said. "But you'll win easy."

"Vote early and often," he said.

Well-dressed people strolled on the deck of the seaport, drinks in hand. My skin was beginning to heat up; I tried to keep from scratching. A vagrant stood on a small concrete platform behind a row of stalls, pissing into the river.

"Ain't too late to change your mind," Gregory said.

"It's years too late," I said.

I stood near my car door with my shirt unbuttoned as Inspector Bruce Browne taped the on button in place so it wouldn't click off accidentally when I sat back. He walked away with a wave, no words for posterity. I sat alone in my own car.

"This is Detective Anthony Ryan," I said. "Shield number seven one two, of the chief of detectives office." I read from the usual form and filled in the blanks. The form was a fading copy of an ancient copy, the print badly speckled, disappearing with each reproduction. The text was a heading for a tape that would later be transcribed and typed for presentation to a DA. A standard script we always used. "The time is thirteen-thirty hours, May 12, 1994. I am about to meet Police Officer Alphonse Guidice, shield number twenty-two seven three, in relation to major case number one one five, slash ninety-four."

When I finished, I ripped the script into shreds and threw it down the sewer. I looked through the rearview mirror at the blue Buick behind me. Inspector Browne gave the thumbs-up sign. He'd heard every word. It hadn't occurred to me until I read the script that tomorrow was Friday the thirteenth.

On the ride up the East River Drive I was aware of my breathing. I tried not to clear my throat or sigh too heavily. Browne and two other IAD cops were behind me in the Buick. And in the distance, behind them, I spotted Gregory's T-bird.

Sonny had told me he'd meet me at a condemned pier, just below the East River heliport. I got off the drive at Twenty-third and made a hard right through the gate, then parked under the curve of the highway. All my dramatic moments were destined to be on the water.

A helicopter was just landing. I covered my eyes as dirt and trash blew in small whirlpools. Noise was going to be a problem. I'd have to control the conversation and spring the bait when the noise was down. I wondered if Sonny had picked the spot for that reason. But he lived in Stuyvesant Town, a few blocks away. He said he always came out here. A group of men in suits climbed out of the copter; another waited to board.

I walked past the landing pad, down a narrow blacktop path alongside the highway abutment. Sonny was out on the pier, hitting red-striped golf balls out into the East River.

"Fucking Ryan," he said.

Sonny had black stitches across his lower lip from his encounter with my head. He wore tan shorts, cheap sneakers, and a grungy black sweatband that said "No Fear." On his shoulder rested the biggest golf club I'd ever seen. I stepped close to him, worried about the copter and the highway and the gulls. He motioned for me to step back, then he smacked a long drive that seemed sure to be heading toward a tanker. It dropped well short.

"I came to apologize," I said, trying to talk above the noise. "I really thought you had something to do with the murders of Santana's dealers."

"I know you did," he said. "I was going to get a piece of rebar as a joke. But I didn't know whether you could still take a fucking joke."

Behind him was a blue bowling bag filled with the red-striped range balls and a white plastic D'Agostino's bag with yellow tees. He wedged another tee in the crack in the rotted wood. He broke a tee with each swing. The copter was still revving. I thought I'd better wait until it left.

"Ever see any of the old retired Five One gang?" I said.

"You know who I did see last winter," Sonny said, shouting above the noise. "Jimmy Rigney. Living in a trailer park in St. Pete."

"There's a character," I said.

"He had me pissing in my pants with stories," Sonny said. "He reminded me that he was the guy who made me my first deuce on the job. From a bodega, on Sunday. I had the foot post on Claremont, right. Rigney is in the sector car and he stops and asks if Pedro took care of me. I say who? He gets out of the car, grabs me by the shirt, and pulls me into this bodega, goes behind the counter, opens the register. The PR that owns the place doesn't say shit. Rigney takes out two bucks, hands it to me, and says, 'Here, this belongs to you. Don't spoil these people.' "

He hit a big banana slice that soared high, then dropped into the water with a tiny white splash.

"Remember the picnic table?" he said. "We laughed our balls off over that one."

A woman jogger in pink spandex pushed a baby in a three-wheel cart down the path. The baby cried, but the woman sang, tuned fully to her own body and her Walkman. The new group had boarded the copter. They'd be taking off any time. Sonny pointed to a barge being muscled upriver by a tug. He made an arcing motion in the air, telling me he was going to land one on the barge.

I'd forgotten the picnic table story. Everybody, including me, saw Sonny take the picnic table. We were working a midnight-to-eight-A.M. tour. Sonny had a foot post next to the park. In full uniform he drove his old Ford Fairlane station wagon into Crotona Park and loaded an immense green picnic table onto the roof. At eight A.M., on that bright Sunday morning, he drove back into the precinct with the picnic table tied securely to his roof and signed out. Then, with that green table, he drove across the George Washington Bridge, up the Palisades Parkway to the backyard of his house in Pearl River. Later, he told everybody it took him two weeks to sand out all the fucks and sucks that had been carved in it.

Sonny hit another ball at a barge; it fell short.

"Fucking Rigney died," Sonny said. "Last month. Doctors said his heart exploded. Fifty-eight years old. Didn't have a pot to piss in."

"Rigney never took care of himself," I said. "I know, I drank with him enough." Then I remembered that all this was being recorded.

"He was already half fucking dead when I saw him in January," Sonny said. "All those guys. It's sad. I mean it. Sitting there. Can't go to the fucking movies until the pension check comes. Living on the balls of their ass. Afraid to buy a fucking steak. Not me. No way."

Sonny hit another ball at the tanker. This too dropped short, a white splash before the gray hull. A beer can tumbled down the path in the wind.

"Rigney told me retiring was the biggest mistake he ever made," Sonny said. "He said he'd sweep the floors if the job would take him back."

"He was too young to retire," I said. "Not without something else to go to."

"What was he going to go to? Kmart, McDonald's? Not me, that's sure as shit. Maybe I'll win big at the track, Ryan. Then I'll retire. A big windfall, hit the fucking number, something like that. Then I'll go."

"I can picture you and Tina in Miami."

"Please," he said. "I can stand that broad for about two hours, no more. I wouldn't spend a whole night with her if you paid me."

Sonny leaned the golf club against his belly and carefully scratched around the stitches in his lip. "I'm just a poor dumb cop," he said. "Going to spend my last years alone and in poverty."

"You're sharper than you'd like people to believe," I said. "I really thought you had everybody fooled. I was sure you were trying to get even with Tito Santana for the murders of Ross and Verdi. I had you pegged wrong."

"Forget it," he said. "You always had me pegged wrong. Even way back."

The copter rose high in the air, swinging south over the river toward the Williamsburg Bridge. I could hear the gulls again. It was as quiet as it was going to be.

"I never figured Francis X. for the rebar murderer," I said. "Never in a million years."

He hit another ball directly at a yacht coasting too near the shore. The ball smashed off the side of the boat and rebounded back into the water. A man in a blue windbreaker appeared from the cabin and looked over at us. Sonny yelled, "Fuck you!" at the yacht, his voice skipping out over the water.

"The Padre was a fucking loony," Sonny said.

"I was worried when he came over to hug me," I said. "Then he started whispering in my ear."

"I thought he was planting a big wet one on you," he said.

"He stunk like hell."

"The prick ain't had a bath since they let him out of Creedmoor. What the fuck was he whispering, anyway?"

I felt my pulse begin to rush. I took a quick, deep breath.

"Something about Santana," I said. "He was rambling. Something about how I should get the rest of the snakes. He said they keep the snake poison in the red house. That old building on the corner opposite the school. Herman Ridder Junior High. In the basement apartment."

Sonny stood there looking at the yacht, wiggling the big driver in his hands. "Fucking loony tunes," he said.

A man in a Greek fisherman's hat stood about fifty feet to our downtown side. He had a surf pole and was casting out into the river.

"I never meant to kill that kid, Ryan," Sonny said. "You never forgave me for that."

"It wasn't a matter of forgiveness," I said. "It was an accident."

"I know that," he said. "I know that very fucking well. But you don't believe it."

"I believe it," I said.

"You're more like me than you want to admit, Ryan."

"Fuck you, Sonny," I said.

The last few moments of tape consisted of Sonny's laughter as I walked back to the car.

I drove back to One Police Plaza and initialed the tape as evidence and gave it to Bruce Browne. Gregory was reading the homicide folder. I handed him the phone number of where I'd be staying in Delaware.

"We're leaving tomorrow morning," I said. I felt awkward, slightly sick to my stomach. I kept thinking I should be feeling good.

"You did the right thing," Gregory said.

"I know. And thanks, I saw you."

"Saw what?" he said, winking and gesturing toward Browne.

"Call me if anything big happens," I said.

I was still awake that night when Delia called. It wasn't even eleven. Sonny didn't wait long to hit the apartment.

"He bit hard," Delia said. "Real hard."

31

I did my part, the rest was up to them. I told myself that for one hundred and twenty miles down the New Jersey Turnpike. In less than three hours we'd crossed the Delaware Memorial Bridge and were in Delaware, bearing left, following signs that said "Seashore Points." I kept rubbing Leigh's leg, until she pushed my hand away, saying I was going to rub the skin off.

"We probably won't see Margaret tonight," Leigh said. "She had to drive Cliff to Virginia to pick up his parents. He has some problem with his license."

"That figures."

"Be nice," she said.

Leigh had cleaned the car, washed the writing off the vinyl trim. It was her car, but whenever I was in it I'd write license plate numbers on the vinyl trim. It was a cop's habit. I was forever seeing crime: a car idling outside a check-cashing place, some mope hanging around a grade school. I'd write the number down and memorize descriptions, just in case. The car had been cleansed of the license plate numbers, but my head was still filled with descriptions.

Although I'd never liked driving, the long stretches of highway were relaxing, the countryside punctuated only by stop signs and ramshackle vegetable stands. Whenever I went on a trip I was always surprised at all the empty space. The farther south we traveled, the more green the grass and trees, the more flowers in bloom. It was like a road trip to spring.

"Could you live here?" Leigh said.

"No," I said.

"Why?"

"Places outside New York lack something, and I don't know what, but it's life sustaining. It's like soul, it can't be explained."

A black man in a wine-colored suit changing the tire on a rusted El Dorado stopped to tip his hat. An elderly white-haired woman in a flowered cotton dress stood in a weed-filled field, bent over from the waist. I asked Leigh what the old woman was doing.

"Picking turnip greens," she said.

"How does she know them from the weeds?"

"The same way you know the BMT from the IRT."

We followed a decrepit blue Ford truck for the last ten miles. Plastic signs on the side advertised "Bob's Mobile Home Repair." The air turned much cooler as we rode down the wide main street of Rehoboth Beach. The sidewalk was lined with short round metal poles sticking from the ground. Leigh said they took the parking meters off the poles after Labor Day and stored them until Memorial Day. I could smell the salt air.

Our motel was right on the boardwalk. About a dozen cars in the parking lot, ours the only one with an antitheft club clamped to the steering wheel. The room smelled musty. The carpet felt damp and sandy.

"What's that thumping noise?" I said as we unpacked.

"The ocean," Leigh said.

"Is it always that loud?"

I walked to the window; the glass was clouded with moisture. I stepped out onto the balcony. Directly below was a boardwalk, beyond that a short tan stretch of beach, then the ocean, immense and dark blue. The surface of the water seemed too calm for the waves to be that loud. An older couple in yellow nylon windbreakers walked a brisk pace into the wind, arms swinging purposefully. "Lewes Volunteer Fire Department" encircled the stenciled logo on their backs.

Later, I sat on the bed reading the paper, listening to the grain report on the news. The surf slapped against the shore. And that night I slept the best I had in years.

In the morning we met at the beach. Everyone, including the priest, was barefoot. The best man wore a T-shirt that said "Teresa has crabs . . . and fresh clams too." Cliff had long sunstreaked hair, pulled back in a ponytail. He kept calling me "Kojak." But Margaret, in a plain white cotton dress, was radiant and looked so much like her mother, it almost brought tears to my eyes.

A woman in a wheelchair with balloon tires played the "Wedding March" on the flute while I walked Margaret toward the sun, toward the white surf, down an aisle of sand.

The reception was held in the VFW, where everybody received T-shirts declaring they'd survived the wedding of Margaret and Cliff. The best man shucked oysters. The bearded disc jockey played everything Springsteen ever recorded and mooned the crowd repeatedly. A keg of beer was floated. My son, Tony, joined Cliff in calling me "Kojak." Then everyone did.

I walked around with a dumb smile on my face. I felt out of it, as I always did in settings where men didn't carry guns and felonious secrets. They were kids trying desperately to be radical, but to me it seemed sweet and harmless, more like a fifties sitcom, where Mom wears a starched apron over her dress and Father truly knows best.

In bed that night Leigh said, "And you didn't want to come."

"I never said that."

"I heard you laugh," she said. "I can't remember the last time I heard you really laugh."

"I can party with the best of them."

"Margaret is really happy," she said.

"I know," I said.

"Everybody loved you, Kojak. You'd go over big down here."

I was asleep when the phone rang, a jangling short bell. I sat up and tried to find it.

"It's me, pally," Gregory said. "We got a megillah going on here."

"What?" The surf was still working outside.

"They're panicking," he said. "Issuing arrest warrants."

"In the middle of the night?" I said.

"Word leaked," he said. "They found out they were set up. They don't want . . . Listen, pally. This is something that happens. It's a bullshit world out there and bullshit happens."

"What, what? Just tell me."

"Sonny ate his gun," he said. "Blew his brains out this afternoon. In the Plaza Hotel. Believe that shit, the Plaza? The PC don't want to take a chance on any more suicides. They're bringing everybody in."

"I'll be right there," I said.

32

I left Leigh in bed, as I'd done so many times, although this was the first time in another state. The roads through Delaware were unsympathetic and dark. But they were empty, and in less than four hours I was across the George Washington Bridge, hearing familiar radio voices speaking my language. At five A.M. city traffic was at its lightest, parking still possible. I found Gregory's T-bird among a pack of NYPD cars near the judges' entrance to the Bronx Supreme Court. I banged on the brown metal door until a precinct cop opened it.

From the moment I stepped off the elevator I could hear noise from the DA's end of the building. Loud clapping, stomping. Hoarse male voices singing: "Fuck em all. . . . Fuck em all. . . . The long and the short and the tall." It sounded like a platoon, but there were only three of them, Shaved Head and two other young cops from Sonny's squad. They were behind the glass partition that ran the length of the corridor, arms around each other like drunken frat brothers. A cadre of stone-faced IAD bosses studied them from the doorway.

Then Shaved Head saw me and leaped toward the glass partition. He slammed against it, screaming, as the others stampeded behind him. I kept walking. He kept yelling, his face contorted, pressed against the partition. IAD bosses tried to pry them away. I didn't hurry or turn away. I made it a point to look directly at each one. Shaved Head leapfrogged the line and ran ahead. He jumped up on a desk, dropped his pants, and pressed his dick against the glass. Joe Gregory pulled me into a side office.

"You got here fast, pally," he said. "Freaking mad-house in there. Three psychos. Never seen nothing like it."

We walked out the back end of a row of computer terminal stations, into the hallway at the other side of the building.

"I hated to call you," he said.

"Tell me about Sonny," I said.

Gregory dropped quarters into a coffee machine. He pressed black, no sugar.

"He got a room at the Plaza," Gregory said. "I told you that, right? Checked in at two-fifteen in the afternoon. About four-twenty somebody called the desk, reported hearing a shot. Security goes in, finds Sonny on the floor of the closet, service revolver in his mouth. He's dressed in full uniform, medals and all."

"Any note?"

"Not in the hotel room," Gregory said. "We're getting a search warrant for his apartment."

He handed me the small paper cup. A sheen of grease floated on top. I could hear Shaved Head screaming my name, swearing my whole family would die.

"I don't think any of these three guys knew what was going on," Gregory said. "Not really. Maybe Shaved Head knew a little, the other two are boobs."

We sat on a dark wooden bench in the hallway. Carved in the seat was a jagged heart, "Emilio 172" in the center.

"Guess who else was here?" Gregory said. "Tina Marquez and her lawyer."

"Her lawyer?"

"Looking for immunity. And she got it. She told us she was the go-between with the Highbridge Boys. She said Sonny threatened to get her probation revoked if she didn't do it. Laid out the whole payoff scheme. How she delivered confiscated drugs to the Highbridge Boys, including what they took from our sting apartment. Names, dates, amounts. Everything."

"She kept records."

"Sonny paid her five hundred bucks a week, but it's not doing her any good. The DA is taking the money. They're seizing her bank account."

"Suspended sentence, probation, counseling. She's home free, again."

"She just thinks she's home free," Gregory said. "She ain't. Remember that little job you gave me, check out Hector's prison status?"

"He's been out, hasn't he?"

"What they call a family ties furlough. They're eligible in their last twenty-four months before parole. Hector is in Mid-Orange up in Warwick, sixteen months to go. You want to guess when he took his furloughs?"

"I don't have to. The dates correspond with the deaths of Verdi and Ross. Sonny Guidice would have died on his next furlough."

"Bingo," he said. "I got State Corrections typing his

blood in the morning. My money says it matches the saliva on the Camel we found at the Verdi scene."

In the conference room, Lieutenant Delia Flamer sat at an immense oak table littered with empty coffee cups. Three silver NYPD shields and three guns, new semiautomatics, were lined up near a cop who was writing on a lined yellow pad. I sat next to Delia. On the opposite side of the table was her ex-husband, who ran covert operations for IAD. He was probably the one who'd set up the sting apartment on Crotona Park East.

"How did Sonny find out?" I said.

"You name it," Delia said. "Too many people in the loop."

"It was a good call, pally," Gregory said. "These guys were running wild. Asshole decides to blow his brains out, that's his business."

"You were right about Guidice from the beginning," Delia said.

"I'm so goddamn smart," I said, and sipped the coffee. It was bitter, already cool.

"You look tired," Delia said.

The first signs of light were filtering through the window. Morning would bring a bad day for Sonny's crew.

"I probably had more sleep than you did," I said.

"Why don't I drive you home, pally?" Gregory said.

"What are you going to do?" I asked.

"Going on that search of Sonny's apartment."

"Not without me."

I stood at the window, waiting for Gregory, looking down at the three cops walking toward the patrol wagon. Their bravado was gone. They were short, disheveled men being led through a gauntlet of cameras and flash bulbs, heads bowed, hands locked behind their backs. They knew this drill, they'd been at the other end when they were the good guys. Now they were playing the title role in the sad procession they themselves named "the perp walk." A few pedestrians walked by on their way to church. The sky was iron gray. A slanting rain was falling. Sorrow avoids the sun.

Gregory drove downtown to Sonny's apartment in Manhattan. He kept a line of chatter going the whole way. Stuyvesant Town was a village of red-brick high-rises a few blocks from the Police Academy, a few blocks from the river. It was an enclave of middle-class families of cops and firemen, Con Ed and Ma Bell workers. We stopped at the office to get a manager to act as a civilian witness to the search. Sonny's eleventh-floor apartment looked out over Fourteenth Street and the lettered avenues called Alphabet City.

Sonny Guidice had three dead-bolt locks on the door and a white cockatoo in a cage. A spear of yellow feathers jutted like a fin from the back of its head. Sonny'd left a note on the cage, saying he'd like the bird to go to Mr. Ferguson in 11K. The apartment was neater than I expected, as if he'd cleaned it, expecting company. Two matching brown corduroy sofas flanked a leather recliner angled to face a big-screen TV.

IAD searched the living room. Gregory and I took the only bedroom. We squeezed by another large TV at the foot of the bed. A bottle of Maalox sat next to the remote control on the nightstand. In the corner was the golf club he'd used on the dock. Gregory began opening dresser drawers. I slid a large flat box from underneath the bed.

The box contained dozens of porno movies, many unopened, still wrapped in plastic. Polaroids of naked women were scattered in the box, women of all sizes and colors. I recognized two: Sonny's late wife, whom I'd once met at a precinct dinner, and a pale blonde, whose sworn statements informed our search warrant.

The photos of Tina Marquez had been taken in his room and were not flattering. Legs spread, she smiled at the cameraman at the foot of the bed. Because of the angle her feet and legs looked huge, out of proportion.

"Bingo," Gregory said. He held up a brown envelope that had been taped to the bottom of the dresser. Inside, a single index card with three sets of numbers, each followed by *L* or *R*.

"A man who owns a combination owns a safe," he said.

Gregory went out to show it to the IAD captain. I stood up and shuffled through the papers on top of his dresser. Taped to the dresser mirror was a yellowing letter.

Dear Officer Guidice

I know you must be living with great sadness and hurt. I want you to know that I forgive you for what happened to my son. I know the Lord forgives you, and I know my son is with the Lord. I miss my beautiful boy, but I know he is in a place that he wouldn't come back from even if he could. He is a lucky one.

Be well, Officer Guidice. Pray to the Lord. Etheleva Hopkins, Bronx, New York.

"You hungry, pally?" Gregory asked later. "You look hungry. We can grab something in Brady's after this."

"I'd like that," I said.

33

The Madison Street Roundtable, a clique of old cops, convened every Sunday morning in Brady's bar. The bar was closed until noon, but Gregory and the rest of the regulars knew to go around back and down the delivery stairs through the basement, then up the inside stairs and through the kitchen. The roundtable was in the back corner of the dining room, under the picture of Willie Sutton.

"I just thought there'd be more money," I said.

"How much you expect?"

We'd found a false wall in Sonny's closet. Behind it was a safe, bolted to the floor, containing just over twenty-eight thousand dollars.

"Quarter of a million," I said.

"Jesus Christ," he said. "I'll take twenty-eight thou tax free. Plus twenty-five he had in legit money markets."

"I thought there'd be more."

"I bet a lot of it went up his nose," Gregory said.

We came through the kitchen and walked into the middle of a Gaelic Mardi Gras, complete with horns and drums. Joe McDarby played "Hail to the Chief" on the accordion. The place was packed, everybody wearing Gregory's shamrock detective badges. Shammy O'Brien threw confetti. A satin kelly green banner, festooned with shamrocks, stretched across the bar front. It looked like a drape; it must have weighed fifty pounds. Large white letters said "Emerald Society," below, in smaller block letters, "The City of New York Police Department." I realized I'd forgotten to ask Gregory about the election.

"Way to go, Mr. President," I said. I shook his hand and stepped back.

Shanahan from Missing Persons was behind the bar, mixing Bloody Marys, his Sunday missal still sticking out of his raincoat pocket. A chorus of red-faced guys sang "For He's a Jolly Good Fellow." Johnny McGuire, the wiretap man, stood on the ice maker with the video camera. The place smelled like stale beer. Dust and cigarette smoke hung in the air like a sorry fog, the noise level going through the roof. It was magic. I knew I'd be drinking before the day was out.

They chanted, "Speech, speech."

Gregory raised a Bloody Mary in the air. "To the world's greatest detectives," he said. "And being Irish don't hurt, either." Everybody cheered and drank, but Gregory wasn't finished. He raised his glass again. "And to the NYPD, and the city of New York. The class of the world. May they live forever." More cheers and imbibing.

On the TV set above our heads a picture flickered, the sound drowned out by celebration. The picture was an old official photo of Sonny Guidice, looking dark and brooding like a young Marlon Brando. Then a graph showing suicide figures in the NYPD: four times the national average. In the last ten years twenty-one NYPD cops had been killed in the line of duty, but sixty-six had taken their own lives.

I felt Gregory's big arm around me, and he was raising his glass again. "And to the greatest partner that ever lived," he said. "That freaking genius who I love, even though he's half a guinea, my partner, Anthony Ryan."

I took my bow with a sweeping flourish, but I knew in my heart I was not a smart man. Those who love you want to create an image to justify their love. My singular pursuit of Sonny Guidice was borne not out of intelligence or objectivity, but out of an unforgiving nature.

Shammy O'Brien started to sing, but the bagpipes overpowered him with a screech and whine that sucked the air out of the room. Five members of the pipe band in kilts and full regalia marched through the dining room and around the brick partition and then stepped down into the bar. Guys cleared stools out of the way. Shanahan saluted. Five times around, maybe six. Then one more time. And again.

My ears were still ringing when they quit. But I heard the words "NYPD police scandal." Everybody heard it and looked up at the TV.

The camera panned the outside of the old Five One Precinct. It looked isolated. Buildings on both sides of the precinct were long gone, burned, or torn down. The scars of the violent separation were evident in the contrast of brick. The newly exposed brick was a pale orange, raw as a wound when the scab was torn away. Above the fourth floor there was an angular slash, and from that point up the walls were a sooty gray, because they'd always faced the elements. From the upper floors of the now demolished apartment buildings, Puerto Rican girls used to throw notes and kisses into the cops' fifth-floor locker room.

"Turn the sound up," Gregory said.

"You'd think after the Knapp Commission everybody learned their lesson," Shammy said. "The hell we went through then. What's the job coming to, anyway?"

"You've got some balls saying that, Shammy," I said.

"My conscience is clear," Wally Spillane said. "Everything I stole I gave to my mother."

I picked up a Bloody Mary and sat it in front of me. A rose-colored light filtered through the stained-glass window onto Gregory's face. He pretended not to see me reach for the glass.

We all watched uniformed cops file out of the Five One Precinct. The day tour, starting on patrol, came down the steps. Reporters moved in, looking for the angriest face, hoping for the stupidest reaction. Most cops ignored them, walking quickly toward radio cars parked in the block. I could hear the TV reporter's nervous breathing as he chased a cop and his story.

"Officer," the reporter said. He'd grabbed a young cop by the arm. "How do you feel about the members of your precinct who were arrested today?"

The cop turned and faced the camera. He looked so young. Like my son, like all of our sons.

"If they're found guilty," he said slowly and very distinctly, as if he wanted everyone to hear, "they should get the chair. They're scum, and we have no place for scum in this job."

Teams from the midnight tour slouched toward the station house after turning the cars over to fresh troops. Arms full of gear, they looked rumpled and weary. The reporter signed off, emphasizing he was reporting live from the South Bronx, as if it were war-torn Sarajevo.

"I got one more toast," President Joseph P. Gregory said. "To that young cop, whoever the hell he was. Welcome. Welcome."

I joined in this toast.

I thought I'd get drunk easily, but the morning turned to afternoon, guys came, went, came back. Brady gave us red quarters for the jukebox. Shammy O'Brien sang "Four Green Fields" twice without interruption. Brady cooked a roast beef; we switched to beer. Shammy fell asleep in the back booth; we switched to gin and tonic. British gin. The election was over.

We left at eight P.M., or ten P.M., maybe midnight. We worked our way north, through bars we remembered, though no one remembered me. Sometime before dawn we found ourselves sitting on the sidewalk outside a White Castle in the Bronx. A driverless city bus idled in front of us. We sat back against the white-tiled wall of the White Castle. All around us were cardboard sleeves emptied of their tiny hamburgers.

"Ever think of getting married again?" I said.

"I am married," he said.

I'd forgotten. Gregory had been separated for over twenty years, but neither he nor Maureen had ever filed for divorce. She claimed it was against her Catholic faith, but Gregory said it was because she thought he'd surely kill himself some fine evening and she'd get the widow's pension.

"You know what I mean," I said. "Bringing another woman home. You're all alone in that big house."

"All I bring home anymore, pally," he said, "is shrimp fried rice and the *Daily News*."

As if on cue, the *News* truck flipped a bundle onto the curb. It tumbled within a few feet of our stash of hamburgers. The front-page picture was Sonny's crew walking to the waiting van.

"I felt bad about that," Gregory said. "But that young cop on TV made me feel better."

What I felt was fortunate. I made a lot of stupid mistakes as a rookie cop. Somehow I got beyond it. It was a matter of maturity, guidance, and luck. I didn't want to admit it, but I was thinking, There but for the grace of God go I.

34

Monday morning arrived like D day, everybody marching off in different directions. Delia went to Mid-Orange Correctional Facility to interview Hector Marquez. Johnny McGuire took half the task force to the Toucan Club to grab Santana. Thirty guys from Bronx Narcotics finalized plans for their simultaneous invasion of Crotona Park, armed with an arsenal of John Doe arrest warrants. Gregory met Tina and her lawyer at the bank. I took a weapons-grade headache to Penn Station to pick up my wife.

Leigh had taken the Metroliner in from Wilmington. I drove my Honda; her car was still at the Bronx DA's Office. I parked in front of an Off Track Betting office west of the Garden. Old women lined the window, just sitting there knitting and reading the racing form. I felt old and stiff myself. My head and chest ached as though I'd been worked over by a pro. I could still taste the belly bombs from the White Castle.

Leigh knew immediately. But she didn't say anything. In fact, she didn't say anything at all for most of the drive home. Gregory was waiting in front of our house. Gregory said, "How's the health?" real cheery, but Leigh walked inside. I carried in the suitcases and told her I had to get to work. I left a note on the table saying that I was sorry and I loved her. I didn't know what else to say.

"What's the big deal?" Gregory said as we drove back to the Bronx. "So you cut loose. You needed to cut loose, the way you let shit build up. Guys like you should be made to cut loose. Once a month, minimum. Doctor's orders."

My hands were still trembling, but I knew they'd steady as the day wore on. On my worst mornings, many years ago, my hands shook so bad, I couldn't get toothpaste on a brush. I had to squirt it into my mouth. Those mornings were probably in Leigh's mind.

"Tina only had six grand in her account," Gregory said. "I suppose you don't think that's a lot of money, either."

"I don't know," I said. "It might be."

"The DA thinks she's playing games. She took eighty-five hundred out two weeks ago. She says she gave it to Sonny. What does that sound like to you?"

"Bullshit."

"Exactly."

We waited for Tina, almost a block away from her apartment. I wanted to pick her up, but Delia had said to watch her until she talked to Hector. We hid in the curve of Crotona Avenue across from an over-the-counter marijuana store disguised as a carry-out food joint. Two layers of bulletproof glass surrounded the pot dealers inside.

Radio cars swooped in and out of the park. The roundup of Santana and his drug dealers was winding down. The bug we'd installed in the Toucan Club's back room turned out to be a gold mine. Besides the drug evidence, the court order had to be amended four times for new crimes: gun charges, stolen property, insurance fraud, and prostitution.

"So what do you figure Tina's role in this is?" Gregory said.

"Femme fatale," I said. "She lured these guys to the spot. Maybe a prearranged meet. Hector killed them. She was costumed to make us look for a hooker. She always wanted to be an actress."

"She got the white gloves from Angel, right?"

"And the Bill Blass dress, too," I said. "Angel figured it out when I showed him the dress. That's where he got the money for the sex change operation. From Tina."

"What about skin color?" he said.

"Makeup."

Uniformed cops were patrolling the street in the wake of the narcotics crackdown. The young cops seemed to be more weighed down than we were, black leather bulging around their hips. When I walked the street we carried the bare essentials: gun, handcuffs, memo book, and nightstick. These kids had all that and more: bulletproof vests, mace canisters, large and bulky radios hooked to their belts. And a leather pouch containing three or four pairs of latex surgical gloves.

Cops carried strange things when I walked the beat. Jimmy Woods carried birdseed for the pigeons. Eddie McCann carried tarot cards and toilet paper in his hat.

Jack Harnett carried hard candy he'd toss to the kids on his post like a WW II soldier liberating some war-torn town. Some cops refused to carry pictures of their families, worrying that they'd fall into the wrong hands. Cigarettes, dental floss, aspirin, inflatable pillows, Tums, quarters for the phone, condoms. I never knew a cop who carried a "drop gun," anticipating he'd be in a bad shooting. I always carried an extra notebook and a small pair of scissors for cutting articles from the paper. Everyone carried too much emotional baggage.

"Tina waltzed in like a movie star today," Gregory said. "The whole enchilada, shades, the outfit. Still had the sleazy lawyer, Raoul. Raoul stands there reading the warrant like he actually knows what the freak he's doing. He's got some act."

Raoul Martinez was a criminal hack who'd lurked around Bronx Criminal Court House for decades. He caught most of his work on the overflow from Legal Aid. The court appointed private attorneys on a rotating basis when Legal Aid was swamped. Martinez was the kind who postponed the case until funds maxed out, then accepted the prosecution's deal.

"Raoul was more worried about his Lexus than his client," Gregory said. "Parked it right outside on Tremont. Kept asking the bank guards to go out and watch it for him."

"You don't mean Tremont."

"Yeah, Tremont," he said. "Parked right outside."

"I thought her bank was on the Concourse up near Fordham."

"You thought wrong. Tremont and Prospect. Banco de Popular."

"I saw her coming out of a bank up there." I remembered her with a shopping bag, running for the bus, the day I visited the Hernandez Funeral Home.

"Probably a branch office," he said.

Two young kids in Oakland Raider gear sat on the shell of a car, passing a cigar back and forth. And laughing at us. They thought we didn't know shit, two old white cops. The cigar was a "blunt," a Phillies or White Owl cigar they'd hollowed out and stuffed with marijuana. Nobody sucked on real cigars like that. But they thought we were schmucks.

"I'll lay money the fat kid gets to Tremont first," Gregory said. "Loser buys lunch."

"You're on," I said.

We jumped out of the car quickly, all business. We hung our shields from our pockets and hustled toward the kids, pulling out handcuffs. The cigar went flying into the air and down onto the Cross-Bronx Expressway. The kids ran in opposite directions, negating the bet.

When we got back in the car, I said, "Let's go back up to that bank. I want to make sure."

The bank on Tremont was a Banco de Popular. The one on the Grand Concourse was an Emigrant Savings Bank, entirely different. All I wanted was one simple piece of information and the Emigrant bureaucrats acted as though they were giving up national security. I made one phone call to Sid Kaye, the head of the Retired Detectives Association. Fifteen minutes later the bank's chief of security was on the phone, telling me war stories. He was the former second whip of the Two Eight Precinct detective squad in Harlem. But then he told me he was sorry. No one by the name Tina Marquez had an account there.

"Good try, pally," Gregory said.

We rode back toward Tina. Gregory was listening to a tape of monks chanting, plus two police radio bands. On Claremont Parkway a block of drug-infested five-story apartment buildings had been replaced by small, attractive red-brick construction. The sign said "Coming Soon! Affordable Two-Family Houses. Procida Construction Corp."

"I gotta rent a tux," Gregory said. "Going to Gracie Mansion next Thursday night. All the presidents of the line and fraternal organizations are invited to some big shebang."

"You probably should buy one. You'll be going to a lot of big shebangs next couple of years."

Across the street, two women sat peacefully gossiping on plastic chairs in front of the Hermanos Fernandez Grocery. It was still a neighborhood of small grocery stores: Vasquez Grocery, Bronx Panamanian Grocery, West Indian-American Grocery.

"When I was a kid," Gregory said, "the only tux in the neighborhood belonged to the undertaker. If you were his size, you were in."

"People in our neighborhood used to borrow folding chairs from the undertaker," I said. "You always knew when there was a christening or confirmation party: all these people would be walking through the streets carrying folding chairs with 'Frankie Flinter's Funeral Home' stenciled on the back."

"Frankie Flinter's Funeral Home," Gregory said. "Say *that* fast ten times."

We followed a *Daily News* truck across Tremont Avenue. I could remember patrolling these streets in the middle of the night when the *Daily News* trucks would pull alongside the radio car and automatically hand two copies marked "Sample" through the window. I knew cops who would chase the truck for blocks if they'd missed their free copy. The same cops chased milk, bagel, beer trucks, all through the night, storing a cache of goodies they'd transfer to their own car trunks before dawn. But all that was in the bad old days, before the Knapp Commission on police corruption.

"Frankie Flinter's Funeral Home," Gregory said. "Some name."

"He should have changed it," I said. "He should have changed it. Let's find a phone. Right now."

The first two phones we stopped at were broken. At the third one, a dead cat sat upright against the coin box, holding the receiver in his paws. I picked it from his paws and dialed Sid Kaye again.

"Ask him if he knows where I can get a deal on a tux," Gregory said.

I asked Sid to check out another name for me, then gave the phone to Gregory. Ten minutes later Sid called back. Gregory had an appointment for a fitting with an ex-cop in the formal-wear business. I had my name.

"This name," Sid said. "Is this not the same name as the guy who runs the Marina del Rey?"

"I'm afraid it's his daughter," I said.

"She got a problem?"

"A big one."

"Well, so long to that contract," Sid said. "Not only does she have an account, she has a safe-deposit box."

"Christina Stohlmeyer, right?" I said.

"You got it," Sid said.

35

Morning sun split the stoop of 719 Crotona Park North into equal sections of light and shade. Gregory and I and two uniformed cops from the Five One climbed the steps to Tina's apartment. The building was quiet except for someone with a hacking cough, and on the second floor—a rooster crowing. The South Bronx was the home of the fighting cock. At one time there'd been a ring in the basement of a building just a few doors down.

The uniformed cops walked heavily behind us, leather gear squeaking. Gregory motioned for the cops to wait on the stairs, then he knocked. Something sizzled in a frying pan in another apartment.

Delia had returned empty-handed from the Mid-Orange Correctional Facility. The scenery was lovely, she said, trees and cows. But Hector Marquez was the Rock of Gibraltar and never budged from his story that he'd spent his furlough time quietly with his wife and kids. No more than that.

* * *

"Who," Tina said as the peephole clicked.

"You know who," Gregory said.

"I'm not dressed," she said.

"We need to talk," Gregory said.

She started unlatching locks. The metal click was the quintessential New York sound. The number of locks served as a rating system to our paranoia. Snap, snap. Only two, a bare Bronx minimum.

She opened the door and hid modestly behind it. We walked in and held it for the uniformed cops. She stared, wide-eyed, at them.

"What's wrong?" she said.

"Get dressed," I said.

"I got my kids."

"Bring them to Angel's mother."

"Oh, no," she said. "Not this time. You better have a fucking warrant."

"As a matter of fact," I said, and handed her the piece of paper that gave us the legal right to go through her possessions. I closed the door, then noticed that some of her possessions were in the living room in cardboard boxes. Apple and orange boxes from the supermarket. The room smelled of fresh fruit.

"Moving?" I said.

"Outta this shithole," she said.

She stood there in black panties and black T-shirt, reading the search warrant. She wore a scarf around her head, as if she'd been working. I ticked off the *Miranda* warnings; I didn't need to read them. The first sentence started with "You have the right . . ."; the last, "If you cannot afford . . ." I knew that when we opened the safety-deposit box in the name of Christina Stohlmeyer, it would show that she could well afford. A box of breakfast cereal was on the kitchen table, a picture of Superman on the front.

"Where's the gun?" I said.

"What gun?" she said.

"Marc Ross's Glock 19."

"How should I know?"

Gregory instructed the uniform cops to start looking through the boxes in the living room. The warrant was specific: the Glock 19, a safe-deposit box key, and Max Factor makeup.

"When was the last time you were in Sonny's apartment?" I said.

"I've been there plenty a times."

"Like last weekend. After Sonny killed himself."

"I had some things I left. Clothes and shit. I knew I'd never get it once you guys vouchered everything."

"Get the kids," I said. "Let's go."

The kids' bedroom was small but packed with toys. Kevin was dressed, ready for school. The girl was watching TV from her bed, chewing on the ear of a stuffed rabbit. Kevin had superhero sheets, blanket, pillowcase, and backpack. Superman, Batman, and Spider-Man were taped to the wall. The girl's bed was covered with stuffed animals. Everything was clean and neat. For whatever else she was, she seemed to be trying to be the good mother.

"Mommy has to go out, honey," she said softly, patting the little girl. "You have to get dressed. You can stay with Lita for a while."

Kevin stared at me, his hair still sprouting upward wildly. Don't look at me, I wanted to say. I can't save you. The only superheroes are taped to your wall.

"Make sure she gets dressed, Kevin," Tina said.

I walked with Tina into her bedroom. Gregory was

in the bathroom, going through shelves of makeup. Some of it was in boxes on the floor.

"You going to watch me dress?" she said.

"That's right," I said.

"Cheap thrill, right?" she said. "Cops . . . Jesus Christ."

I heard the slight break in her voice. She yanked the T-shirt over her head and threw it down. The cone of sunlight accentuated the high blue veins in her arms. Her skin was so pale, the bumps along her spine could have been the bones of her skeleton, bleaching in the sun.

"I want you to listen to me, Tina," I said. "We have people in Warwick, talking to Hector right now. He's going to give you up."

"For what?"

"Don't be stupid. You've got one chance; this is it. Grab the deal before he does."

"Blow it out your ass."

"Is that how a mother talks? You're really concerned about your kids, aren't you?"

"Don't you talk to me about my fucking kids."

I crossed the room quickly to stand next to her and watch her hand as it went into a dresser drawer, expecting to see the flat black finish of the Glock 19. She took out a lacy red bra, pointed it at me, and said, "Bang." Her breathing was deep and quick, her nipples hard. She pressed herself against me, her hand squeezing my cock insistently and roughly.

"Get dressed," I said, grabbing her by the arms, pulling her toward the closet.

"Faggot," she said. "Sonny said you used to be wild. That was bullshit."

"Get dressed," I said.

She didn't put on the bra. She took a blouse from a hanger and laid it across her bed.

"Where we going?" she said.

"The bank."

"I was there yesterday. With the big guy."

"Not the bank on the Concourse, Christina."

"I don't use that name anymore. I told you that."

"We're having your signature checked. We'll do it right."

Dust floated through the sunlight.

"I want my lawyer," she said.

"Be my guest." I pointed to the phone. She picked it up and immediately slammed it back down.

"I had it disconnected yesterday," she said.

"Where's the gun, Tina?"

"I don't know what you're talking about."

"Look at this, pally," Gregory said. "I'm gonna take all this crap." He held up a box filled with small bottles of dark brown liquid and flat plastic cases with puffs and brushes. We were trying to match the tan smear found on the underwear of Officer Paul Verdi.

"Oh, the big man wants to see, too," Tina said. "You pricks want to see me naked. Here, look, go ahead."

Tina stood there with her hands on her hips. The veins in her neck bulged. I could see she was trembling. She glanced at the doorway. Kevin was watching.

"See what you're doing?" I said. "See what you're doing to these kids?"

"What the hell do you know about what I'm doing?" she said. "You have no idea what my life is like."

"You got yourself into this," Gregory said.

"And I'll get myself out," she said. She sat back on the bed, bending over, hugging her knees. She began to cry. "Okay, okay," she said. "Mommy's sorry, Kev honey. Mommy's acting stupid. She's going to get dressed. Everything's okay. Go ahead. You go on. Mommy's okay. Go. Check on your sister, Kev."

Sergeant Drumm and two detectives arrived to take over the search. Tina's kids filed through Angel's mother's open door. Angel's mother's expression never changed. No surprise, no regret. As if she accepted every blessing, every curse, equally, without expectation.

"You can call your lawyer from the station house," I said.

"Call my father," Tina said.

36

It took fourteen hours to get Tina through the system. She was in a van on her way to the Bronx House of Detention. We came downstairs and crossed the courthouse lobby, looking for a pay phone. The lobby had the sad, empty feel of a bus station in the wee hours, the lights dim, the coffee shop closed. It smelled of body odor and fried onions. Ashtrays spilled over onto the floor. Empty coffee cups sat on window ledges.

Gregory called the office; I sat on a ledge and checked the paperwork. We'd found one hundred fifty-seven thousand dollars and a gun in Tina's safe-deposit box. The gun was Marc Ross's Glock 19. She made her deal before we looked in the box. She told us that Hector executed Ross and Verdi, with her as the lure. Hector planned it, waited in ambush. Sonny Guidice was next on their list, but he saved them a bullet. Within an hour of hearing about Sonny's suicide, Tina took the train to

Stuyvesant Town and removed the money from his safe. She said she left enough in there to satisfy us.

We'd called Whitey Stohlmeyer from the Five One Precinct. He came right down with Tina's mom, Helen. Whitey hired a new lawyer, offered his house as bail, and petitioned Social Services for temporary custody of the kids. When we left for Central Booking the scene was tearful, everyone taking the blame. Tina signed her name as Christina.

Worried women whispered in small groups near the phones. Newspapers and cigarette butts littered the floor. Cops passed by, some with handcuffed prisoners, all carrying sheaves of paper. And all younger than we. They dressed like boys of summer in gray sweatshirts, flowered shirts, or Bart Simpson T-shirts and jeans. Gregory and I were in wool suits: dark blue, dark gray.

Gregory bought a paper from the machine and struck up a conversation with several young cops. They were congratulating him, asking him questions. I saw myself at their age and wished there was some way to warn them, to keep them from becoming cynical. Cynicism becomes hate, and that destroys.

For years I clung to a hate for Sonny Guidice. I realized now it was a disdain for myself and what I'd become in those later years in the precinct. The proof was in black and white in the pages of my own memo books.

All New York City patrol officers carried memo books, small notebooks, property of the NYPD, form UF 16. Fifty lined pages, every official act, opened and closed with the signature of a superior officer. We were required to save all our memo books, until retirement or Judgment Day, whichever came first. Mine were kept in two boxes in the basement. Dozens of stacks of yellowing pads, held by rubber bands, packed chronologically. The first went back thirty years.

Last night I opened the boxes because I wanted to reread the account of the shooting that had troubled me for so long. This was it:

June 23, 1968 4 × 12 rmp 2365 Sec G
w/Ptl Guidice meal 1900 ret date Aug 9
1805 hrs to 1645 Bathgate Apt 3a asslt in prgrss
Martin Luther Hopkins M/B/7 DOA, Sgt
Hazzard, ntfd mother Etheleva Hopkins ntfd
Nothing to Report
Ptl A. Ryan #19452

That was all. The brevity of the entry stunned me. For all the detail so dominant in my mind all these years, I'd made a two-line entry. "Nothing to Report"?

I started going back, reading all the memo books, starting with my first day out of the academy. The first book was formal, studentlike. In fact, all the early books were rich and full, the script neat, the entries packed with detail. During my first year on patrol, I filled up twenty-one memo books. The second year, twenty-five. The third, twenty-one. Then eighteen, fourteen, nine. My last year on patrol I used only four memo books the entire year. The writing was so sloppy, I could barely read it. The indifference was obvious. The pages reeked of booze and recklessness.

The problem is cop's eyes. It takes a few years to acquire this occupational disease. Cops learn to see things that other people don't, and it wears us down. Where Leigh sees a man waiting for a bus, I see him loitering in front of a liquor store. Where Leigh smiles upon a loving father doting on his child in a playground, I watch a child molester stalking his prey. The trick for cops is to learn to see both sides, the demons and the angels. It's not easy. Ugliness clings with tenacity.

"You give those guys your autograph?" I asked Gregory.

"Nah," he said. "I was signing them up for the Emerald Society. These young guys are the future."

"You're a real visionary," I said.

"Ain't it the truth," he said. "Let's go home, pally."

As we pushed through the revolving door, I thought there was much to be hopeful about. The winter of numbered snowstorms was finally over. The NYPD was in good hands. The dark blue uniform shirts were coming back; Gregory and I always hated light blue. The Bronx was truly rising from the ashes. Joe Gregory was buying a tux. My children were happy.

Outside, the night was warm, a hint of honeysuckle in the air. Gregory picked a can of grape soda off the roof of the T-bird and tossed it in the trash. A car horn blew. A dark Cadillac pulled in behind us.

"They told me you'd be here," Whitey Stohlmeyer said. "We just got the kids from Social Services."

Tina's little girl was asleep in Helen Stohlmeyer's lap. Kevin was on the backseat, wide awake, holding a McDonald's bag.

"Christina just left," I said. "Check with City Corrections. They'll tell you where she's housed."

"Yeah," he said. "We're going tomorrow. Murray gave me a number to call. He seems like a great lawyer. Thanks."

"He's the best," Gregory said.

"He's working on bail," Whitey said. "We're keeping our fingers crossed."

Kevin was standing up on the backseat, watching me without expression.

"I just wanted to say thanks," Whitey said. "You know what I mean, right?"

"Buy us a drink sometime," Gregory said. "We'll be around the Marina at some cop's racket. We ain't going nowhere."

I asked Whitey to roll the back window down. Then I reached inside my raincoat and took off Gregory's campaign pin, the miniature NYPD detective badge with the shamrock in the center.

"I should have done something a long time ago," Whitey said. "I just hope it's not too late."

I reached in and pinned the badge on Kevin's sweatshirt. Then I saluted him, and I thought I saw a slight smile.

"Maybe we can make a little of it up," Whitey said, gesturing at the kids.

"It's never too late to do the right thing," I said.

37

The induction ceremony for new officers of the NYPD Emerald Society was held upstairs in Gallagher's Steak House in midtown Manhattan, in a room where the thick, dark-paneled walls had absorbed sixty years of state secrets and smoke from fine cigars. We always started with the Pledge of Allegiance, hands over our hearts. The bullshit didn't begin until after the prayer.

Joe Gregory sat on the dais, next to the new police commissioner. Both wore tuxedos—they were leaving early to attend a function at the mayor's residence. Everyone stood and clapped when Gregory accepted the gavel from outgoing president Shammy O'Brien. The gavel was a black-lacquered shillelagh someone's father had actually "brought from Ire-land."

"In true Irish fashion," Gregory said, "I'd like to start with a story."

The story was an old Irish joke, and Shammy O'Brien was the butt. It seemed, Gregory said, that when

O'Brien left the old country for America, he promised old Mrs. Dunne from County Clare that he'd find her son in New York. The Dunne lad had not been heard from in years, and the old lady was at her wits' end. Well, when the boat docked in Manhattan O'Brien rushed toward the first big building he saw and began quizzing everyone in the lobby. No one seemed to know Dunne, so O'Brien stormed into an immense men's room and started banging on the door of every stall. O'Brien was agitated, thinking the job might be much harder than he'd thought. He banged and banged down the entire row of tin doors, screaming, "Are you Dunne? Are you Dunne?"

Finally someone flushed, then told O'Brien to hold his horses, he was done. To which O'Brien drew up his powerful shoulders and screamed, "Then, by God, write your mother!"

"Now Shammy O'Brien himself is done," Gregory said, slapping the blackthorn cudgel against his palm. "And he has no excuse not to write every single citizen of County Clare."

Gregory went on to thank everyone, including me. He didn't have a speech, just a string of yarns we'd all heard before. After one too many war stories Shammy O'Brien rose and made a motion to dispense with the bullshit and adjourn to the bar. Guys jumped over one another to second the motion. Chairs scraped on the wooden floor.

I was sitting along the far wall with Johnny McGuire and Joe McDarby. McGuire unhooked the camera from its tripod; McDarby poured ale into his Guinness, carefully constructing a black and tan. Gregory worked his way toward our table, backslapping, his face shining, a stunningly bright red, as he swung the shillelagh like a nightstick.

"Great speech," I said.

"All lies," he said. "I've the heart of a true politician."

Gregory stared over my head, blinking, as he always did when his mind was going a million miles a minute.

"What time are you due at Gracie Mansion?" I asked.

"Eight-thirty."

"Don't worry. You're going to take this city by storm."

Gregory's beeper went off and he pulled it from his waistband and squinted at the numbers. I wondered if he was going to wear his old ratty raincoat over the tux.

"Someone has to call the office," he said. The sound of broken glass came from the kitchen. The buzz of voices grew louder.

"I'll do it," I said. "You're too important. I guess this is the way it's going to be from now on."

"Unless they dump us, or we croak. Whatever comes first."

"I can see my future now," I said. "You'll be in the tux sipping champagne somewhere; I'll be in some pissy phone booth calling the night desk, or eating cold pizza in the hallway of some crack house. You'll be nibbling caviar in the Russian Tea Room; I'll be alone in the Two Eight Precinct, wolfing down greasy chicken wings, car heater on the blink. . . ."

"Hey, pally," he said. "Are you done?"

Across the floor, Shanahan juggled three cannolis in the air. Brady washed Maalox down with Irish whiskey. Sid Kaye slipped a half-empty bottle into his briefcase.

"Don't say it," I said. "I already know. Write my mother."